# They Call Me Beauty

# They Call Me Beauty

J. Hieb

In The Name Publishing

In loving memory of my Grandmother, Wanda.

# Prologue

I learned from a young age what people wanted me to be: a charming, giggling, bright-eyed beauty. They even called me that when I was young—*Beauty*. So often, in fact, that for some time I thought it was my name. But it's not.

I don't know when I first noticed the voices in my head. Their faces disappeared by the time I hit puberty, but the voices were there, whispering haunting melodies, reminding me of what I am—what I *truly* am.

I think my parents must have suspected something was amiss. At age six, they caught me talking to one of the faces. It had told me that I could take a cookie, that I didn't need to ask. I had laid out all the reasons it was wrong to take the cookie, but the voice was relentless. "I won't lie!" I finally shouted at the fading face, right as Mother's footsteps stopped at my bedroom door.

"Who were you talking to, Beauty?" she'd asked. I told her that I didn't know its name. She had smiled through pursed lips, the way mothers often do when the parenting books fail to give you a warning that your child may talk to invisible forces, ones that apparently direct said child to lie. I think in the end, she convinced herself it was an imaginary friend.

It was not imaginary, and it was not a friend.

Eight of them rotated through my mind, each with its own emotion of focus: anger, greed, pride, fear, offense, lust, loneliness, and oppression. At some point, I started to think of them like Snow White's seven dwarves—only this wasn't a fairy tale, and the worst one wasn't just Grumpy. What I'd given to have just Grumpy.

To that end, I gave each of them a cute name, thinking it would help (it didn't): Annie, Gus, Priscilla, Fred, Oscar, Lucy, Louis, and Opi. Opi was the worst. Thankfully, his presence was also the least frequent, but somehow, he always managed to pull me down under invisible currents, tumbling, cartwheeling, and gasping for air. Even now, I shudder at the thought of Opi showing up.

Why didn't I tell someone, you might ask? Well, the answer is both shockingly simple and mind-blowingly complex at the same time: it was my normal. "That's not complex," you might argue. You might even point a finger at me and tell me that I was delirious, and I won't disagree, but this didn't just happen one day. There was no subtle shift to warn me that something was wrong. My very first memories include the faces. They appear more often in my mind's eye than not when I recall those younger years.

So, yes, I was delirious, and yes, I was probably crazy, but no, these things were not figments of my imagination. They were not some misfiring of my brain, easily controlled by a prescription drug. These things were as real as you or I.

Which might lead you to ask again: *why didn't I tell anyone?* In all honesty...I think a part of me liked them. Well, that's not exactly true. I didn't *like* them, but I was comfortable with them. I'd accepted them as my normal and even trusted them to defend me, to take care of me, to get me what I wanted. I justified my reasoning by saying everyone else probably had an Opi too.

But no, these were my demons. Mine to name, mine to carry, and eventually, mine to send back to the squirming pit of hell to await final judgement.

I'm getting ahead of myself, though. First, I learned to be what I thought I was supposed to be.

# Part I

In the Beginning

1

## Chapter One

I remember one morning, when I was five, maybe six, Mother waking me up to go to school. I loved school and all its noise; the squealing of other children, the bouncing of balls, the chains clacking, and the teachers blowing their whistles helped block out the whispers. But on this day, when my eager little brain was ready to jump out of bed and put on my new white galoshes with the adorable pink ladybugs (which my brother never hesitated to remind me was wrong, ladybugs are *red*)—the first day of school with rain, which I had longed for with the anticipation only a child could have; I had dreamt of jumping in the murky puddles, my socks remaining unscathed by the magic of rubber—on this day, Annie showed up.

Annie didn't like the rain, or galoshes, with or without little pink ladybugs (although she did agree that the ladybugs should be red; she and my brother had that in common).

*Mother comes to my room and sits gently on the edge of my bed. "Wake up, Beauty," she nudges. She does not know that I am awake, or that I am not currently me. I am still there, somewhere down deep, but right now, Annie has the reins.*

*"I don't want to!" Annie screams, kicking out with both feet. One foot catches Mother on the shoulder; the other clips the very edge of her jaw. Mother cries out in pain, reeling away from the bed before tripping over a poorly placed Barbie doll and catching herself on the wall. Annie is gone now, leaving as quickly as she arrived. It's just me left to deal with the hurt look on Mother's face, the way she rubs her tender jaw, a streak of purple foreshadowing what will surely be a nasty bruise.*

*I have two choices: I can tell Mother about Annie, or I can lie.*

*I do not like to lie. Lying is bad. Even at six, I know lying is bad, but if I tell Mother about Annie, Mother will think I am lying anyway, and I'll be punished for lying when I told the truth.*

*I don't like to be punished, so I lie: "Oh, Mommy," I cry out, leaping from the bed and wrapping my chubby arms around her middle, "I'm so sorry." (That's not a lie, I really am very sorry.) "I had a terrible nightmare, and I thought you were a monster coming to get me." (That is a lie—there was no nightmare, just the monster in my mind.)*

*Mother's face softens. I see a glint of skepticism gleam in her pupils, but it's quickly pushed aside in the tight squeeze of her Beauty.*

Annie showed up two more times that day. The first was when Brother and I were playing and she wanted to play with his dinosaur toy (I don't even like dinosaurs, but she remembered how big they were and loved to reminisce). He wouldn't hand it over. Annie stomped and screamed and threw a fit, picking up the dinosaur and smashing it against the wall. The tail and one arm broke off (I should mention here that Annie was much stronger than I was). When Father came upstairs, it was just little old me again, holding tightly to the dinosaur and knowing that a spanking was coming. Annie never got spankings; she never stuck around for them.

The second time was at dinner. Macaroni and cheese was my favorite, but apparently Annie didn't like it.

*Mother sighs, exasperated. "But, Beauty, this is what you asked for."*

*Annie dumps the plate off the table, wailing and kicking her feet. Mother looks at Father; he returns her gaze, and, in a flash, Annie is gone.*

*"I'm sorry, Mommy," I say, sliding off the chair and scooping bits of macaroni off the floor back into my bowl. Mother sighs again and drops to the ground to help scoop up the muck.*

*"Beauty, are you tired?" she asks me. I'm not tired, and I am so hungry, but of course I answer yes. Mothers don't get as angry at you when you're tired, but they do send you to bed, even when you're hungry and don't get to have your favorite dinner because Annie doesn't like it.*

It was mostly Annie in those days. She'd pop up then leave quickly, typically with a mess for me to clean up or, more aptly, lie my way out of. I really don't like lying, but I don't have a choice.

Luckily, the noises at school kept Annie at bay. If it was too quiet, though, she'd show up. Mrs. Alvos, my favorite teacher, seemingly suspected something was amiss, but, like Mother, she kept those thoughts to herself. On the last day of kindergarten, however, I saw the same glimmer of skepticism cross her eyes that I'd seen in Mother's. She knew then that there was something, but she didn't say anything, or if she did, Mother and Father never told me.

On that day, a beautiful June day, it was time to clean the classroom for the end of the school year. All the students had to help. I got third choice of tasks and chose to do the whiteboards.

*I love cleaning whiteboards. I love the way the furry little brush wipes away all traces of ABCs and 123s. I love the way you squirt that little bottle of liquid onto the white and watch as it runs down the board, picking up colors as it goes, leaving a trail of wet whiteness in its wake.*

*Annie, however, does not like cleaning the white board, nor does she like the furry brush and the dripping drops of color. Annie does not want to clean the whiteboard; Annie wants to play in the sun. She loves the sun; it reminds her of her home.*

*Teacher says we must stay and help, and I nod eagerly.* Not now, Annie, *I think, trying hard to pull back control. Annie refuses to give me control, instead letting out an ear-piercing scream, causing all the other children to stop and stare.*

*Annie is the one who yelled, but I am the one who feels the flush of color rising to my cheeks, a single tear sliding from my eye.*

*Annie likes it when the other children look. She likes the way they stare as she makes a scene. She screams once again, only slightly less awful than the first (fortunately, Annie's voice is contained by my small vocal cords, or I imagine the windows would break).*

*Teacher kneels down in front of us. "Now, now," she begins, "we must all participate in cleanup since we all helped to make the mess. You chose the whiteboard." She begins to rise to her feet, taking my elbow softly in her hand to guide me back to my task. Annie moves my foot; it catches Teacher in the shin. She lets out a quiet yelp, and right then, that gleam appears in her eyes, the gleam that says something is not quite right.*

*And just like before, Annie is gone. "Oh, Teacher," I say, dropping to the ground in front of her, "I'm so sorry. I really didn't mean to—it's just so lovely outside. I just—" (the flush returns to my face) "I am just really going to miss you, and school. That's it—I'm just feeling a bit sad." The gleam in her eye is gone. She pats my head and directs me back to my task. The other children stare, but Teacher scurries around, turning their attention away from me and back to their chores.*

How quickly small children forget.

## Chapter Two

One or two years later (I can't remember for sure), Gus showed up. Gus was different from Annie. While Annie would lash out, scream, kick—anything to get attention—Gus was sneaky. Nobody ever saw Gus's actions; they just saw the outcome.

He first showed up when new neighbors moved in across the street. They had two daughters, the first a year older than Brother and the second my age. The girls had different biological fathers. I remember thinking that was weird; how could your sister have a different dad than you?

But I digress. The young girl's name was Rosie. Her dad was her mom's current husband, and that man loved Rosie dearly. He treated Rosie's older sister like an unfortunate obligation, but Rosie was his shining star, his princess, his *everything*, and he went out of his way to show her.

A few weeks after they moved in, Rosie's dad bought her the coolest motorized car I'd ever seen. It was a Barbie convertible, bright pink with headlights that worked. The whole thing was battery-powered, and it lasted forever on a single charge. I watched Rosie out the window, admiring that beautiful car.

That's when Gus showed up. Gus wanted that car. Gus didn't like that Rosie had a car and he didn't. But Gus didn't scream or cry; he just watched. I felt the clenching in my stomach, the yearning for the car. I felt his want.

One day, Rosie left the car outside (she probably had to use the bathroom; why else would you leave your brand-new toy unattended on the sidewalk?). Immediately Gus popped his head up. He checked for Mother and Father; they weren't in sight. Brother was playing an old Nintendo game in the living room; he'd never notice. The field was clear, Gus led me out, one tiny foot in front of the other. I thought we were just going to admire it up close, but no, Gus *wanted* that car. It should have been his. Why did Rosie get that car? Gus told me to get in. *No, I thought, stealing is wrong. Mother says we can't steal.* I tried to fight him, but he was too strong, and it was too pretty. One little arm shot out and took hold of the door, pulling it back. He slid in awkwardly. One little arm pulled the door shut.

I'd never been in such a thing. I'd seen Mother and Father drive, but I was still stuck in a booster seat in the back. I had no idea what any of the buttons or pulls did, but apparently Gus did. It wasn't quite a chariot, but it would do. He turned the key; a slight purr rose from the tiny engine. He moved the little nob behind the steering wheel, and the car jerked forward. I felt my foot push the pedal on the floor, harder and harder, until there was nowhere left to go. I felt my stomach drop; we were moving so quickly, and I was certain we would crash (although looking back, we couldn't have been going more than three or four miles per hour). I heard Rosie yelling behind me and, a short moment later, her father's footsteps. He stopped the vehicle with his foot, catching the rear bumper with his toes. The car lurched to a stop, my small body jerking forward.

In one swift scoop, he had me out of the car, muttering something about grand theft auto (I didn't know what that meant). I suddenly heard Mother's voice, panicked from our house, now two doors down. Rosie's dad carried me beneath his arm the whole way back. Gus was gone.

Mother was displeased, and she didn't hesitate to tell me as much: "That was so *naughty*," she started, "not to mention dangerous! What were you thinking?" I didn't have the heart to respond. I'd already stolen a car; I couldn't lie, too. Mother looked at me, one eyebrow slightly raised, and sent me to my room for a time-out. She said it was to think about what I'd done, but I hadn't done anything. I thought about telling her, but what do you say? *"Sorry, Mother, some unknown force took over my body and made me commit auto theft?"* No, it would just sound like an excuse. So I kept my mouth shut and sat in time-out, thinking about what Gus had done.

As if conjured by the memory, he showed up again, a little bobbing face in the air. You might ask me to prove it, to describe him or draw you a picture. I can't. Of all the people I've known and the non-people I've ever met, Gus was the least exciting. More than that—Gus was boring to look at. There was nothing odd or different about his face. "But he's a demon!" you might argue. "Surely he had horns and forehead ridges and a nose shaped like a mushroom!" But he didn't. It was almost as though a cartoon animator had gotten lazy. There were two eyes, a nose, and a mouth, but that's my full recollection of Gus. Even after seeing him around for years, that is all I can remember.

That night, as he spoke, he told me about all the things he wanted. I was surprised that he wanted such childish things; in my mind, he was a grown-up—a weird, floating, grown-up head. He complained that they didn't have such nice things in his time. He would joke sometimes about shaking chains in cemeteries and running with pigs, but I didn't understand it.

Truth be told, I don't think Annie liked Gus. Of all of them, those two rarely showed up at the same time, although that was not a hard rule. In fact, one November day in the first grade, the two of them were best buds. They still argued some, but it was light-hearted. Mostly, they were having a cheerful good time.

They liked first grade better than kindergarten for the same reason I didn't: it was quieter. Mr. Lopez, my new teacher, demanded that students pay attention. He did not tolerate disobedience or "riffraff." I still don't know exactly what riffraff is. He was scary, and the children obeyed.

On this day in November, a girl in my class named Amanda brought in the most adorable robotic puppy. It was not like the ones you see today—this one was a glorified stuffed toy with a pink leash around its neck that managed to move its head from side to side while its tail moved in the opposite direction, and it would intermittently let out happy woofs. Back then, it was exactly the type of toy a kid would put on their Christmas list to Santa, and I'd planned on doing just that.

Amanda was very gracious with her toy. She walked it around the share circle, giving everybody a chance to pet it. I was so excited when my turn came around.

So was Gus. So was Annie.

As Amanda walked past me, leading the dog by its pink leash, I felt my fingers reach deeply into its white fur and knew I was in for trouble. Gus wanted that puppy, and he was going to get it. Gus turned my fingers into steel vices and yanked that toy backwards hard, sending me and Amanda both spiraling across the floor. Amanda squealed as her arm bent backwards unnaturally. Just like Annie, Gus was stronger than I am.

Mr. Lopez rushed to Amanda, who was whimpering quietly, tears streaming, eyes wide. Her shoulder had popped out of place. He gently patted her hand, telling her to stay very still, before turning to me. "YOU," he roared, leaving her side and marching to where I lay, crumpled in a ball with the puppy close to my midsection. "Give it up now!"

Gus didn't want to, and Annie didn't like his tone. She screamed her ear-splitting, mind-numbing, window-shattering (if she had vocal cords other than my own) scream.

Mr. Lopez did not like that scream. The children watched as he directed me: "You will give that toy back, and you will go to the principal's office. We're calling your parents." By that time, reinforcements had arrived. One teacher led Amanda to the principal's office while the second approached me.

Annie didn't like the second teacher, not one bit. As the teacher pulled me to my feet, Annie buckled my knees and sent me falling to the ground once again.

Mr. Lopez was not impressed. "Up! Now!" he snapped. The children huddled closer together, slowly inching away from Mr. Lopez and myself. Annie was not impressed by Mr. Lopez, nor would she be deterred. She remained on the floor, sprawled out her (my) legs, and began her tantrum. Wildly and with enthusiasm, she kicked and screamed, even lifting my head off the floor and dropping it back down with a thump that sent black spots to my eyes.

Teacher Number Two moved the other children out of the classroom for an impromptu recess. I heard her mention the principal's name while Mr. Lopez pulled up a tiny chair and sat, watching as Annie thrashed about. Finally, despite Annie's protests, my little body gave out, no longer able to carry on with the fit. I could feel a knot forming where my head had met with the laminate flooring. I laid there, looking up at Mr. Lopez, and he sat, looking down at me.

I found it amusing that Mr. Lopez, who was not a small man, was sitting on that little itty-bitty chair. So did Gus. He liked the chair. I stifled a smile; best not to laugh now.

Annie was gone. Gus was gone.

For what felt like an eternity, I laid there. I didn't think an apology would work on Mr. Lopez, so I decided to save it for Mother and the principal. As he sat, I watched his eyes moving, thinking. He must have been considering all the possibilities that would send a child into such a fit. Abuse? Physical or sexual? Trouble at home? Perhaps divorce? He was going down the list, staring at me as I stared back, seeing and not seeing me at the same time.

The click-clack of a woman's heels on laminate interrupted our staring contest, and Mr. Lopez shook his head, clearing away those thoughts and lifting himself from the chair with a grunt.

*Ms. Reed is there now. She's the principal, a stern lady who wears brown all the time. She doesn't wear makeup like Mother, but she's not an unattractive lady. She doesn't smile, however. She doesn't drop down to the ground beside me (I'm not certain her brown pencil skirt would let her anyway). No, she doesn't do any of that. In fact, she doesn't acknowledge me at all. Instead, she stands five or so feet away from me, whispering with Mr. Lopez.*

*"No, this is a first," I hear him say.*

*"Trouble at home?"*

*"Not that I know of. Should we call CPS?"*

*"No no, not yet. If there's no sign of trouble, we'll talk to the parents first." She finally looks down at me, and I gaze up at her. The knot on my head is thump-thumping to the rhythm of my heartbeat, echoing like a drum in my ears.*

*She doesn't say a word for several moments. When she does, it's "Up." I oblige.*

*The walk to her office is a long one. Mr. Lopez doesn't come. He must stay behind and get the lesson back on schedule. There is math to be done, after all. I wish he'd come; he's scary, but at least he's familiar. I've never been to the principal's office before.*

*We walk in silence down brightly lit hallways covered in colorful artwork: watercolor turkeys, self-portraits, and crayon- traced ABCs. A few doors even show the beginnings of Christmas decorations, though we've yet to celebrate Thanksgiving. One door bears a lovely construction-art rendition of a Christmas bulb. It twinkles and sparkles in the light, covered in glitter and sequins.*

*Gus likes glitter and sequins.* No, no, no, *I think to myself, fighting to keep my arm down as it rises to pull the craft off the doorway. As it brushes the colorful paper, the bell rings, and the classroom door opens, pulling the decoration from his reach.*

*Annie does not like that Gus did not get his decoration. They are friends today. Annie slows my feet down until I feel like I'm walking through cement, each step slower and slower. Ms. Reed is now two full strides ahead of me as more children pour out of classrooms, crowding the halls in a river of puffy coats, mittens, scarves, and pouf-topped hats.*

*Ms. Reed looks down and realizes that I'm not beside her anymore. She looks around and spots me, slowly moving one foot in front of the other, and her mouth flattens to a thin scowl.*

*Annie does not like Ms. Reed. Gus wants to go to recess with the other children. I want to go home and cry, tell Mother everything, give it all up. But I can't. The noise of the children quiets Annie and Gus, and the weight on my feet is removed. I skip-step to Ms. Reed, who is looking at me with a grim, thin mouth.*

*She's not amused. Neither am I. But Annie is.*

*In her office, she points me to a chair and orders that I sit still.*

*"Will you play some music?" I ask, almost begging, knowing that the river of children will soon empty to the playground and Annie and Gus will return full force.*

*"Do you think you deserve music?" she asks in turn. Her face is stern, but her boney white hands are wringing together. She's nervous, but I don't know why. She's an adult*

*—unless she knows about Gus and Annie, unless she knows how strong they are, how much stronger than me they are. For a moment, I feel hopeful. If she knows, then maybe, just maybe, she can help.*

*She turns her back on me and turns on her radio. The thick sound of jazz music flows through the tiny office, filling every nook and corner. I ask if I can sit closer to the radio, promising not to touch, and she nods a quick yes.*

*I don't like jazz; I can already tell. But I do like that it helps to keep their voices away.*

Mother showed up some time later. When she came through the office door, her face was pinched with worry. She'd clearly thought something had happened to me. I couldn't meet her eyes, so I dropped my gaze to the floor, counting the squares I could see around the thick pewter rug. I counted to forty-six before I ran out of squares. I couldn't count that high last year, so I was pretty impressed with myself. Then I noticed the silence in the room.

*Mother and Ms. Reed have stopped talking. They're looking at me. I look back and forth between them, not entirely sure what's expected of me. "Well?" Ms. Reed prods. "What have you got to say?"*

*I let out a meek, "Sorry," which clearly does not satisfy her.*

*Mother looks at me. "You don't need to apologize to us. You need to explain what happened."*

*I don't know how to explain, so instead, I panic. "I didn't mean to!" I cry, which is true—I really didn't mean to yank back on a toy with enough force to pull a girl's shoulder out of socket. I try to get more words out, but my mouth and nose are filling with mucus. I just need them to understand that it's not my fault.*

*Mother pulls me into her lap and offers me a tissue. I curl into a ball and bury my face in her chest. It's safe there.*

*I hear them talk about me some more. Ms. Reed asks about life at home, if there's been any big changes—divorce, pregnancy—that would cause me to act out this way. Mother insists that there aren't. I hear Ms. Reed clicking her tongue.*

*"You're not going to like my next question," she states matter-of-factly, "but unfortunately, I must ask." She pauses, giving Mother a chance to interject. Mother doesn't. "Is there any abuse? I don't think—" she breaks off, clicking her tongue against the roof of her mouth once more. "Well, I suppose what I'm trying to say is, there aren't signs of physical abuse, so I must ask—the men in her life, are they...?"*

*I feel Mother tense. She holds me a bit tighter and puts one hand up, palm facing Ms. Reed. "Let me stop you right there. I know my girl, and I would know if something like* that*"—she draws the word out as if unwilling to acknowledge what it is they are speaking of— "were happening. Besides, the only men in her life are her brother and her father, and they would never do something like that. In fact, just last summer, one of the neighbors lifted her off the ground, and her father about decked him for it. I ask you, Ms. Reed," she says in the same drawn-out* *way,* "does that sound like the kind of environment where a child would be abused?

"Well, there are so many times when the mother is not aware, and with her unknown background..." *Ms. Reed teeters off. Something in Mother's eye must have stopped her. I bet it's the same look she gives Brother when he says a swear word. I don't why she's glaring at the principal, though; I don't know what an unknown background is, either.*

"Now, you listen, and you listen very closely. If you ever so much as suggest any sort of abuse again, I will sue you and this entire school district for slander."

"I'm not suggesting your husband—I'm just saying there might be someone you don't know about—or something from before..." *Ms. Reed says the words fast, without a breath, as though trying to get them all out before Mother can cut her off.*

*Before what? I think, still unsure what they're talking about.*

"You are out of line." *Mother's voice has dropped in volume. The words are barely above a whisper, but they're weighted heavily, and Ms. Reed sighs in defeat. Mother stands prepared to leave.*

"Will you..." *Ms. Reed pauses again. Hesitant. Mother's threat has clearly been received.* "...will you at least let her talk to someone? Not me, not even necessarily the school counselor, if you prefer but please, find a doctor, a pastor,* something, *and let her talk. The behavior, I can understand. Kids being kids, I understand. Tantrums,* *lashing out..." She trails off, then takes a deep breath before finishing, "I am certain she didn't mean to hurt that child, but what I don't understand is how she laid on the floor, unmoving, for nearly twenty minutes. Does that sound normal to you?"*

*Mother does not honor Ms. Reed with a response. Instead, she turns abruptly on her heel with me cradled in her arms and marches out of the office.*

That night, Mother and Father approached me about the incident. Father sat on my bed while Mother leaned against the door frame.

*"Come on, Beauty. Can you just tell me what's got you acting out?" Gus's face dances behind Father's head, but he doesn't seem to notice. Neither does Mother.*

*What can I say? I do not have the mental capacity to explain what I'm seeing, what I'm experiencing. Instead, I cry. I cry because I don't understand, because I don't know how to explain. I cry because I am frustrated—not sad, but angry, and scared, and lonely—so lonely with all the things I see and feel that no one else does.*

*Father lifts me gently in his arms and rocks me. I hear Gus mocking me as I fall asleep. He wants to be rocked; he can never be rocked. He tries to take over, but Father is too big and strong. Not even Gus is as big and strong as Father.*

Something changed after that. I can't really explain it, but everywhere I went, I could feel eyes on me. They watched me at school, at bedtime, during my playtime with the neighborhood kids. I think Mother talked to Father about having me go to a shrink (I didn't know what a shrink was, but I thought it might be a lizard). Father smirked at the thought. What on earth would a six-year-old have to say to a shrink?

"We really don't know her past," I overheard Mother say one night, which seemed weird to me. If anybody knew, it should be them, shouldn't it?

Father disagreed, insisting that I was too young. When Mother suggested a priest, he nearly blew a gasket. I heard him yelling over my favorite nightly cartoon, "If nothing's happened to her yet, it's bound to if you send her into the hands of those bastards! Don't you watch the news?" I army-crawled across the floor, peeking my head around the corner into the kitchen. Mother had a glass of wine, Father a small tumbler of whiskey.

"You know they aren't all like that," Mother countered, taking a sip. I liked the way the wine glass created a mosaic of color on the kitchen tile when the small chandler overhead bounced light off its faux crystals through glass. I stared at the dancing colors, mesmerized, waiting for Father to answer.

"If even one..." He paused to take of his own glossy liquid. "If even *one* of them...well...you know what I'm saying. You see it on the news all the time."

"Alright," Mother relented, "maybe not a Catholic priest. Maybe—oh hell, I don't know—Baptists? What about them? Are they any better?"

"You don't even believe in God," Father scoffed at her. "Why would you want to send her to a place that's going to force religion down her throat and probably try to exorcize her at the first sign of trouble?"

"I thought you wanted to get back into church?"

"I do. I miss it. But it's one thing to go and enjoy a service, and another to send our daughter to some unknown man who's going to do who-knows-what to her!" He took a breath, leaned back from my mother. "Maybe, if this behavior keeps up, and I'm comfortable enough with a specific pastor, we'll talk about it," he conceded, before adding, "but not a priest."

*Mother tips the glass up to her lips. She keeps the liquid in her mouth for a moment, almost like a cow chewing cud. She finally swallows and continues, "Something just doesn't seem right. I love her dearly, with all my heart, but I just wish we knew more."*

*Father nods in agreement, I wonder what it is they want to know more about. Maybe they know about the floating heads after all. Maybe they just want to learn more before telling me.*

*Father pushes back from his chair and walks to the freezer, where he pulls out a carton of strawberry ice cream. I hate strawberry ice cream, but apparently Gus does not.*

*"I don't know how you eat that with whiskey," Mother says, twirling the wine glass in her hands. The red shadows dance once more against the tile. I try to watch, but Gus forces my attention to the ice cream. In one short move, he pushes me up off my belly and over the kitchen threshold. Mother jumps, spilling some of her wine on the table and floor. I don't know why, but the drops remind me of blood.*

*Father begins to laugh. He holds out his big arms and invites me to sit with him.*

*Gus is gone. I think maybe Gus is afraid of Father. Come to think of it, Annie never shows up when Father is around, either. They have both misbehaved in front of Mother, but never Father. I look up at him. He's a very strong man. He does roofing for a living. I don't know what that means, but I do know that he's gone during the day and always home by dinner. His hands are big, the size of mitts. Maybe that's why they're so afraid of him—he could crush their weird, floating heads with his giant hands.*

*The thought makes me giggle. Father's skin is tanned from being in the sun all day. Even in winter, he has a tan. His hair is dark, unlike mine. Mine is gold, made from King Midas, Mother says, whose touch turned my hair and skin to gold. Father said I was made by God. I don't really know who either of those people are.*

*As I sit on his lap and watch him eat strawberry ice cream, I think some more about why* they *are afraid.*

3

## Chapter Three

The next month and a half passed with little incident. Even I couldn't blame Gus for stealing the turkey leg after Brother called dibs at Thanksgiving, and Annie only threw one fit during that time. I spent more and more time with Father. Instead of playing in my room after school, I'd sit by his feet and read my little books. *They* left me alone when I was there, but it upset them. At night, they'd both talk in my head simultaneously, murmuring in some language unfamiliar to me. It made sleep nearly impossible. I started playing jazz music to block them out. I still didn't like jazz, neither did Gus and Annie, but it kept them quiet. At least for a while.

During Christmas break, they got restless. I could feel it or, rather, I could hear it. The murmurs in that foreign language become louder, more urgent. Gus longed for all the new toys at the mall. He even slipped a small round stone into my pocket while we were out finishing our Christmas shopping. The guilt ate away at me, and I told Father about it before we left. Well, sort of. I told him I found it in my pocket. Father asked me if I put it in my pocket, and I lied, saying I had. He reminded me that stealing was wrong and made me take it back and apologize to the clerk.

Then Father told me about grace. He bought the stone for me and told me that, even though I didn't deserve it, I could have it because he loved me. Gus wasn't happy. Gus didn't want to have the stone anymore. Whatever grace was, Gus hated it.

That same night, Gus and Annie got into a fight. Gus wanted Annie to stand up for him at the mall. He thought she should have done something, but Annie said that it was a stupid rock. They yelled in my mind. Whatever brief friendship they had ended that night.

Their incessant arguments droned on, making sleep impossible. Giving up, I walked down the carpeted hallway to Mother and Father's room and tugged at his pajama sleeve. His eyes squinted open, a bit of surprise on the edge of his sleep. "What is it, Beauty?" he asked. I couldn't bring myself to tell him, so instead I said that I was scared (not entirely a lie) and asked if I could sleep in their bed. He lifted me up and over his body and placed me on the bed between them. Mother stirred but didn't wake. I shifted until my body was under the blankets and waited for Gus and Annie to start up again. They didn't. Finally, I was able to sleep, listening to the rhythmic breathing of Father's slumber.

Father let me sleep in bed with him and Mother until after Christmas. He then explained that, with school starting up again, we needed to get me back to being a big girl. Gus and Annie were giddy, thrilled to be alone with me again. They weren't scared of me like they were of Father.

That was the night Gus told me to steal the cookie. Annie had been quiet for a few days; it had mostly been Gus showing up, wanting things, feeling as though he deserved them and demanding that I take them. That particular night, though, he didn't make me do it; instead, he tried to convince me to do it myself.

With his floating head hovering up in the corner where the wall met the ceiling, he talked about the cookies—how good they were, how much we deserved one. I couldn't disagree; they were after all delicious cookies. He said I should take one, but I reminded him that Mother had said none tonight. He said that Mother didn't know what she was talking about; that she just wanted the cookies all to herself.

I almost believed him. But Mother was Mother, and I was me, and I knew it was bad to steal. Gus said that the cookies were technically mine, which made sense. Just like this was my house, those were my cookies. Then I remembered that, if I took the cookie, I'd have to lie to avoid punishment, and I would not lie.

It was then, as I firmly reminded Gus that I wouldn't lie, that Mother appeared at the door.

She stopped in the door way and asked me who I was talking to. I told her I didn't know, which was true—I didn't know Gus's true name at that point, and it would be a few more years before I'd give him (or any of them) a name. She looked concerned; I saw it in her eyes. She glanced at the corner where I was looking, then shook her head and left the room. A few minutes later, Father came down and said it was bedtime. As he tucked me into bed, he said that tonight we were going to try something new, a thing called prayer.

I didn't know what that was. He told me that prayer was just talking to God, thanking Him for all the things that He's given us and asking Him to guide us. I asked if Mother would come pray with us, but he said that she talked to God in her own way. I didn't believe him; their conversation about the priest was still fresh in my mind, and I remembered him saying Mother didn't believe in God. Why would you talk to something you didn't believe in?

Father said a prayer with me and tucked me into bed. That night, instead of the jazz music, he played a station that talked about God and Jesus and somebody called Lord. I didn't understand most of the words, but I did like the music. It was better than the jazz, at least.

Interestingly, I think Gus and Annie preferred the jazz. It might have kept them at bay, but at least it wasn't about God. They *hated* the God man. They begged me to turn the radio off, yet neither one could make me do so.

I decided I liked that music. I decided to listen to it more.

# Chapter Four

Things settled down for the rest of the year. My seventh birthday came and went. Annie and Gus still showed up periodically, but less often, and never while the radio was turned to the Jesus music. I even learned some of the songs, and when they did show up, I would sing as loud as my little voice could. They still weren't scared of me like they were of Father, but something about those songs made them leave. I thought the God man might have some sort of power. I decided to ask Father.

When I did, Mother rolled her eyes. She didn't believe in the God man or the Jesus that Father talked about. He told me how Jesus died on the cross to save us and forgive our sins. I didn't understand most of what he said (cross? sin?), but I nodded along as if I did.

Father told Mother that he was going to take me to church. Mother rolled her eyes again and reminded him that he had thrown a fit when she wanted to take me to a priest. Father countered, saying he wouldn't take me to the Catholic church but instead would find one that's "nondegominatal" (I don't know what that means). Mother finally relented and agreed to let Father take me.

*The following Sunday, Mother dresses me in my favorite dress, the one I wore for Easter. I'm not usually allowed to wear it for fear I'll get it dirty. She puts tiny, ruffled socks on my feet and lets me wear my nice shoes, the shiny black ones with a strap across the top. I like that I can see my face in them, even if it is a blown-up, balloon-looking face.*

*Gus and Annie are not happy. They say I shouldn't go to the church place. They say it's a bad place full of bad people. Hypocrites! they yell in unison. I don't know what that word means. Even though they aren't friends right now, they both agree that the church place is a bad place. They tell me about the hypocrites they used to know. They have funny names and are called Pharisees (whatever that means).*

*I feel moisture begin to form in the palms of my hand and wipe them vigorously together, my fingers turning pink. The excitement turns to something else, something hard that sits in my stomach. I don't want to go anymore. I don't want to meet the God man. I don't want to know hipacritz, and I most definitely do not want to see any funny-named-Pharisees. I'm trying to tell Mother that I don't want to go when Annie decides to help. She throws a fit, stomping, kicking the wall, throwing the hairbrush at Mother. Mother is not amused by the display.*

*I feel warmth wash over my face. I don't like it when Annie acts this way because Mother looks at me disapprovingly. I really want to please Mother. I want to be a good girl, but Annie won't let me.*

*Father hears the yelling and comes up to my room. Annie is gone; it's just me now. He squats down and takes my hand in his.*

*"Beauty, what's the matter?" he asks, a look of concern in his eyes. He's so patient. Mother gets annoyed, but Father doesn't. When I don't answer, he tries again, this time pulling me closer so our noses are almost touching. I want to giggle—his nose is so big in my eyes—but it doesn't seem right to giggle right now. Annie made a mess, and I have to clean it up. "Beauty?" he says again, the question oozing from the end of my name.*

*"I don't want to go to the church place!" All my fear bursts out. "I don't want to know about the God man! I don't want to see the hipacritz!"*

*Father looks up at Mother, then back to me. "Why don't you want to go, and who told you about hypocrites?"*

*I don't know how to answer. I can't tell him about Gus and Annie—his look of patience will disappear, and he'll look at me with annoyance like Mother does. "I don't know," I answer.*

*He doesn't believe me; I know he doesn't. "Okay. Forget about the hypocrites—why don't you want to go to church?"*

*His question pulls me up short. I have to think for minute about this because I really don't know. Annie and Gus said it was a bad place, but can it really be all that bad if the Jesus man lives there? I drop my head, my eyes fixed on one shiny black shoe (the other had been kicked off during Annie's fit).*

*"I'm scared," I finally whisper to my face in the shoe.*

*Father gently lifts my chin with his finger until my eyes meet his again. "There's no reason to be scared. Why don't we go this one time, and if you don't like it, we can leave?"*

*That seems like a good plan to me. I wait for Annie to show up again, but she's scared of Father. I wonder again what it is that scares them, but I'm sure it's because he's so big and strong—even stronger than Gus.*

*In the car, Father plays the same music that I listen to at night. I like the song and hum along. The trip is a quick one, but the whole way I'm filled with worry and excitement. What is the church place like? What do they do there? Will I get to see the Jesus man? I'd really like to see him, although I'm worried he's a zombie. Father said he was raised from the dead after three days. In the movies, when something raises from the dead, it's a zombie. I don't want to meet a zombie.*

*Worry has turned into full-blown fright by the time we get to the church. I expect that we'll walk into the building and be overtaken by zombies. Mother was right; I shouldn't have watched that movie.*

*When Father pulls me out of my booster seat, I see the church for the first time. It's not much to look at. A brown building with a high-pitched roof and pretty flowers lining the sidewalk. There are people going inside. They're dressed up in their nice Easter clothes, too. They don't look like zombies.*

*Father sets me on the ground and takes my hand. These people seem nice. Too nice. They smile and wave to each other and even to Father and me. I hope these aren't the hipacritz. I try to look at them closely, just to see if I can tell if they're zombies or hipacritz. I can't tell, and Mother always says it's rude to stare, so I drop my eyes and watch my face in my shoes as I walk.*

*When we get to the door, a tall, bald man is holding it open and greeting people. He seems nice. He shakes Father's hand and then offers his hand to me to shake. I look to Father, unsure of what I'm supposed to do. The man can sense my hesitation and instead asks for a high five. I can do a high five.*

*We go through another set of doors, passing more smiling people, and enter a big open space. There are tons of people standing around, eating donuts and drinking from little paper cups. They all look lovely, not like zombies. No, I don't think they're zombies. But maybe the Jesus man is.*

*Father talks for a moment with a man he knows, one of his crewmen. Apparently Crewman is the one who told him about this church. He offers us seats next to them during "service". The only service I've ever been to was my Nana's funeral. I wonder if church is a funeral for the Jesus man.*

*I see kids running around and want to go play with them, but I worry that they might be the hipacritz. Can a kid be a hipacritz? I don't know. I want donuts, but I don't want to interrupt his talk with Crewman. It's rude to interrupt—probably wrong, like stealing or lying. Instead, I hold tightly to Father's hand.*

*Finally, it's time to go through the wooden doors into the sanctuary (this place feels like it has its own language; maybe it's where they keep the Jesus man's body). We go through the door, leaving the donuts behind, and I see that the sanctuary is just a big room with rows and rows of chairs, all facing the stage up front. A young man with nice hair steps up to a microphone and welcomes everybody. He says it's time to worship the Lord. I don't know who the Lord is; maybe he's a friend of the God man and the Jesus man. Father follows Crewman to a seat a few rows back from the front. The rest of the band is now on stage, and they begin to sing a song. It's a song I know from the radio; I like this song.*

*I can't see the band over the tall people in front of me, so I drop down to my knees and scramble to the aisle (Mother wouldn't be pleased; she'd say it's improper to crawl on the floor in a dress). I don't want to leave Father's side, but I do want to see if the man at the microphone, the one with nice hair, is the Jesus man.*

*The song is about the Jesus man, how he died on the cross and how his blood (ew) covers us and makes us clean. I hope that they don't pour blood on us. I don't think that would make me clean; I think it would make me red and ruin my dress, and then Mother would be mad.*

*I watch the band from the aisle, sitting crisscross. A beautiful, red-headed lady is singing now. I like her voice. She sways along to the song, raising one hand in the air and calling out for her Father—the Jesus man? She says she's so thankful for all that we've been given and that his Spirit is welcome in this place. My ears perk up at that. I think Gus and Annie are bad spirits (they've been awfully quiet here, too), but maybe there are good spirits, too? I want to ask Father, but his eyes are closed, and he's swaying to the song, just like the lady.*

*By the time the next song begins, I've decided that I like this church place. This seems like a good place to be. The redheaded lady and the nice-haired man sing a song together. It's beautiful, and I feel something in my chest stirring. I can't really describe what it is, but it fills the place that Gus and Annie usually occupy. They aren't here right now. I don't think they're welcome in this place like the other spirit, the holey one. I wonder for a minute how a spirit could have holes but decide it doesn't matter; as long as this good spirit seems to be stronger than Gus and Annie, I like the good spirit.*

*The song ends, and the redhead invites everyone to say hello to the people around them while the nice-haired man strums his guitar. I'm pretty sure he's not the Jesus man, that'd just be weird. What type of man sings a song about himself? Probably a hipacritz. Father turns to me and says I can go back to the children's church now, but I start to worry. I don't want to. What if the holey spirit isn't in children's church? What if Annie shows up? What if all the children look at me and know that I'm bad? No. I don't want to go to the children's church. I want to be in this big room, where Father and the holey spirit keep Gus and Annie away.*

*I beg Father to let me stay. He says that I'll be bored. "I'll be good," I promise, pleading with him. He finally relents, and I climb back into the chair next to him. With everyone sitting, and with my head at the right angle, I can just manage to see the stage over the head of the woman in front of me.*

*The nice-haired man finishes playing guitar, and another man walks up the steps. He takes the microphone and says that we should give a shout of praise to the Lord. The room eagerly obliges, and I do too. It's fun to whoop indoors. Mother wouldn't like this; we have to use indoor voices at home.*

*Once the cheering dies off, the man welcomes the room. He mentions that he sees some new faces and that he's excited to get to know us. I don't really want to get to know him, though—he might be the Jesus man; he might be a zombie. He doesn't look like a zombie, though. He's wearing a light blue blazer (the type that Father wears when his boss has a dinner party), dark colored pants, and shiny shoes. I wonder if he can see his face in his shoes like I can in mine. The maybe-Jesus man talks about the upcoming baptism and communion (two more words I don't know) and reminds us that anybody who wants to be baptized or volunteer for communion should stop by the visitor's center and sign up.*

*Then the preacher starts to talk about the Jesus man. He tells us to open our bibles to Mark, chapter something.*

*I don't know who Mark is or what a chapter is, unless it's like the chapter books at school, which I haven't read yet. He starts to talk about how Jesus had disciples and how they went with him from town to town.*

*This is boring. Maybe I should have gone to the children's church.*

*I'm leaning my head back and drifting into sleep when, suddenly, I hear the maybe-Jesus man (although I'm seriously doubting it at this point) talk about the real Jesus man encountering someone possessed with an impure spirit—a demon. I sit up straight in my chair and listen intently as the preacher shares of the demon man living in the tombs and how nobody could bind him, not even with chains. This man would cry out and cut himself, but then, when he saw the real Jesus man, he had shouted, "What do you want with me, Jesus, Son of the Most High God? In God's name, don't torture me!"*

*Jesus had said, "Come out of this man, you impure spirit." Okay, so the Jesus man is the son of the God man and, like the God man, has some sort of power over the demons. I'm still not entirely sure what a demon is, but I'm pretty sure Gus and Annie are both it. It would explain why they don't like the church. Maybe the hipacritz aren't actually bad things, then. Maybe they just hate the hipacritz because they belong to the place where Gus and Annie can't go.*

*I like this place. I want to live here. The definitely-not-Jesus man on stage says that Jesus sent the legions into pigs, then the pigs ran off a cliff (I stifle a giggle at the image). He emphasizes that the Jesus man has authority over demons and impure spirits. I'm not entirely sure what authority is, but Mother says I have to respect it and listen to it. The Jesus man must be the boss, then. Over the demons? Maybe that means he is the boss over Gus and Annie. I wonder if I can find his office after the service. If he's the boss, then he must have an office, right?*

*When the not-Jesus man on stage finishes talking about the pigs, he says that, by the power of the holey spirit, we have the same authority over demons that the Jesus man had. He says that the holey spirit lives in us, and, with his power, we can cast out demons. I like the sound of that, although I don't know what "cast out" means. He asks the band to come back to the stage, where they play a light melody as he finishes. He tells us that God the Father loves his children so much that he sent his Son (the Jesus man) to the cross to die for our sins (I look quickly towards my father, hoping he doesn't get any ideas about sending me to die) and that, if we choose to accept it, his holey spirit would fill us as well. He tells us all to bow our heads and close our eyes, then says that, if we want to accept the holey spirit into our lives, we can do it right now by repeating the words after him. He asks the whole church to do the repeat thing. I don't know exactly what he's saying, but I try to keep up. He asks for anybody who needs to accept the holey spirit to lift their hands, assuring us that everybody else has their eyes closed.*

*I don't lift my hand. I already have two of these things; I need to learn more about them before I start inviting more in. But I think I'd like to come back next Sunday.*

*The band plays a happy song to wrap things up. They hoot and jump and lift their hands to the God man (he must live in the attic). Then, another man, not the not-Jesus man, but still probably not Jesus, climbs the steps. He thanks everyone for coming and tells us to have a blessed week. I don't know what that means, but it sounds nice, I nod in agreement. Yes, a blessed week.*

*Father talks to Crewman some more while I stand behind him, looking around the room. Above the stage, there's a big wooden T. Without thinking, I push through torrents of people heading the opposite direction to stand at the base of the stage and look up at it. The second not-Jesus man, the one who shared the story about the pigs and demons and the holey spirit, comes to my side and asks what I'm looking at. I tell him and ask him what the T is. He says it's a cross, like the one where Jesus lost his life. He introduces himself as Pastor Tim and says he has a daughter my same age; her name is Katie, she's home sick today, but he's sure that, if we come back next Sunday, she'd love to play with me after church. I say I'll have to ask Father, and he says he'd love to meet him, so I take him to where Father has just finished talking with Crewman.*

*Pastor Tim introduces himself to Father and says that he's so happy we could make it. They talk about things I don't really understand, and Father says that we'll be back next week. My stomach rumbles; I wish that I had one of those donuts. Father notices the noise and asks if I'm hungry, I nod. He thanks Pastor Tim, assuring him once again that we'll be back, then takes my hand to guide me to the car.*

*Back outside, the sun is shining high in the sky, and it's warm enough to take off my jacket. I fold it neatly and put it on the seat beside me. Father says this is a good sign. He says this summer will be a long one and that it will be a wonderful time.*

*We eat at McDonalds, and Gus and Annie don't show up once. I don't know what it is about this Jesus man's authority, but they don't like him, or the church, or Father. I get a chicken McNuggets Happy Meal with a coke. Mother doesn't like it when I have coke, but Father says I deserve it for behaving. Over the table, a fry dripping with ketchup in one hand, he asks what I thought of the service.*

*I'm hesitant to respond. I like the church place, and I'm glad there weren't any zombies, but the best part was that there was no Gus and no Annie. I can't exactly tell him that, so instead I say through a mouthful of nugget, "I like the Jesus man. I think I'd like to go back."*

*Father laughs, a big hearty laugh that fills the room with joy. "I like the Jesus man, too! I think we will go back."*

That night, Gus and Annie returned, and they weren't happy. They yelled and screamed in my mind in their weird language, although sometimes I caught bits and pieces in English, things like, *We'll stop it* and *We can't let this happen* and *This one is ours.* I heard a third voice, but I didn't recognize it. I turned up the radio, but it didn't help this time. They were too angry, fueled by their hatred of the Jesus man and the God man. I thought maybe they were worried the Jesus man would tell them to go into pigs. I hoped he would.

# Chapter Five

A few nights later, Mother and Father called Brother and me to the living room. They said they had great news: Mother was pregnant. We were going to have a little brother or sister.

My heart practically leapt from my chest. I hoped it would be a sister; it'd be like having a little baby doll. Oh, how I hoped for a sister.

Gus did not want a baby. He did not want to share Mother and Father's attention.

*Gus lashes out. It's unlike Gus to behave this way— Annie, yes, but not Gus, and especially not when Father is around. Gus moves my feet and storms us out of the room. I turn my head to look back as we climb the first step and see Father's shocked face. I don't like seeing it, but Gus doesn't care. Gus stomps, one foot in front of the other, down the hallway and slams my bedroom door. He yanks books off the shelves, throws stuffed animals all over. He does not want to share Mother and Father with a baby.*

They won't love us anymore, *he hisses in my mind. All their attention will go to this new baby. We'll be old news—nothing, capootz. No more Beauty.*

*Standing with piles of books and toys askew around me, I feel my shoulders drop. I don't want to go capootz. I hear a low whimper escape my lips and fight back the tears that threaten to run from my eyes.*

*I hear heavy footsteps outside the door. Gus leaves (of course he does; they always do), and I drop in a puddle on the floor, surrounded by the chaos he's left in his wake.*

*Father raps the door gently and twists the handle, saying, "Beauty, I'm coming in." I see his face tighten as he takes in the mess. He's disappointed. I hate disappointing him; I hate that Gus makes him disappointed in me. "Come sit on the bed," Father commands. I obey. "Beauty, what was that about?"*

*I don't know how to answer because, while I'm very excited for a baby sister, I can't tell him Gus isn't. Instead, I repeat what Gus said to me: "You won't love me anymore."*

*Father's face softens. "Beauty, we will always love you. You are God's special gift to us." I feel my lip begin to quiver, and I push my face into his chest and cry. I don't want Gus to be right; I want to believe Father, but babies are so cute, and I'm almost eight—what if they can't love me and the baby?*

*I hear him speak through my stifled sobs, "Did we love Brother any less when you came along?" I hadn't thought of that. I pull my face back, wiping my eyes with the back of my hand, and shake my head. They hadn't. Brother is a boy, and boys are gross, yet for reasons I can't understand, they love Brother just as much. If they can still love Brother...*

*Hope fills my soul. I look up at Father again. He's so strong and patient. "You'll still love me?" I ask. He nods. "Then I hope it's a baby sister." I say. A smile fills his face.*

That night, after Father tucked me in, the new voice grew louder. Her bobbing head appeared, just as nondescript as Gus's. Her voice reminded me of the teenage girls in movies. She warned me that I would have to be better than the baby if Mother and Father were going to keep loving me. She said that I had to *prove* that I was better.

This new voice was Priscilla (though I wouldn't call her that for a few more years) and she had what Mother called "a bad attitude". Priscilla loved to brag, telling me how she had taken down kings. However, Priscilla didn't like it when she noticed Mother glowing, or when Mother and Father would talk about things like baby names or where to put a crib. She would demand that I get their attention, making me spin around all silly-like or climb up on Father's lap and get in his face. Her favorite thing to do was to spill things on purpose so that Mother and Father had to stop what they were doing to help clean up.

Father said I was misbehaving. I agreed—I was not acting like a lady. Not like a Beauty.

## Chapter Six

Priscilla's presence continued to grow over the next several weeks. School was almost out; the sun was staying in the sky longer, and the days were growing warm. Father and I still went to church on Sundays (I joined Pastor Tim's daughter, Katie, in children's church; turns out the God man was there, too) while Saturdays were spent at the park with Mother and Brother.

It was in this season, one Thursday after school, that I came home to Father's truck in the driveway. It wasn't like him to be home so early.

*When I get inside, the lights are off. I hear a weird noise coming from upstairs. I climb the steps quietly, hoping they won't squeak under my weight. At the top of the stairs, I hear Mother weeping and Father telling her it's alright. He says, that they can try again. I don't know what that means, and before he can say anything more, Father spots me in the hall. He stands and walks to the door, and I think he's going to say hello, but he shuts it instead, silencing Mother's weeping.*

*Father's action makes Priscilla mad. She stomps and screams and wails. She does not like that he did not greet us. She does not like that he shut us out. She wants to be important, demands to be important.*

*Father opens the door. His face is hard, and his jaw is clenched tight. His eyes stare at me, unblinking. I'm not used to seeing that look; it scares me.*

*Priscilla disappears as Father takes my arm firmly. Without a word, he drags me down the hall to my room, picks me up, and sets me on my bed. "You will not move," he growls. Then he leaves the room, shutting the door firmly behind him.*

*Priscilla's head reappears, bobbing in the corner near where the wall meets the ceiling. I'm surprised it's not Gus. I think I expected Gus, what with Mother getting all Father's attention; he doesn't like that. But no, it's Priscilla. She tells me that I wasn't good enough, that I must be better. Then she blames Mother, saying this is all her fault, with her weeping and wailing. She says Mother is just hormonal. I don't know what that means; I don't understand anything that's happening*

*That night, Mother doesn't come down from her room. Father's face is still hard when he gets me from my room. He tells me that I may sit at the table and do my homework while he makes dinner—macaroni and cheese, my favorite.*

*Priscilla says loudly that macaroni and cheese is for children, whereas at nearly eight, I'm practically grown and don't eat children's food.*

*"Enough!" Father roars, his voice filling the whole house. "I'm sick and tired of your whining! Not everything is about you." His voice drips with disdain. I don't know how to make him understand—I know that Priscilla is being naughty; I'm very hungry and really do want macaroni and cheese, but Father just sends me to bed. He says if I'm only capable of complaining, then he doesn't want to be around me.*

*In my room, Priscilla again blames Mother and the baby. Gus is there too—not his head, just his voice. He agrees with Priscilla; I think they're friends. I want to turn on the radio, but Father said I was not to leave the bed. Instead, I dig under the covers and pull the pillows over my head, but the pillows can't block out their voices in my mind.*

*They hate Mother. They hate the baby. Most of all, they hate Father. They try to convince me that he is bad. I don't believe it, though. I know they are scared of him, but he's not bad to me. Priscilla reminds me how he treated us.* How dare he send us you to your room without food, *she hisses. I want to tell her it's her fault. I want to tell her that maybe, if she'd just eaten the food, we'd be full and comfortable and not banished to bed, but I don't. It's bad enough that they're yelling in my head—I don't need them yelling at me too.*

The next day, Father kept us home from school. Grandma came to stay with us while Father took Mother to the doctor. Grandma's face was grim. I didn't understand what was happening, and she wouldn't tell me. Priscilla didn't like that; Priscilla thought we deserved to be told. She wasn't scared of Grandma, not like she was of Father. She demanded to know what was going on and threatened to scream if she wasn't told.

*Grandma sighs that she's too old for this, and warns me that, if I don't behave, I'll be sent to my room. Priscilla insists that she's not a child, but Grandma says that's exactly what I am, so Priscilla lets out a blood-curdling scream. She doesn't seem to be as limited by my vocal cords as Annie is.*

*The noise comes from deep in my chest and grates against my ears. Grandma's hands are clasped tightly over her ears. I can see her mouth moving, ordering me to stop. Then Brother comes running down the stairs, grabs a couch pillow, and swings it at my head.*

*Priscilla is gone. I'm on the ground in shock, Brother standing over me. He's twelve and has gotten very tall. "Shut UP, you stupid head!" he growls at me. "Don't you know anything? Mother lost the baby." I don't know what that means—how could she lose it? He sees the confusion on my face, and his shoulders drop. I'm only seven; that's easy to forget when Priscilla is demanding that I'm not a child. But I feel like a child right now—so very, very small. I start to cry. Brother thinks I'm hurt.*

*I'm not hurt. I am hurt.*

*Priscilla continues to hiss in my mind. I don't like her.*

*Brother stands awkwardly to the side while Grandma comes and lifts me from the floor. "You can't behave like that, Beauty," she reprimands. "That's a very ugly way to behave. Your mother and father are very sad right now, and they need you to behave. If you want to be treated like a big girl, you need to act like one."*

*I don't really want to be treated like a big girl. I don't want to know why a curtain of sadness has fallen over the house. I don't know how the baby got lost. I don't want Grandma to be here; I want Father. I don't want to hear Mother weep.*

*I nod anyway.*

*Grandma asks if we'd like sandwiches for lunch. Priscilla does not want sandwiches, and I do not want to deal with her, so I shake my head and climb the stairs to my room. I turn the radio on to the Jesus music and bury my head under my pillow once more. But it doesn't work on Priscilla; she doesn't stop talking.*

Brother came to my room a short while later to apologize. I cried. Unsure of what to do, he left, only to return minutes later with a brownie for me. He set the plate on my bed. I cried again.

Later, I heard Mother and Father come home. I didn't want to see them. I didn't want to know what was so bad that Mother cried and had to go to the doctor. I had heard about cancer—my friend Cynthia's dad had it. He had to go to the doctor a lot. Did Mother have cancer? Was that how she had lost the baby? Would it somehow make her and Father lose me too?

Gus was happy there wasn't going to be a baby. He liked being the baby.

*Sometime later, after Grandma has left, I hear Father calling from the bottom of the stairs, telling Brother and me to come down. I don't want to go. This is it; I know they're going to tell me that Mother has cancer. I don't know what cancer is, but I know I don't want her to have it.*

*I hear Brother's door open and close. His room is further down the hall than mine; if he can hear Father call, then so can I. I drop my feet to the floor, moving slowly. There's no Gus, no Annie, no Priscilla, but there is a new voice. I don't recognize it, but I feel it: fear. A fear that bites at my gut. I don't want to go out the door; I don't want to go down the stairs; I don't want to hear that Mother has cancer.*

*Footprints approach my door—light, not heavy like Father's. Brother opens my door. "Come on," he beckons. The fear isn't gone, but somehow, with Brother in the room, it's not as bad. I follow him down the stairs. He's so much taller than I am that I have to jog to keep pace with him.*

*Mother is sitting at the kitchen table, Father standing beside her. Whatever makeup she'd had on is now stained black under her eyes. She wipes a tissue over her face. Father squeezes her shoulder.*

*"I can't," she says simply. Instead, Father tells Brother and me to sit at the table. They did this same thing when Nana died, only that time it was Father's face puffy from emotion.*

*The new voice is back. It's quiet, unlike the others. He doesn't say much, just that this is it—this is when they tell us that Mother has cancer, that she is going to die.*

*Father sits beside Mother and takes her hand. "We lost the baby," he says simply. I watch Brother nod his head knowingly and do the same, even though I don't know, don't understand. But something in my face must give me away because Father asks me if I understand what that means, locking my eyes in his gaze.*

*I don't, but it doesn't seem right to admit, so Brother says what I can't: "No, she's stupid. She doesn't know." Father turns his gaze to Brother. If daggers could come out of eyes, it would have happened that day.*

*I'm still nodding, but I don't know why. Mother starts to tremble in her chair. Brother, knowingly, gets up and gets a glass and a bottle of wine. I think wine is some sort of cure for grown-ups.*

*Mother sets the glass on the table with shaking hands. She takes Brother's hand in her own briefly. I don't think she can speak to thank him, so this small gesture will have to do. She tries to meet my eyes, and she can't. The new voice tells me this is my fault, I've made Mother sad. That doesn't make sense to me, but she won't look at me, so maybe the voice is right. Father takes her free hand again and squeezes, as if putting his strength into her. He goes on to tell me that the baby has gone to heaven—it won't be coming to live with us after all.*

*Mother rolls her eyes at his choice of words. She quickly finishes her glass of wine and pours another. Father tries to explain what he expects of us: we are to be good children; we are to behave and not cause any grief while he's at work. Mother finishes her second glass and pours a third.*

*The shaking in her hand has stopped, but her tongue seems thick. The tears start again. I wonder why they sent the baby to heaven instead of bringing it home.*

*Eventually, she can't stay anymore, and she stumbles to her room, leaving the three of us at the table, Brother with a knowing look on his face, Father's eyes soft and gleaming. He assures us that we'll be okay, Mother just needs time.*

*I leave the kitchen and sit on the floor in the living room with a Barbie doll. The new voice whispers that Mother won't be fine. It says that this is my fault. It gnaws at my intestines, twisting and turning, until a hard ball forms. I want to cry, but I don't know why. Crying seems like the right thing to do. I really wanted that baby—a sister. An adorable little sister, as cute as a doll.*

*Gus, of course, is thrilled that there's not a baby. Priscilla hears Brother and Father talking and is upset that we're not included. We're big now, she demands, and despite my efforts, she drags me back to the kitchen.*

*I overhear Father saying Mother has a hostile 'room' (whatever that means). He explains that when Brother was born, there were complications that led to an emergency c-section. He says the scar tissue from that made it impossible for Mother to carry the baby. It seems odd to me that Mother would have trouble carrying a baby; she still carries me from time to time.*

*Priscilla is still upset. She wants to stomp and scream, to demand to be a part of this conversation, but she doesn't drag me forward. She tries, one slow step after another, right to the archway into the kitchen, but she can't carry me across the threshold to the tile. I stand, bare feet in the thick carpet, and Father looks up. There's sadness in his eyes that I've never seen before.*

*"Come here, Beauty," he says, patting his lap. Priscilla doesn't want to. The new voice says it's not right, I'm in trouble, not to go. But somehow, in his gaze, I see a sort of need in Father's eye. He needs me to comfort him, and the voices can't stop him. Even this new voice is afraid of him.*

*I wonder again what type of power Father has over them.*

The following day was Sunday. I was excited for the church place. All night, the new voice (Fred) had murmured, telling me that Mother had cancer, that that's what C-section meant. I told myself he was lying, but I still couldn't unclench the knot in my gut. I needed the holey spirit again. I needed the voices to stop. I made a plan: I'll sit in the big room with Father, listen to not-Jesus talk about the real Jesus, and maybe just fall asleep. I hadn't sleep well at all.

*I pull a lavender dress from my closet. Not the Easter dress I wore that first week—this dress has a soft floral design and lace on the sleeves. I think I wore it for the first day of school. It feels tight, just a little too small. I put on a pair of white leggings and grab my soft white sandals. They're made of gel and have glitter. I grab my hairbrush and a lavender bow and head down to the kitchen where Mother is sipping a cup of coffee. There are dark circles under her eyes, and her whole face is puffy. When I take the hairbrush and bow to her, she stares at them, as though not sure what I want from her.*

"It's Sunday," I say, trusting that to explain it all.

Father comes to the kitchen and sees me. "Beauty, leave your mother alone."

I don't understand. "Can I wear a bow for church?" I ask. Father looks to Mother. Her face has twisted, almost a snarl.

"You aren't going to that place," she hisses. I don't know how to respond. Priscilla doesn't like that Mother is talking down to us; Annie is ready to put up a fight; but they're hesitant. I wonder what would have happened if Father wasn't in the room.

He glances at me, then her. "Will it really hurt?" he asks. "I'm going anyway—why don't I just take her with me?"

Mother looks at me pointedly, a look that tells me to leave the room. Priscilla is unhappy; she drags my feet as I try to walk away. She's not bold, but she's putting up as much of a fight as she dares in Father's presence.

"Scoot," he says. I do—out the archway, back to the carpet, where Priscilla promptly freezes my feet. I'm stuck like concrete, like in the movies where the bad guy seals the other guy in concrete shoes, only I'm not being dropped to the bottom of the deep blue. Instead, I'm stuck eavesdropping. Not that I mind.

Mother says she doesn't want me at "that place". Father tries to argue, but she cuts him off: "You really want her to go to a place that worships some fake man in the sky?" (I thought the God man was in the attic at church, never *thought he'd be in the sky; that seems dangerous, with planes and birds and whatnot).*

*"He's not fake," Father rebuts.*

*Something in Mother's voice changes—it's high-pitched, almost desperate. "So your God would let this happen to us?" she squeaks.*

*Father doesn't respond. I hear the tap-tap of his shoes on the tile. He nearly runs into me coming out of the kitchen. I pretend like I'm walking past the arch. Priscilla is gone.*

*"Beauty," he begins, "this week you're going to stay home with Mother." Priscilla and Annie are thrilled, somewhere down deep inside me; they don't want me to go to the church place.*

*"But," I whine, "I want to see the Jesus man."*

*Father sighs. "Sometimes," he says, "mothers feel like they don't have control, and that can make them sad. When they feel that way, it's best to let them control the small things, like you going to church. Just give it some time. You'll be going with me again in no time."*

I never did.

# Chapter Seven

Several months passed, and the new voice became a frequent companion. Fred wasn't like the others; he held me from the inside—never bursting out, never making a scene. I think he was the boss of the others. Like with Father, when Fred was around, they stayed away. He often showed up in my dreams, or what Mother called night terrors. Of all of them, he was the only one who had a face that you would describe as a demon's.

In my dreams, he took me to the heaven place. The baby was there. It was sad. It asked why it couldn't have Mother and Father and told me it was my fault it was gone. I don't think it was really the baby, though; Fred often liked to play dress up in my dreams. He also liked to make me fall from things. He'd tell me that Mother was mad at me, that it was my fault, and then send me tumbling off a cliff, over a balcony, or sinking to the bottom of a pool.

In one particularly bad nightmare, he sent me backwards off the high diving board at the middle school, where Brother had swim meets. It was so high, and I fell down, down, down into the pool. Looking up, I saw at the inky faces of the spectators who'd come to cheer on the swimmers, but they took no notice of me. I kept going down, until my back hit the bottom of the pool. I felt my lungs burning, overwhelming fire forming in my chest, until finally, unable to hold it anymore, I gulped in the chlorinated water.

Gasping, I flung up from my bed. My sheets were soaked; I'd wet my pants.

Priscilla's bobbling head showed up. She shamed me, told me what a stupid child I was to have wet the bed at my age, no less. A new pit formed in my stomach. What would Mother think? Priscilla didn't have to say much more to send me spiraling to clean up the mess. I quickly pulled the sheets and comforter off the bed and snuck past their room, slowly down the dark steps (the sun had not come up yet) and to the laundry. I'd never started laundry before, but it didn't seem like it would be too hard. Briefly, I wondered if I should wake Mother, but then Priscilla reminded me how mad she'd be, how she'd look at me and call me a baby or maybe even a bad girl.

So, I pulled the stepstool from beside the refrigerator and dragged it to the laundry room. Carefully I climbed it, my arms full of the pungent sheets. I dropped them in and turned the dial like I'd seen Mother do a hundred times. I scooped out the white sandy stuff and dumped it in—adding a second scoop, just to be sure. I paused, then I took off my pajamas and underwear and threw those in too. Naked, I stood in the laundry room, feet on cold tile, watching as the machine filled with water and bubbles.

As soon as I was certain the sheets were sufficiently saturated, I closed the lid and stepped down.

I pulled fresh underwear and a night shirt from a basket on the floor and dressed again. Priscilla reminded me that I'm gross, disgusting, shameful to Mother. Bed-wetting at our age? She'd asked, but it wasn't a question; it was an accusation. Fred showed up too, fretting that Mother would be furious, Father disappointed. He insisted that we needed to stay up, wait until the load was done, put the sheets in the dyer and get them back on my bed before Mother and Father woke. I peeked into the kitchen. The microwave showed 3:48. How long would this take?

I waited as long as I could, trying hard to keep my eyes open, but eventually, I fell asleep on the cold tile, using one of Father's sweaters as a pillow.

I woke to my parents looking down at me, concerned. Blinking the sleep from my eyes, I peered back and forth between their faces. This was it. They were going to be so mad at me. I knew I'd failed; I was supposed to stay awake, to put the sheets in the dryer, but now they'd know.

*"Beauty?" Mother asks (she looks tired, so tired). "Why are you down here? Why are you sleeping on the floor?"*

*Fred returns, back to his tricks. He doesn't seem to mind that Father is there—not today, at least. He clutches my lungs, like he had in the dream. Don't look at them. They are so mad, he says in my mind.*

*Father, in the way that he so often does, drops to the floor beside me. "Beauty, what are you doing?" His eyes are mixed with curiosity and concern.*

*"I made a mess," is all I can muster. Mother looks around the kitchen, then takes a few steps backwards to look in the living room. When she sees it, clean as always, she shakes her head no at Father.*

*"What mess?" he asks me.*

Bed-wetting? At your age? *Priscilla's disgusted voice echoes in my mind.*

*"Beauty?" Father asks again. I want to tell them; I really do. I'm desperate to tell them about the dream, about falling deeper and deeper until I can't breathe, but Fred's captured my tongue, stopped my lungs from working as they should. My face is getting tight.*

*I'm a bad girl, a very bad girl.*

*"Beauty, breath!" Father demands, and it breaks Fred's control over me. He isn't gone, but he can't hold me any longer.*

*Father has his hands on my shoulders, his eyes searching mine, pleading silently for me to explain. Finally, I let out a short cry. I'm so embarrassed. I almost break; I almost tell them everything, but Fred whispers to me that they'd lock me up, put me in the looney bin, just like they did to old Aunt Arlene. I didn't want to go to the looney bin. So instead, I say that I had a bad dream (which is true). I say that I was drowning (which is true) and that I wet myself (which is true), but I don't tell them about the face, the floating heads, or the cement shoes. No I don't tell about that.*

*Mother stifles a laugh. That seems like a weird response to me.*

"You're not mad?" I ask.

"Oh, Beauty," she says, pulling me up to her and running her hand through my curls. "No, I'm not mad. I just wish you would have woken us. We could have helped." Now I'm even more confused. Priscilla said she'd be mad, but she's not. "How about a bubble bath?" she asks. "A birthday bubble bath."

That's right. It's my birthday. I'm eight years old today.

Chapter Eight

Things stayed much the same for the next several years. I'd have random, unexplainable outbursts, which lead to quick glances between Mother and Father, looks that asked what was really going on. Annie and Gus became less and less vocal, but Priscilla and Fred picked up the slack. Priscilla was always outspoken and eager to be heard, whereas Fred was quieter, stirring somewhere deep. But Fred was the boss. At times, he'd silence Priscilla, preferring to allow his weight to hold me down or push me back. Other times, he'd sit back and allow her outbursts, content to whisper in my mind how it made me theirs.

Around age thirteen, Oscar showed up. He wasn't as bad as Fred, but he did seem to take everything seriously—and personally. Mother excused it, saying it was typical teenage behavior, but Father was skeptical. Oscar would have me stomping up the stairs at the slightest look or adverse tone, often (more like usually) when I didn't want to go stomping up the stairs. That was the point at which Brother gave up on me—and who could blame him? He told Mother once that they'd picked a dud and should have returned me. I didn't understand what he meant, but Oscar and Priscilla were both outraged and screamed at him

I thought a lot about church and the Jesus man over those years, but Mother was relentlessly against it, saying that he took the baby to the Heaven place, that it was *his* fault. That didn't seem like something the Jesus man would do, but she was so sure, and Oscar agreed. We couldn't go to the Jesus man's house if he was a taker of babies. Fred also thought it would make Mother hate us, so I settled for listening to the songs about Jesus when Mother wasn't around. It helped keep the voices at bay, although it no longer silenced them completely.

In August, Mother's father passed away. They weren't close and, according to Brother, hadn't been since I was born. Brother said it was because "Good ol' Gramps" couldn't handle that I was mixed (I didn't fully understand that either…mixed with what?) and said that Gramps had used a word that sent Mother out the door, never to return. When I asked what the word was, Brother started to tell me, but Father caught him in the act and silenced him with one look. Father said that I was his golden girl, kissed by the sun, but that some people didn't understand that. He said that old-school thinkers had it in their mind that things ought to be a certain way and that I pushed those boundaries. For a brief moment, I was certain that he knew about the voices, their floating heads and deep whispers. I thought to ask, but Fred reminded me of the looney bin.

It seemed strange that they wanted to drive all the way to Oregon for the funeral of someone Mother hadn't seen in over ten years, but Father said that even though he was a crotchety old jerk, he was still Mother's dad, and we would all be going to support her—not for him.

So, we packed our bags, loaded the truck, and settled in for the ten-hour drive. The *others* were not happy (*others* seemed like safe thing to call them; besides, I still wasn't exactly sure what they were and was starting to think I did belong in the looney bin).

The first few hours were fine. I had my snacks and a book, Brother had his game, and Father and Mother chatted, their voices barely carrying to the backseat. Father even had the radio set on an oldies station. It was almost relaxing until Brother pushed his backpack into my space.

It should not have been a big deal. But to Oscar, it was unacceptable, an outrage, the crime of the century, and he made sure everybody in the car knew it. Thirteen-year-old vocal cords are much stronger than those of a six-year-old, and Oscar used every bit of their strength to scream and yell at Brother, whose face showed both shock and anger. Oscar let out a few words that I'm certainly not allowed to say, implying that Brother was the child of an unmarried mother (to put it nicely). I don't know what all was said or how long it went on for—I went into a weird, semi-conscious blackout. I knew what was happening in the most general of senses, but I remained outside of it.

Finally, I heard Father's voice—so calm, so quiet. "Beauty," he said, again and again. Not mad, not panicked, just calm. "Beauty."

His face slowly came into focus. Oscar was gone. Fred was laughing, if you could call it that. Priscilla was embarrassed. I blinked, looking around the car. Mother had tears in her eyes, Brother's face was bent in a grimace, and his body was pushed back into the car seat as far as it could. I glanced out the window and saw that we were stopped on the side of the highway. I turned my eyes back to Father, who was saying something. "What?" I mumbled, still feeling dazed.

"You need to apologize," he repeated. Priscilla hated that. Why should we have to apologize when Oscar did it? I felt my lips tighten as Priscilla prepared to fight back (although I wasn't sure I had any power left in my throat), but Father saw it and immediately jumped from the car. He opened my door, unbuckled me before I even realized what was happening, and pulled me into a giant bear hug, squeezing me so tightly that I could barely breathe.

It took a moment, but Priscilla eventually relented, and my body relaxed in his arms. As he held me, swaying from side to side, I could hear Mother telling Brother that this age was very hard for girls, that I had hormones now and it might be time for her to talk to me about them. Brother asked why they hadn't just given me back when they had the chance, and Mother scoffed, claiming that as soon as they saw me, they knew I was theirs.

That didn't make any sense. Of course I was theirs.

After several minutes, Father released me. Part of me wished we could have just stayed that way forever. The others didn't like Father, and for those brief moments, it was almost like they didn't exist. Father whispered that all was forgiven, that we were going to let this go for Mother's sake, but that we would have a conversation when we got home.

The rest of the drive was uneventful. Brother avoided eye contact with me. Mother's voice was cheery—too cheery, the type of forced cheer people put on when they don't know what else to do. Father turned the radio up and sang loudly (and poorly) to the sounds of the 80s. He wanted to play worship music, but Mother argued that nobody wanted to listen to that "Hallmark crap."

When we got to the hotel, Priscilla turned up again, this time over the sleeping arrangement. The room had two queens, and she felt very strongly that she deserved one. I tried to talk her out of it in my mind. The pull-out couch probably had fewer people who had slept on it, it was much cleaner, blah blah. She would have none of it. Brother argued that, as the eldest, he got the bed. Mother tried to reason with me, saying that I was the smallest and would be more comfortable on the pull-out than anyone else and that Brother was in fact the oldest.

Priscilla would hear none of it. She locked us in the bathroom after slamming the door shut. Oscar appeared in the bathroom, a floating head in the corner. At that point, it was rare for them to show up as heads, but apparently, the bed situation was worth it. He and Priscilla fed off each other, each pleading their case for why I should get the bed. It felt like an episode of Jerry Springer, with me caught in the middle. Eventually, Priscilla was so upset by the situation that she started howling. The childlike wails of a spoiled child came out of my mouth. I felt frozen, stuck, as I listened to her cries.

After some time, I heard a quiet tapping on the door. Priscilla relented long enough for me to open it. Father was on the other side. This time, the calm was gone from his eyes, and exhaustion was written on his face. "Beauty," he asked, "how many blowups are we going to have on this trip?"

I wanted to apologize. I wanted to plead with him not to give up on me, to beg him to pick me up and rock me, just one more time. Instead, my head fell. Priscilla was gone. Oscar's head no longer floated above the toilet. It was just me.

"Your mother and I will take the pull-out bed. Now, can we please go get dinner in peace? With no more outbursts?"

I slowly nodded my head and scooted by him without making any contact. The hotel room was empty. Apparently, Mother and Brother had decided to sit this one out in the car. We found a local diner and ate in near silence. I knew it was my fault, and I wanted to tell them how sorry I was, but Priscilla wouldn't let me. Priscilla said that we won.

Sometimes winning just didn't feel worth it.

After dinner, we drove back to the hotel in silence. We got ready for bed in silence. Father pulled out the pull-out bed and helped Mother make it in silence. Brother turned on the TV and found an old movie, one of Mother's favorites, and played it. It was the only noise in the room since we had returned.

I laid in that queen-sized bed and hated every moment of it. I didn't want this. I knew Father's body ached from his job and felt an overwhelming sadness at the thought of him sleeping on such an uncomfortable bed.

I wanted to jump up and apologize, to give up the bed and let my parents be comfortable, but Priscilla and Oscar kept me down. I felt glued to the mattress, unable to move and barely able to breathe.

When the movie ended, Brother turned off the TV, and I heard faint murmurings coming from Mother and Father.

"Do you think this is normal?" asked Mother.

"I'm honestly not sure anymore. It seemed like these outbursts were starting to pass at one point, but now they're worse than before," Father replied.

"Maybe it's just hormones?"

"You're the expert on that, " Father joked. "I know we talked about it a few years back, but what about counseling? Or maybe we try church again? She did really well when we were going to church."

I could hear the disgust in Mother's voice: "You know I don't want her going back to that place. And how can we send her to counseling without telling her everything?" Not telling me what?

"You're right, but maybe it's time. There's so much we don't know. What if something that happened before is impacting her now?" Before what?

"Maybe we give it just a bit longer, see if she grows out of it. If not, we may need more than just a counselor."

Father sighed. "Alright. But not too long."

That night, I met Louis for the first time. He bore with him a silent heaviness—a feeling of complete isolation, despite being surrounded by my family.

9

# Chapter Nine

The next day, at my grandfather's funeral, it was just the four of us and two old men from his combat unit in the army. Both of them gave me an odd look when we walked in and greeted Mother, Father, and Brother without extending a hand to me.

"Well, at least she's got her beauty," one of them scoffed as he walked away. I could feel Father tense up, like a lion ready to pounce, but Mother put her hand on his shoulder, gently pulling him back. She asked me if I was alright, which seemed like a strange question to ask. All the man did was comment on my looks; the whole family called me Beauty, so why was this any different? Their reaction implied that I missed something, but I wasn't sure what it was.

We walked to the front of the empty room, where the open casket lay. A wreath of flowers hung on one side, a picture of Grandfather, unsmiling, on the other.

"I thought Carol was coming," Father said, referring to my mother's sister.

"No," Mother responded, "she found an old Christmas card with a note where he was... well, being himself, and changed her mind. I think she hated him even more than I did." I don't know how, but somehow, I felt like the *others* would have liked Grandfather.

The lights dimmed, and the community center's minister stepped up to the wobbly microphone to begin the eulogy. For a moment, I wondered if he was the Jesus man from church, but it quickly passed. While the minister droned on about war and honor, Fred and Louis speculated about my own funeral. Fred worried that nobody would come while Louis whispered that I was just a burden on everyone around me. He reminded me of the night before when I was laying in bed, wishing that any one of my family members would notice my pleas for attention. He warned me that I was alone. Fred added it would be easier if I were the one in that coffin. How much better would Mother and Father and Brother be if I were just gone?

Priscilla showed up as well. She reminded me about the heaven baby, the one Mother had wanted so badly—more than she wanted me. They all began to talk at the same time, sometimes in English, sometimes their native language, always overlapping each other. Their words jumbled in my mind, swishing and turning like a tornado. They blamed me, scolded me, laughed at me, and told me I should just end it.

There, at my grandfather's funeral, I thought about suicide for the first time.

Tears rolled over my cheeks, slowly, then faster and faster, splattering on my folded hands. I dropped my head to hide from Mother, who was studying me from the corner of her eye. In my mind, I cried out for help, for comfort, for *something*, but once again, my silent pleas went unanswered.

*See?* Louis asked, his voice now the only one talking. *If they really cared, they would know that you needed them. But nobody knows, and nobody cares. They wouldn't even show up to your funeral if you died right now.*

With that, he was gone.

The minister's voice faded back in. He was saying some sort of prayer, commending Grandfather's spirit to the Lord. I kept my head down, trying as hard as I could to stifle the sounds that threatened to come out of my mouth, begging the tears to stop.

As soon as the minister uttered, "Amen," I felt Mother and Father shuffling to stand and collect their belongings. I quickly wiped my eyes on my sweater and hoped that they weren't too swollen. When I finally looked up, Mother's eyes were puffy, and her mascara was smudged. She had been crying, too. I suddenly felt a weight lift. It was normal to cry at funerals, I realized, even if you weren't close with the deceased.

As we walked down the aisle, one of the old men approached us again, causing Father to pull me in tightly. For a moment, I felt relieved, comforted by his strength. Then the old man said, "You know he never approved of *that*." Gesturing at me.

"Say one more word..." Father growled, staring into the old man's eyes. Daring him.

He instead turned to Mother. "I'm just saying. You had a choice, and you chose wrong. Ten years without talking to your own daddy... it's a damn shame." Father stepped forward, his hands clenched into tight fists, but Mother quickly jumped between them.

"The only shame here, Harold, is you showing up to an eleven a.m. funeral with whiskey on your breath." She held her head high as her eyes met his, unwavering. "Besides, I'd wager I didn't miss much of anything. Looking at you and Dan in your rumpled clothes and those deep bags under your eyes, I'd guess the three of you did nothing but drink for these past ten years anyway. Now, if you don't mind, I'm leaving with my family—the one I *chose* and would *choose* again." She pushed past him, her shoulder catching his, forcing him to step back.

With a smirk, Father followed, ushering Brother and me towards the door. He nodded stiffly to the other old man, presumably Dan, and we left.

"Way to go, Mom!" cheered Brother once we were outside. I still didn't know what had happened or why Harold didn't like me—maybe he just didn't like daughters—but I was thankful that Mother had chosen Brother and me over them.

The relief didn't last, though. All was well through lunch and the first part of the ride home. Then Fred showed up, and he brought Louis with him. I'm not sure they were exactly friends, but Fred certainly seemed to like him more than Oscar (which of course sent Oscar running to Priscilla, and those two together were something else—but I digress). The two of them chatted the rest of the ride home.

They continued their dialogue about my death. Louis pointed to the car door handle. *Pull it,* he hissed. *End it all right now. You'll slide out, and they won't even notice you're gone.* My mind fixated on that handle. The rest of the drive, all I could do was to stare at it. I memorized every part of it: the way the silver had smudged on the lever, the specks of some unknown substance (ice cream, if I had to guess) across the handle and part of the door, the shape of it that made me think of wings. I pictured doing what they said and pulling it, rolling out of the car, but rather than falling, two of my own wings unfurled, and I took flight. In this vision, they couldn't follow me. I looked down at them as they sat in the car, door bouncing open and closed, their muddled faces looking up at me, mouths hanging open in shock.

A pothole in the road pulled me from the sky and back to reality, where their voices caused a dull ache to form at my temple.

That night, home again, I crawled into Mother and Father's bed, something I hadn't done in years. The space in my head was getting smaller and smaller, and the voices louder and louder. Annie, Gus, Priscilla, Oscar, Fred, and now Louis, all crowded in there. But the worst was yet to come.

For several nights, I slept in their bed until, after one particularly brutal kick to Mother's shin, I was sent back to my own bed. Father delivered the news; no doubt Mother had flashbacks to the time I (or rather, Annie) kicked her in the jaw and wasn't willing to risk additional bodily harm.

Father tap-tap-tapped on my open door. I was finishing up the schoolwork I'd missed while gone for the funeral.

"Beauty," he began, coming into the room, "you know you are always welcome when you need us, and our door is always open for you, but you're just too big now to move into our bed full time. I'm sure your grandfather's funeral upset you—it upset us all—but it's time to sleep back in your own bed."

I waited. Surely one of the others would show up here. Being told what to do? Not getting what we want? But no, it was just me (this was the first time I realized that they weren't really about me).

"Beauty?" he asked. I realized that I hadn't responded—I was so used to someone else doing it for me.

"Um," I stammered. I didn't know how to respond. They were quiet when I was near him. With six of them crammed in there now, there was a constant barrage of noise in my mind, demanding, threatening, reminding, holding me hostage. But when I was with Father, there was silence. Peace.

"'Um' isn't a response," he joked, looking into my eyes, knowing that there was something, but not knowing what. "Talk to me, girl."

I wanted to. I was desperate to. For the second (maybe third) time in my life, I was ready to spill it all. To tell him about all of them, the way their words wrapped around my wrists and ankles, invisible chains that held me up like a marionette doll, making me stomp and scream. Their symbolic hands up my backside, forcing words out of my mouth, while floating heads took a sip of water from the corner and bowed to the audience. I wanted to tell him how I was my very own freakshow, with six ringmasters controlling my every act. Cue the circus music.

I stared at him, longing for him to understand somehow without my having to say it. I knew it wouldn't make sense—there's no way to make floating heads sound logical—but I needed him to know. Truthfully, on some level, I think he did. I think he noticed something in my eyes, the way my mouth twitched, trying so hard to form words.

But I couldn't. My lips were pressed firmly together by something greater than myself. Fred's voice warned from a great distance of the nut house. Louis chimed in about how I'd always be alone. How I deserved to be alone. Oscar was just mad that they dared to kick me out of their room, even though he didn't want to be in there in the first place.

"Okay," was all I could muster. He searched my face, trying hard to pull something from me. I watched as his eyes narrowed (for a moment, I thought that one of them had goofed, shown themselves to him—a tiny glimmer that didn't belong). But then his shoulders fell.

"Okay," he echoed, pushing himself up off the bed. "Well, good night, then." As he walked towards the door, I could feel the words forming somewhere in my heart. Priscilla could feel them too. She stuck out my jaw defiantly and locked my mouth closed.

But I knew. I knew if I didn't say something then, I would never be able to say anything. I forced my mouth open; she forced it shut. Teeth ground through the smooth surface of my lip. I tasted blood and experienced an urgency I'd never felt before.

"Father!" I nearly shouted. "I—I think I'm afraid." He stopped in the doorway. Looked back at me. Tried to decide if he should come back or stay put, as though maybe if it was his distance that had allowed me to open up (if only he knew the truth).

He settled against the doorjamb. "Scared? Of what?"

"Of them."

"Of who?"

"The *others*." It was the first time I'd ever referred to them as anything out loud. They were furious, shouting what I can only imagine were curse words in their native tongue.

"Oooh. I see," he said, stepping back into the room. "Beauty," he sighed, "there will always be people who don't like you or understand you for a variety of reasons. Harold and Dan—well, they just come from a different time and a different place." He took a breath, collected himself, then continued. "It's not an excuse. They shouldn't judge you for any reason. What's important is that you know who you are. You are my daughter. You are Mother's daughter. No matter what, *that* is who you are. If that's not enough, just remember what you learned in Sunday school."

"About Jesus?" I asked, unsure where this was going or what *they* had to do with Harold or Dan.

"Yup, and God. You are God's daughter, and that makes you a princess. So when people like Harold and Dan have something to say about you, you just remember who you belong to. First, they gotta go through me. If I can't take them on, they have to go through your Father God, and nobody is going to win that battle." He chuckled at himself. I still didn't know what Harold and Dan had to do with any of this, but I thought that maybe Father's words would apply to the *others* anyway. "Just remember to pray, Beauty. He hears you, just like I do. Even sometimes when it doesn't seem like there's anybody out there, *He is.*" Father emphasized those last words like they held all the power in the world. Pray? That's what the pastors and Sunday school teachers do (not to mention the weird families at McDonalds after church).

"How would you like it if we prayed together right now?" he offered. I wasn't sure how to answer, so I nodded slowly. "Okay, take my hands." I did, and he began: "Our dearest Heavenly

Father, we come before You tonight with hearts full of gratitude for everything that You've done for us and the way You've bought and kept us together. Tonight, as our little Beauty is feeling some fear, we ask that You comfort her with Your goodness and Your light and plant the truth in her heart that fear cannot exist in the light. We banish her fear in Your name and pray protection over her and over our family and our house. Amen."

I felt him squeeze my hands but dared not open my eyes. The voices that had fought so diligently through the prayer were silenced. I felt light for the first time in years but was afraid that the moment I opened my eyes, they'd be back.

"Beauty?" Father nudged. I finally opened my eyes and looked at him. His face was so calm, so gentle. "If you need to come in our room, you can, but why don't you try sleeping in here tonight? We'll turn on some worship music and leave the hallway light on."

"Okay," I agreed, fighting back tears of relief.

That night, I learned that the others hated prayer. While it didn't keep them away forever, it certainly gave me temporary peace. I sensed, not for the first time, that they hated the God man and the Jesus man. I just didn't know why.

For a while, things were better. I found that a prayer timed just right could silence them—at least Annie, Fred, and Louis. The others were more difficult to control. I learned to mitigate the outbursts, which made it easier to blame puberty and hormones (when Mother had the talk with me, I don't think she realized she was giving me the greatest excuse I could have asked for).

I finally started to feel some semblance of normal. I finally started to breathe. Until...

# Part II

**When Everything Changed**

10

# Chapter Ten

Two years later, everything changed.

Several weeks after my fifteenth birthday, I noticed a change in Father. It was the type of change that had happened over several months, but you don't necessarily notice when you lived with that person. I'd gone away to a school retreat over the weekend, and when I came back, he didn't look like himself. He seemed smaller to me. His face was tight; there were wrinkles around his eyes, and his brows were furrowed. He tried to smile when I got in the car, but it didn't seem real. When we got home, he tried to lift my bag out of the trunk but couldn't. He looked at me sheepishly, and I knew I had to play it off.

"The bus driver said mine was the heaviest of all!" I joked, pulling it from his hand.

Fred showed up, that gnawing feeling deep in my stomach warning me that something was wrong—something was definitely wrong. Priscilla and Oscar showed up too, saying that we'd been lied to, that Mother and Father knew what was happening and they'd kept it from us.

They didn't seem to be scared of Father anymore.

Once inside, Father went straight to his chair, practically falling into it. His breathing was labored. I ran up the stairs, skipping two at a time. Mother sat on the edge of their bed, folding laundry and watching a soap opera.

"Mom!" I cried out, breathing heavy myself. "I think there's something wrong with Dad. Hurry!"

Mother raced down the stairs and dropped to the floor next to Father's chair. I lingered awkwardly in the doorway, watching her. She whispered gently to him, moving her hand over his forehead and resting her fingers on his wrist.

"Beauty," she spoke softly, "call 911." I froze, paralyzed by confusion. What did this mean? What was happening? In that moment, Opi made his appearance.

Opi was like nothing I can explain or expect you to understand. He pinned me to my spot—heart racing, forehead clammy, sweat clawing its way down my back, breath catching in my throat.

"Beauty, look at me." Mother's voice was gentle. I could hear Father's labored breathing, and my eyes were glued to his face, taking in every feature: the width of his nose, his strong jaw, his high forehead. "Beauty, I need you to look at me." I tried to move my eyes to her, but I couldn't. Opi warned me, said I needed to remember this; he urged that this was the end.

One last time, Mother called to me, her voice pleading with me, so I forced my eyes to meet hers. "Call 911," she repeated.

Finally able to move, I ran to the kitchen phone and did as she asked.

When the operator asked what my emergency was, I hesitated, unsure how to respond, not wanting to say what I feared. "I think he's dying," I managed. She asked my name, my age, and who was dying and said that an ambulance was on the way. Then she asked more questions about Father, and I didn't know how to respond. *How long has he been sick, what were his symptoms*—all questions that I should have been able to answer. Was I that self-involved that I hadn't noticed an illness eating away at my father? The weight hung heavily on my shoulders.

When the EMTs arrived, they hooked Father up to their oxygen machine and took his temperature. They assured us that there was no outward evidence of trauma. They asked how long he'd been like this, and Mother answered, saying he'd been feeling worn out lately but assumed he'd caught a bug.

While she talked with them, I was trapped in a mental cage, as Fred and Opi assaulted me with their declarations of 'truth.' They reminded me of my failure as a daughter; that this was *my* fault; that I could have done something to prevent this; that Mother would never forgive me; that I would be abandoned again; that I would lose my family again. My knees buckled under me, and I saw the world flash upward as they whispered to me that this was the end. His end.

When I woke, one of the EMTs stood over me. "Just a panic attack," he determined. "No need to load her up. Let's get her to the couch, then we need to get him to the hospital."

*Just had to be the center of attention, didn't you?* Fred accused. The paramedics moved me gently to the couch. Mother sat near me, holding my hand.

"Beauty, you need to be strong," she implored. "Brother is at a wrestling match—I need you to call the school and tell them what's happened. He can come pick you up and bring you to the hospital. I'm going to ride with Father in the ambulance. Beauty, do you understand? I *need* you to be strong," she repeated.

I slowly nodded my head, forcing my brain to take in what she'd said, and just like that, they left, rushing Father to the hospital.

I called Brother and told him what had happened. Then I just drifted around the house, a shadow clinging to my mind. I was filled with an expectant sort of dread, the type that tells you everything is about to fall apart. It wasn't just fear; it was a weight that pushed me down into the deepest part of my mind, the part where nightmares live.

It was Opi.

When it was Fred, you knew. He was subtle, not acting out like Annie or Gus or even Priscilla, but you always know when it was him holding on. You'd be less likely to cross a street because he'd warn you that you could get hit by a car. You wouldn't join the talent show to sing your favorite song because he'd said that everyone would judge you. He'd make your heart race when the teacher called on students to answer questions and you knew you hadn't studied enough.

Opi, on the other hand, sucked everything out of you. I should have been sad, but I wasn't. I should have been mad, but I wasn't. I couldn't figure out what I was, so I wandered, stopping multiple times through my impromptu trip down memory lane.

Here was where I fell and tore up my knee, and Father kissed it better. *This time, he's falling and there's nothing you can do.*

Here was where I broke my favorite glass doll, and he painstakingly glued it back together. *When he's gone, you'll be like that doll was. Shattered. Broken.*

Here was where he told me they'd lost the baby. *The baby that probably would have noticed he was ill.*

Here was where he sipped his whiskey and kept the floating heads at bay. *When he's gone, you'll be ours, forever.*

Every stop, every memory, was perverted by Opi. For what felt like hours, he pulled me apart, piece by piece. He turned me into a puddle of tar, bending and folding under the weight of my own failure as a daughter and the crushing reality of the darkness that I knew would crash down on me fully once Father wasn't there to stop it.

Eventually, Brother arrived, rushing through the door, looking all the ways I should have: his face was puffy, although he tried to hide it, and his eyes were heavy with grief.

"Have you talked to Mom?" he demanded when he found me standing in the kitchen. I shook my head listlessly in response. "Well, come on then! Let's go find out what's happening."

The drive to the hospital was a quick one. Brother wouldn't look at me (*It's your fault,* Fred whispered). Annie didn't like that. She stared defiantly at him, then, without warning, threw my hand down on the horn. Startled, Brother jerked and twisted the wheel hard to the right.

The blaring of car horns around us muted the string of curses directed at me. "What the *hell* is your problem, Beaut?" I didn't know how to respond. I wanted to say I'm sorry, to explain everything and tell him it wasn't my fault, but the look in his eyes was of such contempt that I turned away and gazed out the window instead. I can recognize now, all these years later, that Brother was doing everything in his power to hold it together. He was trying to be strong and stoic for me, not blaming me as Fred and Annie led me to believe—but again, I digress.

When we reached the hospital, Brother jumped out of the car without a word. I followed him slowly, Annie dragging my feet the whole way up to the Guest Services counter (an odd name if you ask me; I don't know that "guest" is the right term for someone hooked up to ventilators or undergoing surgery). By the time I got there, the woman behind the counter was telling Brother that Father was in room 389. Brother thanked her and moved towards the elevator. This time, it was Fred who slowed my steps. *What will we see when we get to the room? Will it be like on TV? Will Father be on life support? Will we have to pull the plug?* I felt my heart racing and beads of sweat popping out on my forehead.

"Beauty," Brother called from the elevator, holding open its doors. I tried to pick up my pace, but I couldn't. It felt like there were anchors attached to my feet, each one weighing fifty pounds. My mind raced like Opi was stirring it with a wooden spoon, adding in ingredients like dread, doubt, and hopelessness.

Sighing, Brother left the elevator and came to me. "Beauty," he said, almost tender, "I know you're scared. I'm scared too, but we have to be brave for Father and Mother." He gently took my hand and led me to the elevator doors, which had dinged shut behind him. His hand felt so cool and calm compared to mine. I'm honestly surprised he didn't let go when he felt how clammy my palms were. I suppose he worried I might bolt if given the chance (Fred was disappointed it wasn't an option).

I don't think she'd ever admit it, but Priscilla helped that day. She refused to let Brother see us melt into a ball on the ground and insisted we act grown up about this. Fred and Annie didn't like her approach, but, somehow, she won. She held my head high when I couldn't and kept back the tears that threatened to spill (I said earlier that I relied on the heads, and this is one of those times where it might start to make a bit of sense to you, even though it shouldn't).

When the elevator dinged open, Brother led me down a long, fluorescently lit corridor that reeked of antiseptic and something else, that sinister smell that all medical places have. The door to room 389 was open, and we could hear the murmurings of Mother and Father, along with another, unfamiliar voice. It was deep and rich, the type of voice that instantly calms you. Brother released my hand and walked with determined steps into the room, me on his heels.

Father was laying in the bed, his upper half elevated. He had IVs hooked into his wrist, monitors on his chest and finger, and an oxygen tube flowing into his nostrils. Heavy bags weighed the skin below his eyes, and his lips trembled when he tried to bring them up into a smile. A male nurse, the owner of the other voice, slipped by me and out the door as I felt panic begin to wash over me.

I froze, unable to walk any further into the room. *This is it,* Opi seethed. I saw his form, shadowy and ominous, just inside the bathroom door. Part of me wanted to reach out and touch him, but I knew that if I did, I would be sucked into his ink and never seen again. A scream worked its way into my throat, crawling up from my lungs. I held my breath, fighting to keep it in. My face felt like a balloon right before it pops, stretched and about ready to burst.

Then I felt a quick, hard pinch on the back of my arm. Brother had returned from Father's bed and got the back of my arm between his finger and thumb. The bite of the pinch brought tears to my eyes, and Priscilla and Annie complained loudly in my head, but it snapped me out of whatever trance Opi had put over me.

"Come in, Beauty," Mother beckoned me. Father's eyes were nearly begging. He needed his Beauty. I hesitated to walk closer, not knowing what Priscilla and Annie had in mind, but his presence, although weak, forced them back into whatever place inside of me that they hid. I moved slowly towards his outstretched hand, taking it in my own. Brother grabbed a chair and pushed it towards me. I sat.

"So...what is this?" I asked through trembling lips, staring steadfastly down and admiring the thinness of the skin on Father's hands and the blueness of the veins that ran below it.

"They aren't quite sure," Mother hedged, but the wetness of her eyes betrayed her. I knew it, and so did Brother.

"Just tell us already," he demanded, stomping his foot, reminding me very much of Annie. Mother sighed deeply, looking to Father for wisdom.

"Let's just wait until the doctor comes in," he suggested. "He should be here soon."

"Soon" in doctor's time apparently meant at least forty-five minutes—a fact Brother was all too eager to point out several times. Each time, Mother sighed and gave some excuse, but I was with Brother on this one. How could it take this long when there was clearly something seriously wrong?

When he finally made an appearance, Dr. Smith was not what I expected or wanted to see. His small frame was hunched, his eyes worn, his gray hair too long and hanging loosely around his ears. This was not the kind of doctor I was used to seeing on TV (and if they did show one like him, he was usually the one you didn't want). Where was the lusciously-haired, overly confident, ready-to-take-on-the-world doctor? I wanted *him*, not this weak-looking man in front of me.

Dr. Smith introduced himself to Brother and me, then turned his attention to Father. "It's what we feared," he started, bedside manner out the window. Both their faces fell, Mother's with sorrow, Father's with defeat. Whatever "it" was, it was the worst news expected.

"AML?" Father asked, despite knowing the answer. Doctor Smith nodded. I saw Father's eyes dart to Mother, whose gaze remained fixed on the doctor as though waiting for balloons to fall and for him to shout, "April Fools!"

"What's AML?" I asked. Mother continued to stare at the doctor while Father's eyes dropped to his hands. "What's AML?" I asked again, this time louder, nearly shrill.

"Beauty," Brother tried to admonish me, but I could tell he wanted to know too. The doctor looked at Mother, then Father, then me. It was bad; I knew it. My mind felt faint, like it had zoomed itself out, the words and the thoughts so small that I had to squint to pull them together.

"Please?" I begged.

"AML," the doctor began, "is Acute Myeloid Leukemia." I saw Mother shiver from the corner of my eye. "It's a type of blood cancer that starts in the bone marrow—where other types of cells come from. When AML cells begin to multiply, they crowd out those other, healthy cells. They can move from there into the blood and, in some cases like your father's, to other parts of the body—in his case, the spinal cord." He turned to face Father. "Which explains the weakness you've been feeling over the past several months."

*Months?* My mind screamed. *Months?!* How could this happen for months without my knowing—without *anybody* knowing?

"So, what does that mean?" Brother asked. "Cancer is bad, but...like, he's going to be fine, right?" He looked for reassurance from Mother, whose trail of tears had run down her face and was now wetting the front of her shirt.

"It's not good," the doctor responded bluntly. "It can be hard to catch early, and in situations where it's already spread, we need extra-aggressive measures to fight back. We'll test each of your bone marrow to see if there's a match. Otherwise, he'll go on the register. In the meantime, we'll begin chemotherapy, which should hopefully help with the pressure on his spine and relieve some pain, but I should warn you, it comes with its own downfalls." He looked at each of us in turn. "Chemotherapy is hard, and you all need to be prepared for that."

"What does that mean?" Brother asked again. "Is...is he going to die?"

Doctor Smith looked to Mother. There was grief in his eyes, but his gaze was steady, the type that comes from having to tell bad news to too many families too many times. "It's hard to say. The five-year survival rate is about twenty-six percent."

"What does that mean?" Brother whispered this time.

"It means that around twenty-six percent of people live at least five years after the cancer is found."

"Five years?" I asked. "Just five years?"

"Well," the doctor glanced towards Mother again, "that's an average for the condition. It doesn't consider specific stages and individual scenarios—"

"*What does it mean?*" Brother cut him off. "Stop skirting around the issue and tell us the"—I won't repeat the word he used here— "truth!"

"Brother!" Father admonished. His authority, although weak, dropped Brother's shoulders and forced him to take a step back.

"I'm sorry," Brother responded, this time soft, quiet. Afraid.

Mother, who'd wept silently this whole time, finally mustered the strength to speak: "It means that our time with Father is limited, even with treatment."

"Take my marrow," I blurted out. "You can have it—all of it."

Father looked at me, his eyes so soft. "Beauty," he said. "Oh, my Beauty."

"What?" I asked. "He said the bone marrow could work. I'm young; I'm healthy. Take mine."

"I...don't think you'll be a match," the doctor interjected.

"I don't understand—I'm family. Family is supposed to match, right?" I felt like I was missing something. They all stared at me.

"How are you so dumb?" Brother finally asked.

"Brother!" Father roared.

"Brother," Mother whispered.

The doctor's eyes darted between each of us. His feet pedaled the floor uncomfortably. "I—I'm going to let you all discuss this. I'll be back later to discuss next steps." He quickly skirted past us and out of the room.

"You're not really that dumb, are you, Beaut?" asked Brother. I didn't know how to respond. I could feel *them* laughing in the background—Annie and Priscilla, Fred and Opi. All of them were in on this; they knew what I didn't.

I felt a flush rise to my cheeks. I was embarrassed, and angry, and lost—so very, very lost. "I... I don't understand."

"Beauty, come sit," Father said, patting the hospital bed. He looked so fragile; I worried that I'd break him if I accidentally bumped him too hard. "Sit," he said again, this time not asking. I moved slowly towards the bed. Brother stood by Mother and put his arm around her.

What was I missing?

"You see, Beauty, we won't match. You are our family, and nothing will change that, but you didn't come to us like Brother did. You came from our hearts." I stared at him, confused. This didn't make any sense. I was fifteen; I knew where babies came from, and it certainly wasn't the heart.

When I didn't interject, he continued: "After Brother was born, your mother had a very hard time. She was rushed into an emergency c-section and the surgery was hard on her. She was dealing with serious postpartum depression and told me that she didn't ever want to go through that again. When we did think about having another child, well, that's when we found out that the surgery left scarring. We were told that we wouldn't be able to conceive again. We had always wanted one boy and one girl, so when Brother was two, we started looking into adoption."

My heart fell. My belonging, my identity, my *home,* swept out from beneath me.

After a heavy pause, Mother spoke up: "When we heard about you, we just had to have you. You were technically a refugee, so we were able to bypass some of the regulations that come with adopting from another country. By the time the adoption was complete, you were already in the States, so we were able to meet you in person." Her eyes bore into me, pleading. "The moment we saw you, we knew you were ours. There was no question that *you* were the little girl we wanted so desperately. The system was so overcrowded that they let us bring you home a week later, as soon as final home checks were complete. You were so beautiful and so happy, despite everything."

*"Everything"? What is "everything"?*

I still couldn't speak. My mind was a tornado of thoughts. *Who was I? Where did I come from, outside of the States?*

"To be honest, Beaut, we all kind of thought you'd figure it out—you know, because..." Brother trailed off, raising his hand toward me. "...you know..."—I didn't know— "Well, you're kind of...brown." Brown? I wasn't brown. Father said I was kissed by the sun, but it was just a tan. My face betrayed me. "Oh my god.

You really didn't know?" Brother moved away from Mother to a chair beneath the window.

"I think that's enough for now," Mother said firmly. "We'll share more with you later. We have some files with general information about your birth parents. We kept them thinking that you might ask, that someday you might want to know. Do you want to ask us anything?"

What I wanted was to scream. *Who am I?* I waited for the voices to chime in, but there was nothing—just absolute emptiness.

My father was dying, and he wasn't even my father. I was in shock, but I wasn't even *me*. Nothing felt real. Nothing felt true. "Where am I from?" was all I could muster.

"You were born in Africa, but your mother was a Swedish missionary. Your father... well... we'll let you read about him," Mother answered.

I looked to Father. His eyes were so tired. "When?"

"When you were about two," he answered.

"Two?!" I yelled, shocking Father, who jerked and gasped when the movement pulled at the IV in his arm. I jumped up from the bed, glanced at Mother, then sprinted from the room.

I ran to the stairwell. Up the stairs. Through long corridors. Past open doors with sick people. Past open doors with families gathered. Past tired nurses, weary wives, loud children.

I ran.

11

# Chapter Eleven

Finally, my breath sporadic, I ran out of space to run. At the end of a long hallway, I found a door, left slightly ajar. A broom closet. I nestled into a corner between gallons of paint and boxes of supplies, and there, I cried.

I wept for my father, who wasn't my own. I wept for a past I never knew. I wept because, somehow, everyone knew, yet it never even occurred to me that I could belong to anybody else.

*Except us.*

At last, the faces showed up. Opi hovered above like a dark cloud, ominous, lingering. The others shouted in their native language. I didn't know what they were saying, but I knew that they were gloating, telling me I was *theirs*, that they'd known it all along. *See how the Jesus man let you down?* Annie said. It was the only thing said that I could understand.

I don't know how long I was in there, but I do know I nearly scared the life out of an old janitor. I must have been half asleep because I remember having to open my eyes when I heard him, but I don't remember falling asleep or when the voices fell silent.

"You must be the girl they're looking for," he grumbled, pulling me to my feet. He walked me silently to the nurse's station and dropped me off with an unceremonious "Here" to the young blonde behind the desk before turning and walking away.

The nurse, annoyed, looked me up and down once before calling to a large older lady, who came around the corner and roughly grabbed my arm to pull me behind her. I do believe, had there been any room in my mind, that Annie would have responded with a vengeance, but even she couldn't claim control through the swirling and spinning of my emotions.

I don't remember much of the rest of that day. Walking back to my father's room felt like I was stuck in slow motion, the world breezing by, unaware of the bomb that had been dropped in its midst. Once in his room, I couldn't bear to look at anyone. I sat in a chair, my head down, while the large lady berated my parents for letting me run around the hospital "like it's some sort of jungle gym." My father tried to say something to me—I remember the weary disappointment in his voice—but the words never registered. Brother had already left, so Mother called Grandmother to pick me up.

On the ride home, Grandmother admonished me for my behavior, reminding me that the world didn't revolve around me, that this was no time for attention-seeking behavior, that my father was *dying*. I resisted the temptation to remind her that he was not my father.

As I sat in the car of my not-grandmother, listening to her drone on and on about my not-mother and what she was going through, I thought, for the second time, of taking my life. I pictured reaching out, grabbing the steering wheel, jerking into oncoming traffic. "Just a tragic accident," they'd say. I didn't do it—probably because not-Grandmother was in the car too—but to say I was tempted would be an understatement.

That night, as I lay in bed, Louis showed up. He often appeared in times like these, when you would find yourself begging the universe for your grandmother, who was watching *The Late Show* in the other room (and who was also not your grandmother), to somehow read your mind, to understand that you needed her desperately—to understand that you felt so broken and lost and that you just needed her to come lay with you.

But she didn't, and that's when Louis would show up. Louis would remind you that you were all alone in this. He'd offer to comfort you, but he was just another weight—a heavy weight, one that pulls your heart somewhere deep into your stomach.

# Chapter Twelve

Louis was my constant companion for the next eight months. As my mother wept and my father deteriorated before me, Louis told me that this would be my life forever. Fred often accompanied Louis. Opi contented himself with appearing only in my dreams, where he told me that when Father was gone, I'd be his. There would be no hope, no light—just the inky darkness where Opi resided.

Since Mother spent most of her time at the hospital (Father had been moved into something called hospice), I was stuck with Brother during the week and Grandmother on the weekends. Brother mostly ignored me while Grandmother constantly reminded me of Mother's pain: "Don't be selfish right now, Beauty. This isn't about you." Yeah, sure. The only father I'd ever known was dying, but clearly I was not a part of this scenario at all (I should say here that Priscilla *hated* my grandmother, although, if I'm to be honest, I probably did too during that time ).

As I prepared for my adoptive father's death, I found I wanted to know more about where I came from. I thought that maybe, if I knew about them, if I found them, I wouldn't be lonely anymore. Mother had mentioned a file at the hospital, and when I asked, she begrudgingly gave it to me. I spent hours, days, weeks, months pouring over it, trying to learn more about who I was.

Like Mother said, my biological mother, Tindra Lundberg, was a Swedish missionary, and she was beautiful. On the nights when Louis lingered, I stared at the picture of her from the file. She had a straight nose, thin but wide lips, beautiful blonde hair, and striking blue eyes. She was like one of the Barbies I'd favored as a child.

My biological father had a mixed heritage: his mother was Egyptian, and his father was from Sudan. He was a handsome man, although his face looked like it had been put in an editing program and stretched the wrong way a little bit. His forehead was high, his cheeks a bit narrower, and his chin wide. His skin was just a few shades darker than my own. I kicked myself multiple times while reviewing the file for never noticing the difference between my skin and my family's—although, to be fair, Father had never let me think that I was different - and with Swedish and Egyptian genes, I was quite light.

The thing that stood out the most were his eyes. They were lovely, nearly golden, like he held the entirety of Egypt's ancient fortune in them. His irises were enclosed in a thick dark ring that brought to mind a lion. The most shocking part about them, though, was how hard they were. There was no joy in them—no life, no love. He looked like a man who had been born to death, and, according to the file, he was.

Amani Ibrahim. Born to Farid Ibrahim and Anippe Darwish. Unwanted by his mother's family—a wealthy family in Egypt, whose only daughter had fallen in love with an older man with ties to extremist organizations. According to the Department of Homeland Security, Farid's activities were never verified, but they believed that he had been sent to Egypt as a spy for the Sudanese government. In fact, this speculation, along with my biological father's own actions, nearly prevented me from receiving refugee status.

Since my grandmother, Anippe, was only fifteen when he was born, her family rejected my father and sent Amani away as an infant to live with Farid. My father never forgot their rejection, and he spent the remaining years of his life avenging it.

Amani quickly rose in the ranks of the Sudanese militant forces, who were quick to step in between various leaders and wars and made a name for himself as a violent and angry man. He used his resources mercilessly, even going so far as to kill his maternal grandfather in an act of revenge—a crime that put him on the run from both Sudanese and Egyptian authorities. He eventually landed him in the southern region of Chad, where my mother was part of a missionary outreach. Immediately smitten, my father exchanged letters with her, calling her his "ukulukula," or butterfly. In her own letters, she admitted that she found him intriguing—her "ljuv riddare," or sweet knight.

Looking at his picture, it was hard to imagine anything sweet about him. It was hard to imagine him feeling anything other than hatred.

When the church found the letters, they confronted Tindra about the flirtations. She had admitted that she had become intimate with him and was promptly kicked out of the mission-ary program. They made plans for her to return to Sweden; Amani had other plans, ones which would land him on several governments' Most Wanted lists.

This may seem like a lot of information for an adoption file, but you have to remember that I didn't come from "normal" (if there is such a thing) circumstances. The further I read, the more dire my reading materials, much of which had been provided by Chad and Swedish authorities and compiled by DHS, became.

The night before Tindra was set to leave, Amani kidnapped her from her tent, with a troop of local boys he'd managed to sway to his cause. In the dead of night, the troop entered the missionary camp and slaughtered all but three of its occupants with machetes. Tents were burned, supplies and funds stolen, and my mother taken.

Those who survived recounted something akin to a horror story. They described the men as shadows, faces partially covered by heavy hoods, eyes darkened by charcoal, and an excitement described as "djävulsk"—devilish. At some point, those faces began haunting my dreams. I've wondered many times if my biological father's face from that night was the same face that Opi wore all those years that he plagued me.

For three years, my mother's location was unknown. Her family pleaded with various governments to find her, begging them to send military forces after her. Their letters and requests went unanswered. At some point, they reached out to Anippe's family to see if they would use their influence to sway action. Anippe's uncle refused and demanded that they stay away; how-ever, Anippe herself felt differently. Over the years she'd kept track of Farid, who had since left his various extremist groups and was raising goats in South Africa. In secret she sent him a note, explaining the crimes of their son.

Farid, who had himself been touched by missionaries, quickly took action. Using the influence he still held, he tracked down my father, who had found a home in Uganda, where he held rank with the Lord's Resistance Army. One of Kony's commanders was a friend from Farid's youth, and he permitted my grandfather to enter the camp and speak with his son, promising that he would leave the camp alive, although he could make no such promises for my mother.

Farid was shocked when he discovered that Amani had married the Swede and conceived a child, now nearly age two. When he saw them, his heart was demolished. The woman before him was nothing like the images he'd received from Anippe. In his own account, he described her as broken, her face bruised and scarred, her body bent like that of an old woman. The atrocities committed to her would never truly be known, but they were there, written on her body.

Disgusted, Farid demanded that Amani let the woman and her child free, but his son refused. In his official interview, Farid said that the child—me—had no life and no joy. I had simply sat in a dark corner silently. Even when bribed with a treat, I stayed in my place, an old, dirty blanket woven between my fingers and a thumb in my mouth, bearing the same bruises and scars as my mother.

Amani allowed my grandfather to stay in the camp for one night but promised that his life was not guaranteed past the next morning.

That night, Farid took matters into his own hands. He snuck into the cabin of his son and found me asleep on a dirty mat in the bathroom. He picked me up, noticing immediately how light I was for my age and, without waking me, tied me to his chest under his jacket. He then crept through the small house, looking for my mother. Two doors down from the bathroom, another door was slightly opened. He entered the room silently and was looking around, trying to discern shadow from human, when he saw movement and the flash of a blade to his right. Protecting the child strapped to him, he turned his body away; the knife's tip glanced against his jaw and neck before digging down his shoulder and back.

There were pictures in the folder, accompanying his account, and the images were brutal. Another slice split his right forearm to the bone, and the final opened his cheek. When asked how he escaped, Farid simply said he didn't have a choice. One child's life had already been ruined by his actions; he couldn't live in a world where he let another suffer from them. He described a sort of supernatural surge of energy washing over him. As his son brought the knife down again, aiming for his heart (unaware that the little girl was resting there), Farid shoved off his heels, jamming his injured shoulder into his son and pushing them both through the window. Farid rolled hard to his left, his bloodied arm cupping the child and pulling her away from the earth. As the two men scrambled to their feet, flashlights and lanterns began to flare around them.

The interviewers wrote at this point in the interview that Farid was sobbing, his words switching between English, Arabic, and a blend of other languages. What they gathered through the sobs was that he could not get to the woman - my mother. He swore that he'd tried to find her and that he would have tried again if he wasn't certain that she would be punished for any further attempts. He blamed himself for everything. Eventually they pulled my grandmother, who hadn't seen him since shortly after my father's conception, from her own interview to calm him and translate the rest of his story, although there wasn't much left to tell.

Farid had run and run until he was able to steal a jeep, the child, whom he called Zahrati Aldhaabila (my wilted flower), still strapped to his chest. He drove for nearly thirty-five hours straight, stopping just once to purchase food and milk and to nap briefly. At one point, the interviewer noted that Anippe didn't want to translate what Farid was saying. He wrote in this notes that "They argued in an unknown language until she finally agreed. She then looked up, taking the hand of her once-lover, and said, 'He says he couldn't stop because the devil was after him.'"

There were several newspaper articles tucked in the folder as well. After translating one headline—*Tifl Altaabie Shaytan 'unqidhat*, "child of the devil rescued"—I decided to stop learning my history for a while.

The voices hated this idea. They needed me to know from where I came and to whom I belonged, promising that I would be his again. I searched for any indication that my father was found and prosecuted, but authorities never found him.

*They* assured me that *he* would find *me*.

Curious about my grandfather, I decided to conduct a quick search for him. It turned out that he'd married Anippe mere weeks after my rescue. Based on refugee papers, they'd wanted to keep me, but Farid worried that as long as I was in Africa, my father would find me. My mother's parents blamed Farid for failing to rescue her and blaming me for her death refused to see me. Eight months after I was sent to the United States, Farid was killed. According to media outlets at the time, hooded raiders attacked the goat farm at night, slitting the necks of the livestock and Farid before burning the property to the ground. Anippe had been tied to a post, naked, to watch the property burn. Six months later, she took her own life. In her note, she told her family that she had "given birth to hell" and "could never be forgiven for that."

There was a picture included. In it, a beautiful woman clung to the arm of a rugged goat farmer with stitches down his jaw, a bandage around his forearm, a sleeping child on his chest, and a mournful smile that carried the weight of the nightmares that he'd seen. The nightmares I'd lived.

# Chapter Thirteen

Ten months after receiving his prognosis, only a few weeks from my sixteenth birthday, Father went to be with his Jesus man. I don't think that we ever really get to mourn the loss of our innocence, but I know that, that day, I lost whatever small amount was left for me. I felt nothing at his funeral.

Nothing when Mother wept.

Nothing when his body was lowered into the ground.

Nothing when Brother, barely eighteen, read a eulogy.

*Nothing.* Somehow, the inky black place where Opi lived had become comfortable. It was the only place where I felt I belonged. After all, my birth mother was most likely dead; my birth father, a monster; biological grandparents, dead or didn't want me; adoptive father, dead. Brother didn't want me, and, as Fred and Louis often reminded me, I was nothing but a burden on Mother.

She tried to talk to me, but I don't think she knew what to say. She knew that I'd read some of the file, that everything I ever knew to be true was a lie. In her own grief, she wasn't able to push past herself to get into my world, or at least the world that I came from. At some point, she gave up—not that I blame her. She called a therapist and started sending me twice a week, three times when I had outbursts. Annie loved every bit of this. Now she didn't have to hide in the shadows; she had an excuse. Each time she took control, I saw Mother's shoulders drop a bit more and felt Annie's strength grow. She reminded me of a warrior. When she took over in a rage, I could feel my heart pound to an ancient beat.

For the first few weeks, the therapist, Beatrice, read my files and encouraged me to do the same, but I couldn't stomach it. When she tried to go through my medical records, a new voice showed up—Lucy. She pretended to be good and innocent, but she wasn't. She postured as love, but she wasn't.

At Beatrice's insistence, I returned to the records. In them, I had to confront what was done to me in that camp. I'd been used and abused in every way as a child. The records showed horrific physical abuse and indication that sexual abuse had recently begun. *See, you've always been mine*, Lucy whispered. Beatrice tried to get me to interact with my emotions, but I couldn't. I knew then that I was bad. My grandmother knew it of her son, and I knew it of me.

I remember one night, a few months after Father's death and several days after Beatrice made me read the files, I jerked awake, my lungs on fire. Opi had led me back to the camp, showed me who my father was, and what he was capable of. I was suddenly surrounded by men in masks, eyes darkened as they shook torches to the sky. The air was heavy with their shouts and yips of excitement. I knew I needed to hide, but my feet were glued to the ground. Then I was somehow one of them, the voices inside me rising with their own yips of excitement.

I tried to call for Father—I needed him to hold them back—but he was gone, and they knew it. It was as though they were swirling about me, *in* me, screaming in their native tongue, sucking the life from me. The beat-beat-beat of my heart matched Annie's drum. I felt my arms suction to my sides and my body wrap in invisible binds. I struggled and fought but couldn't get free. Suddenly, my eyes popped open, a scream strangled in my throat. I struggled in my sheets before falling out of bed with a thump. Pushing my body up, I ran to my bathroom, not caring how much noise I made, and stuck my head in the sink. "Shut up, shut up, SHUT UP!" I screamed.

When I lifted my head and looked at my reflection in the mirror, I realized for the first time that the Heterochromia that some might say made my appearance striking, displayed in my eyes a contrast between my biological parents. I had one blue eye like *hers* and one golden like *his*. My own eyes reflected the battle between good and evil.

I knew I had to get rid of it.

I yanked on the drawer handles, nearly dislodging them in my fervor. I tore through every item until I found what I was so desperate for. Thin and cold between my fingers, the light over the sink reflected from it in flashes. That night, I took a razor blade between my fingertips with the intention of gouging out his eye.

Mother, who must have been woken by my yelling, raced through the door right as the blade touched my eyelid. Her eyes widened when she realized what was happening, and she quickly grabbed my arm. While she tried to pull my arm back, I pushed harder, landing the razor on my eyebrow and pulling it down my cheek.

Mother yelled for Brother, who came pounding down the hallway and stood in the door. "Stop her!" Mother screamed. Brother pushed his way in and grabbed my wrist, right before the blade made its second contact with my face. He held my arm, suspended in the air, and looked to Mother for guidance. Mother stood, unsure of what to do next. I sobbed, the salty tears stinging my cheek and riding the flood of blood down my face onto my nightshirt. Suddenly, Mother ran from the bathroom. When she returned, she was on the phone. In a half whisper, her voice repeatedly breaking, she described the scene in the bathroom. Brother stood stoically, still holding my arm, simultaneously keeping me from collapsing to the floor and from making any other attempts to harm myself.

Mother ended the call, and what felt like years passed as we waited, frozen in place: Brother's wide hand clasped around my wrist, holding it high above my head; Mother, leaning against the door, exhausted in all the various ways; and me, half slumped over the counter, blood now slowly spilling from my eyebrow and cheek slowing as it began to clot over my eye.

Finally, the doorbell rang, and Mother left the bathroom without a word. When she returned, Beatrice was with her, along with two men in white scrubs. One stepped in for Brother, taking my wrist and gently removing the blade. With that, I finally crumpled, my fall only slowed by the man's grip on my arm.

Beatrice came and knelt beside me in the bathroom, Brother was now hugging Mother outside the door.

"Beauty," she said with so much kindness, "I think maybe you need to come stay with us for a couple of days. You're not in any trouble—we just want to make sure you're all right because, right now, it doesn't seem like you are. Beauty, can you look at me?"

I slowly looked up, squinting, one eye blurred by blood. She really did have a kind face. *It's a trap!* Fred yelled. *Don't go with her—you'll never escape!*

"Beauty, can you come with us? Just for a little bit. We can get you cleaned up, get you some stitches, and then we can talk about what happened, okay?"

"I have his eye," was my response. I don't think she really understood, but she nodded anyway and helped the men lift me to my feet. "Beauty, Marcos here is going to take a quick look at your face to see if we need to go to the hospital"—*That's where they killed him!* Fred yelled—"and give you a quick shot to help you feel better. I'm going to talk to your mom for a minute and help pack up a few of your things, just enough for a couple of days."

While Marcos cleaned up my face—no hospital for me; luckily the razor had completely missed my eyeball—Mother and Beatrice whispered in the hall. I didn't catch much, but I did hear that Mother would have to sign some papers and that she would not be allowed to see me "at first". I heard Mother sob, but she agreed. Their voices vanished for a moment, and then they were back, this time right outside the bathroom door.

"Just tell her goodbye for a few days and that you'll visit as soon as you can," instructed Beatrice.

"Okay," Mother managed through another sob.

"Let's clean your face up first—here's a tissue. You must be strong for her. I know it's hard with everything you've gone through, but you need to be her support right now." With that, they came through the door.

"Okay, Beauty," Beatrice said brightly, "it's about time to go. I've got your bags—your mom showed me your favorite pajamas, so we'll get changed into those later. I also grabbed some of your CDs and the stuffed bunny from your bed, so you'll have those tonight as well. We can play some music to help you sleep. Let's say goodnight and head out."

I may have nodded; I may not have. I felt Mother embrace me, her face still damp and her body trembling. I don't remember most of what she said to me, but I do know she reminded me that I came from her heart. Brother didn't say anything as Marcos and the other man led me down the stairs, out the door, and into a white van.

That was the last day I was in my father's house. I don't think I ever looked back.

# Part III

The Time I'd Rather Not Mention

14

# Chapter Fourteen

When the van finally stopped, it was at a large wrought iron gate. Not-Marcos clicked the intercom button and stated, "Patient intake." The gates beeped open, and the van slowly pulled forward. We drove for several minutes down a long, winding road, shrubs bordering both sides, grass neatly mowed in the moonlight. As the van slowed once more, a large, white sign declared *White Pines Psychiatric Care*, which humored me as I hadn't seen a single tree, let alone a white pine, on the premises.

We parked in front of a looming building, and Beatrice (who'd been in another car behind us) opened my door. "We're here," she declared (as if that weren't obvious). I still didn't entirely understand what "here" was, but I learned rather quickly.

Marcos and not-Marcos each took an elbow and guided me down the stone walkway to the door, with Beatrice hovering behind. Once inside, she shooed the men away; within the walls, I was apparently less of a flight risk. The foyer was large and open with stone pillars and large windows with bars across them.

There were off-white, almost yellow chairs and couches around a coffee table covered in magazines—an unsuccessful attempt to put visitors at ease and disguise what was held within. In one corner was a large, L-shaped kiosk, its base covered in wooden panels and the top outlined in plexiglass to the ceiling. As we neared, a small window slid open, and a heavy-set, middle-aged woman poked her head through.

"Well, this one's young," she observed in a gravelly voice, marred by years of smoking.

"That's enough, Marge," Beatrice scolded.

"I'm just speaking the truth."

"Well, how about less of your uninvited *'truth'* and more *checking in?*"

Marge remained unpleasant throughout the remainder of what Beatrice called the intake process. Beatrice explained each step to me, but between the pain in my face and whatever they'd given me in the bathroom, I couldn't comprehend any of it. I nodded each time she asked me if I understood, though, then followed as she beeped us through a door to the right of Marge and down long halls with doors on either side. She ushered me to an elevator, the doors clicking open when she ran her badge over their sensor and motioned for me to step inside. I heard Fred somewhere in the background yelling that it was a trap, but his voice was muddled, like he was screaming in a pool. Annie tried to hold my feet down, but somehow, I was able to stay in control, and so I stepped in. Beatrice followed, and the elevator went up.

"How are you doing?" she asked, her voice filled with the same kindness as at the house.

"I feel like I'm floating in Opi's ink," I answered.

Both of her eyebrows shot up. "Beauty, who is Opi?"

I giggled—not a cute giggle, an evil-witch-watching-the-princess-take-a-bite-of-the-poison-fruit giggle. Hesitancy crossed Beatrice's face for the first time since I'd met her, like she was changing her mind about me.

"Beauty, who is Opi?" she asked again, this time taking my shoulders in her hands gently and looking directly into my eyes. I heard the doors slide open, but she didn't loosen her grip on me.

I knew *they* were telling me not to. I was about to spill all the secrets. *They* knew it too. I don't know what muffled them, but regardless, when they all yelled at the same time, it was piercing. My eyes squeezed shut, shooting pain across my face as the dried blood cracked under the pressure of my squinched face.

"He is the darkness," I managed through gritted teeth

A helpless look on her face, Beatrice clicked a red button on the elevator panel, one hand still on my shoulder.

"That was quick." The gravelly voice of Marge filled the elevator.

"Please send Dr. Oliver and Marcos to floor six." Beatrice led me from the elevator and set me on a bench outside the door. Moments later, the doors opened again, and Marcos stepped out, followed by another man in a green sweater vest and tan corduroy pants under a long, white lab coat. His blonde hair was speckled with gray and swept back from his face while fashionable glasses highlighted his bright green eyes. He was a handsome man, the epitome of the TV show doctor I'd wanted so desperately that day in my father's hospital room.

*I think he likes us,* Lucy murmured, her voice deep and muddled at the back of my mind.

"Marcos, please stay with Beauty for a moment while I speak with Dr. Oliver," Beatrice asked, stepping away from me so Marcos could assume his perch. She took the handsome doctor's arm and led him several feet away, but despite the distance and their low voices, people are never as good at whispering as they think. I heard her tell him about Opi and ask about antipsychotics. He shook his head, saying it was too early for such extreme measures: "Suicide watch and a sedative tonight. We'll start group and personal therapy tomorrow. Then, if we need to go that route, we can revisit medication." I could tell Beatrice was unhappy with the decision, but reluctantly she agreed.

Turning back to me, she nodded to Marcos, who took a step back, and plastered a smile on her face. "Okay, Beauty, let's go to your room. Andrew has already taken your bags up and unpacked for you. We'll get you a sleep aid and into bed. After everything that's happened, I bet you're ready for some good rest."

Ignoring her, I blurted out, "Hello," to the doctor (I suspect Lucy had something to do with this outburst, although I'm not sure how, seeing as the rest remained subdued).

Beatrice took in a quick breath, her eyes glancing between me and the doctor.

"Hello, Beauty," he smiled, stretching out a hand. "I'm Dr. Oliver. I'll be one of your doctors while you're with us." I stared at his hand. I didn't want to touch it, but *she* did. My own stretched out, brushing his. That was all Lucy could muster; my hand dropped, and I looked to the floor. Beatrice looked at him meaningfully, as if to say, "See?".

"Well, good night. I'll see you tomorrow," he said, stepping back into the elevator.

Beatrice gently took my arm again, nodding once more to Marcos (the non-verbal communication at this place was like a choreographed dance, each participant knowing the next step with the slightest of cues). She led me down another hall and, after a right turn, guided me into an open door. "Here we are." She led me to the bed and pointed to the pajamas laid out. "I know they aren't yours, but it's policy your first few nights with us." I picked them up. They were soft, but they smelt too new, almost chemically. "You can get changed and brush your teeth in the bathroom"—she motioned to a small room adjacent—"and I'll be back in a moment with a nurse to help get you in bed."

She stepped out of the room, closing the door behind her. I walked to the door to lock it, but there were no locks or chains. I moved to the bathroom with the pajamas in my hand. In the small room, I clicked on the light to find only a small sink and a toilet—no tub, no shower, and no door. I quickly slid into the pajamas, nearly falling when my head began to spin again. I was thankful that there was no mirror. While part of me was curious to see my face, I wasn't ready to see *his* eye in this place.

I picked up the toothbrush provided, still neatly packaged. It was soft, like a child's toothbrush. Next to it was an unopened package of toothpaste, deodorant, and face/body wipes. Brushing my teeth, I finally started to feel the fog lift from my mind. On one hand, it was nice that the urge simply to sit down was fading, but it also meant that *they* were back and louder than ever, as if all of their screams into the waves were breaking against the shore of my mind, assaulting it all at once.

They accused me, words pointing like fingers. *Traitor*, they hissed. *They mustn't know. They already think you're crazy. If they know, you'll never leave this place. If you tell them about us, they'll never believe you.*

She *left you here. What sort of mother would do that?*

*They don't care about you. They'll lock you up forever.*

By the time Beatrice came back with the nurse, I was curled up in a corner, grasping my head, fighting the migraine rising at the back of my neck and shooting behind my eyes as each word they spoke struck like a blow.

"Beauty?" Beatrice asked, hurrying across the threshold. "Here, dear, let's get you to bed." Bedtime was evidently synonymous with three pills from a small, white cup and a sip of water from a plastic bottle. The pills stopped at the back of my throat, gagging me. My stomach retched. *They* were fighting this. They didn't like the pills. Annie abruptly threw my weight against Beatrice while Fred stuck my feet to the ground like cement boots, making me a leaning tower that fell into her slight frame.

Beatrice took it like a wall. Solid. This must not be unusual behavior to her. The nurse quickly pulled me back, pushing me onto the bed. The three pills fell from my mouth. I looked at the nurse, locked eyes with her, pleading for her to see that this wasn't me, begging her to know that I didn't want this to happen. Then Annie was in my eyes. I believe, to this day, that the nurse saw the switch. She had that look in her eye, the same one Mother had all those years ago when she caught me arguing with *them* over a cookie.

What came next was Annie with the power of a sixteen-year old's lungs. I felt it start in my stomach, then it rose to my lungs; I begged for them to explode before the sound could travel further but to no avail. My lips parted, and a shrill, banshee-esque shriek escaped. It only lasted a moment, though, before I felt a pinch in my arm—the nurse had brought a back-up to the pills. The sting overloaded my mind as the world began to melt away. I felt them tuck me gently into bed, planting me between cool sheets before pulling the scratchy comforter over the top.

"Her mother mentioned episodes like this to me in our first session," I heard Beatrice confide quietly.

"There's something different with this one," the nurse agreed.

*See...* they whispered as the world faded to black.

# Chapter Fifteen

"Beauty, your mother said that you told her you had 'his eye'. Who did you mean?"

I sat in an overstuffed chair in Dr. Oliver's office, which was surprisingly comfortable, though he clearly had a thing for boats. I'd never seen a boat up close, but he had pictures on his walls of him posing in front of a large one. Father would say a boat like that was a fool's dream—no purpose, just a money suck. I could see that someone was cropped out of the photos. An arm was on his shoulder, and light, wispy hair could be seen against his navy shirt collar. *We can dye our hair,* Lucy, whose voice was still new to me, felt the need to remind me.

"Beauty?" he asked again, breaking through wandering thoughts. "Whose eye do you have?"

I hesitated, unwilling to disclose my past. I didn't want him to know that I was a monster.

"This is a safe place, Beauty. We just want to help you, and we can't do that if you don't let us understand. Beatrice mentioned Opi—is that whose eye you have? Opi's?"

I shuddered, knowing that I'd broken the unspoken rule made all those years ago, when the first floating head showed up. I didn't respond, hoping that he'd change the subject. I'd found that most people were uncomfortable with silence and were quick to fill it.

Unfortunately, he seemed to know this as well.

When finally, I couldn't take it anymore, I broke. I burst out of my seat, yelling, "My father, okay? Well, not my father-father. My adoptive father was good, but my biological father—he was *evil*. And...he's in me," I finally admitted.

He nodded. "Okay. Tell me more."

"I don't want to!" I paced while my words settled in the room. "I didn't want to know— I shouldn't have *had* to know. My father shouldn't have gotten sick—there shouldn't have been stupid tests—I should have been able to go on living with him, safe. But now I know, and you can't unknow what you know."

Dr. Oliver gestured to the seat, directing me to sit down. "Beauty, when we talked with your mother, she mentioned some other...incidents...from before, going back into your childhood. Do you know what I'm talking about?" I nodded. "Is it possible that, even though you didn't know about your biological parents, what happened in that camp had an effect on you?"

*He knew.* He wasn't supposed to know; I knew that Beatrice knew, but not Dr. Oliver. I stared at him for a moment before whispering, "You probably think I'm a slut."

He stared back, mouth twitching and hands tightening. "Beauty, no. You have to know that nothing that happened was your fault. You were a baby. Nobody could ever look at what you experienced and think anything badly of you."

"But I am *him*."

"No, Beauty. You are *you*. He was him. That was just one part of your story. And even during that time, you had a mother caring for you and loving you the best that she could. Think about what your grandparents went through to save you. That's part of your story as well. Do you see that?"

"And what did that get them?" I demanded. "My grandfather was killed by his own son. My grandmother took her own life. *That* is my story—what I'm from. And *they* won't let me forget it."

"Who, Beauty? Who doesn't let you forget?" But without the sedative, they were too strong for me. Fred sucked the air from my lungs; Annie pushed my back into the chair; even Priscilla and Oscar showed up, clenching my hands so tightly my nails pierced my palms and screwing my eyes shut. I was trapped in a cage they built.

"Beauty? Beauty, are you alright?" I heard him set his notepad down and come to me, felt his hand on my wrist, checking my pulse. "Open your eyes—breathe, Beauty. Breathe!" Despite his commands, they refused to let up. "Beauty!" Dr. Oliver sounded panicked now. "I need some help in here!"

I felt my mind fading away. My lungs burned, pleading for air. A memory of Father flashed through my mind. How had he ended this with a word when no one else could? Not Mother, or Beatrice, or even Dr. Oliver.

I could hear hustling all around me, then felt the familiar sting of a needle in my arm. Immediately, I was released. My lungs opened and filled with warm, sweet air. My eyes fluttered open and looked from face to face around me. Six or so nurses and orderlies stared back.

"What happened?" one of them asked.

"I honestly don't know," Dr. Oliver responded. "Maybe a panic attack?" He searched my face, hand still on my wrist. Lucy felt it; Lucy felt him. "Do you need to be done for today, Beauty?" he asked. I nodded while Lucy grasped his hand. "Okay. Let's get you to your room for a nap before lunch." He shook his hand out of Lucy's grip, much to her dismay.

As one of the nurses led me back to my room, Lucy looked back towards his office, fighting me for control. The door was partially open, and we watched as Beatrice stepped through.

"Maybe *she's* the slut," Lucy whispered from my lips. The nurse looked back, then to me, one eyebrow raised. He didn't respond; they rarely did.

16 |

# Chapter Sixteen

For the remainder of my time at White Pines, I had two constant companions: Lucy and Louis. Lucy liked the way people looked at us. At sixteen, she knew we looked more like a woman than a girl, and she used it to her advantage. She got us extra treats, extra servings of meals, and cigarettes. I don't smoke; I hate smoking, but Lucy didn't. Lucy thought it made us look older, more mature. She liked looking mature. She liked being the crazy, pretty girl. Most of all, she liked Dr. Oliver, and she was determined to lure him in. She likes him. Despite the twenty or thirty years between us (although, to be fair, Lucy was technically older; you'd think that being a whatever-she-was, she'd have outgrown that sort of behavior, but evidently not).

Louis, on the other hand, was like a shadow. He rarely stepped in, rarely acted out. He was just there, reminding me that I was alone. That, no matter how many people Lucy lured into her orbit, at night, when the drugs were taken and the lights were out, it was just me in this place. Well, me and *them*. Whatever concoction the doctors gave kept most of them at bay. They still tried to talk through it, to control me, but they couldn't break through the fog. While Lucy could break in periodically, if the situation was right, Louis was content to just linger, and Opi...he came and went as he pleased. His heavy presence was always near. Silent. Hovering.

After the initial seventy-two hours under suicide watch, I was moved to a full-size room and was allowed to see Mother. In a matter of days, she had become a ripple of the strong, confident woman she once was. I think, between Father's death and dealing with me, she just felt hopeless. For the second time, I wondered if other people had voices too. Whatever voice spoke to her pulled her eyes and smile down. The heaviness was obvious—or maybe she just wasn't used to it like I was.

She brought more of my belongings from home, along with a few decorations— "to brighten up the room." As if a few positive phrases and floral print could somehow take away the fact that I was where I was. I loved her for wanting to be there for me, but I hated her when she left. *What type of mother leaves their own daughter?* they asked. *Your real mother must have been killed by that monster—you know, the one in you.*

The nurses, as if on cue, filled the room in her absence. They oohed and aahed over the new decorations, and one even added a small succulent to the pile. After helping me unpack (something Mother wasn't allowed to do; I assume they needed to check for anything that I could hurt myself with), they suggested that I take a bubble bath in my new, private bathroom. Still no razor, mirror, or glass bottles, but at least I now had a tub (apparently, it's quite difficult to intentionally drown oneself, so a bath wasn't a concern). They packed my new pink–and-rose-gold shower caddy with the soaps, shampoos, and conditioners Mother had bought me and loaded the tub with lavender bubble bath.

They then left me—door propped open, of course—and I slithered into the bubbly heat. The floral scent filled my nostrils, bubbles tickled my skin, and the tension slowly eased from my neck. As my mind began to empty, I felt it—a presence in the room.

My eyes burst open, and I looked around, searching for the eyes that made my skin crawl, but the room was empty.

*Look at you.*

I jerked my attention to the toilet seat, where the voice came from.

*You're disgusting. No wonder nobody loves you.*

I stared at the porcelain, fighting to catch a glimpse of her. The voice was Lucy's, but unlike Fred and Annie, there was no floating head to accompany it. Rather, there was the idea of a presence, like heat waves rising from the asphalt on a hot summer day—visible for a moment, but as soon as you look at them, they're gone.

I lowered my body lower into the water, letting it fill my ears until there was a tiny *bloop*, and the noise around me muffled to a whisper. I heard a single drop fall from the faucet with a tink, then the relief of silence. For a moment.

*Nice try,* she said, her voice sultry and soft. *I don't know why you always fight me. I just want to take care of you. I just want you to be loved. You could really be something, but not like this, not if you're the size of a whale. If you lost a little weight, they'd want you. They'd love you.*

I squeezed my eyes shut and lowered my head further into the water until bubbles tickled at my nose. It still wasn't enough.

*Just let me handle it. All you need is love. I can get it for you. Trust me, I know just what to do.*

With that, my head went below the water. Heat and bubbles stung my sinuses. Like in the dreams I'd had as a child, I was stuck, caught below. *She* was holding me down. To this day, I think, more than anything, she just wanted me to surrender (really, they all did), and she almost succeeded—until my mother's face flashed on the back of my eyelids, followed by my father's voice, spoken loudly from some memory: *Come now, Beauty. Time to get up. Beauty. Look at me, Beauty.*

*She's mine!* Opi roared back, trying to silence the voice of my father.

*Look up,* Father commanded once again. *Breathe, Beauty.* Some force, greater than Lucy, propelled me from the water. I burst through the bubbles, arms flailing, coughing violently, snot and water shooting from my nose.

"You okay in there?" Nurse Addison asked. I hadn't heard her come back into the room.

"I'm fine!" I lied. Lucy was gone; it was just me again. I quickly dried off and changed into pink pajamas.

Addison met me at the bed with a little cup of little pills and a little water bottle. "Here you go," she said, holding her hand out, watching as I took the little cup and swallowed the pills with a little sip from the little bottle. She then bid me goodnight, gesturing towards the bed, and I realized then how much better it was to be surrounded by my things—like I was somehow a bit closer to home. A bit closer to Mother.

Her face flashed again through my mind, this time with a memory of the two of us flying down a slide. I had been so afraid, but she had been so strong and so comforting. I remembered her smile, bright and warm—something I hadn't seen since Father's death.

*"The memories you miss the most are the ones you don't have."* If that's not a something people say, it should be. It's what I thought that first day I saw Mother, and it's what I continued to think every time after. Through that summer, I daydreamed about how I should be spending the time before my senior year camping with my family or shopping at the mall. During the school year, I daydreamed about making new friends, going to prom, having my first kiss (Lucy especially liked to think about that last one). But every time I saw Mother, that life seemed further away.

She seemed further away.

Within the first year, I found I could barely remember Father's smile. I clung to it, tracing the lines over and over in my mind. I remembered how he could chase *them* away, how they cowered in his presence. Mother couldn't do that. I mourned the time, so long ago, when I could climb into her lap and feel safe. Now, each time she was with me, she touched me less; she leaned back more.

*She knows what you are,* they said. *She knows that you belong to him.*

I think, for the first time, I fully believed them. Well, maybe not the first time. I had believed them before, but I had never been willing to fully surrender to them, to their truth. But now, I gave myself over to them, day after day. When Lucy moved my arm to brush another patient or nurse, I didn't fight her. When Opi flooded my mind with ink, I let him. I was floating in an endless ocean. If I ever thought to paddle, they threw waves at me, pushing me back. If I tried to leave my lifeboat, they pulled me under, sucking the air from my lungs.

Dr. Oliver tried to help. We met once a day, twice on Wednesdays, and he asked me more about Opi. He wanted me to talk about my biological parents, but how could I talk about things I couldn't explain or didn't know? Lucy appeared often during our sessions. She asked about his love life, asked if he liked us. I must give him credit, though. Maybe it comes with being a psychologist, but he took every word she spoke and turned it back to his initial question.

It never dissuaded her, though.

# Chapter Seventeen

Nearly eight months in, there was a mix-up with my medication. Whatever they'd been giving me that kept the voices at bay, I didn't get it. I woke up to *them* and months of their rage, spinning like a hurricane in my mind. It started with Annie, who materialized with a southern accent and all the explosive rage of Aileen Wuornos. Oscar showed up later in the day when another patient took the last turkey sandwich—an offense which sent him over the edge. Annie immediately sided with him, whereas Priscilla didn't really care all that much until she saw the look the patient gave us when he was called out (for what it's worth, Fred just wanted to go back to the room and to skip the rest of the day).

Annie disagreed with this approach, and quickly ripped the tray from the other patient. The stunned look on his face just fueled her rage, and she slammed the tray to the ground and stomped on it with my feet. I tried to fight her; I lost. Two orderlies stepped in, including a newer employee who was often the target of Lucy's flirtations. He took Annie's flying fist to the shoulder, and when he pulled my arm down, she hissed at him, seething spittle flying everywhere.

He stared at me, hurt and confused, looking as though he didn't recognize me, before leading me back to my room, wherein any object that could be used to harm myself or anybody else was removed: sneakers, shoelaces, pens, etc.

I tried to tell them it wasn't me. But *they* had my face.

An emergency session with Dr. Oliver was scheduled. To my surprise, I found Mother sitting in one of his chairs as well. Her hands were folded together, clasped so tightly that her knuckles were white. He invited me to sit, and the large orderly behind me made sure that I obeyed.

"Maddox," Dr. Oliver directed him, "please wait in the hall-way. You can leave the door cracked."

Once Maddox left, the door left slightly ajar behind him, Dr. Oliver sat in his red leather chair across from us. He looked to Mother, folded his hands neatly in his lap, then looked at me. Frustrated tears formed in my eyes. I knew they thought that this was me. I wanted to tell them. I wanted to explain that it wasn't me, that it was *them*. I felt once more like that child sitting in the principal's office, desperate for someone to understand, to see that it wasn't me, it was *them*.

"Beauty, we are concerned," he began matter-of-factly. "We found out that there was a mix-up with your medication today—and I take responsibility for that—but regardless, your behavior today was...well...not what we expected, to put it lightly. Some of our staff, like Maddox, are reluctant to work with you. I have to say, despite his size, Maddox is a teddy bear and has never, I mean never, expressed this sort of concern. As I was saying to your mother, we've been holding off on an official diagnosis because your symptoms don't follow the patterns that we typically expect to see." He looked to my mother. She caught my eye for a moment before dropping her gaze.

Dr. Oliver then expanded: "Take, for example, multiple personality disorder, or dissociative identity disorder. True cases are very rare. In the psych community, we consider them unicorns. We've had a few nurses tell us that they've seen your face change. Your expression, mannerisms, even the way you speak. They want me to diagnose and treat you for DID, but I'm not convinced."

Once again, he paused and glanced at Mother, his eyes asking for input. She continued to stare at her hands, refusing to make eye contact with him. Or me. Recognizing her reluctance, he continued, "Your mother told me that you've experienced these outbursts"—I watched her flinch from the corner of my eye—"since you were quite young. She said that she and your father discussed therapy early in your life, but your father preferred a more religious method." I remembered the Jesus man. So did *they*. I could feel them wiggling, anxious about whatever would come next. I met his gaze, hopeful. "I don't want to treat you for something that I truly don't believe you have, but we need a diagnosis to move forward with treatment. Based on what we've seen over the past few months, I am diagnosing you with borderline personality disorder with borderline Schizophrenic tendencies. Technically, you're too young for a conclusive diagnosis of Schizophrenia, but I think it's important we document this now." His prognosis complete, Dr. Oliver looked once more to Mother.

As did I. I needed Mother to look at me, to pull me close and offer me strength, just like she had on that slide so many years before. To see me as her little girl in light of this verdict, not as a monster beside her, within arm's length and yet somehow a million miles away.

But she couldn't, and she didn't. Looking back, I can understand. She knew my history, where I came from, but she bore this burden as her own failure.

Something in me gave up that day. If my mother couldn't see me for more than what *they* made me, it made sense to become what they said I was.

When she didn't respond, Dr. Oliver once again focused on me. "We've decided to treat you with anti-depressants and anti-psychotics. We are also going to up your therapy to twice a day on Tuesdays and Thursdays. The rest of the week, we'll continue our morning appointments, and you'll begin attending group therapy. I'm hopeful that we've caught this early enough to allow you to have a somewhat normal life." If he expected a reaction from me, he didn't get it. I stared back at him. Silent. "Furthermore, although your mother disagrees, we'd like to invite you to join our Sunday chapel services. I know how important your father was to you and how important his faith was to him. It's possible his passing may have contributed to your current state. I'm hoping that church will help you reconnect with who he was and what he meant to you."

I could *feel* Mother roll her eyes. I don't know what she had against the Jesus man or his father God, but whatever it was, *they* agreed with her. I suddenly felt a sharp pain in my palms and looked down to see blood forming at my fingertips.

"Maddox," Dr. Oliver called, "come quickly, and grab the first aid kit from my desk." He pried my fingers loose, four perfect rounded imprints on each palm slowly disappearing beneath the blood. Maddox handed him the first aid kit and a wet towel. Dr. Oliver wiped my palms gently—*Told you he likes us,* Lucy insisted—and wrapped a thin bandage across each palm with a neat knot on the back. Once he was satisfied with the placement of the bandages and security of the knots, he took both my hands and looked deeply into my eyes. I could tell he was searching for something (probably *them*) before he said, "I'm not giving up on you, Beauty." I heard a faint whimper from Mother's chair. "I'm going to give you a small shot. You've had a rough day already, and it might take a bit for the previous medication to clear your system before we can get you back on the right prescriptions. In the meantime, I want you to rest. Maddox will take you back to your room where Nurse Addison is waiting."

I nodded and let Maddox guide me from the room. As soon as we were out the door, Mother finally let out the grief that she'd managed to stuff into some hidden corner of her heart. "It's not your fault," I heard Dr. Oliver say. "With her sort of history, there's no knowing what demons haunt her. I said I'm not going to give up on her, and I meant it." Although he meant demons in the generic way, the moment he said it, a lightbulb turned on in my soul.

Demons. I had called them that once before.

*Oh, you wish,* Lucy whispered, her hand suddenly stroking that of Maddox, the now increasingly uncomfortable teddy bear.

*We're all you, dear. I do have to give props to your mom, though— barely widowed and already moving in on the hunky doctor. Don't worry, we'll show her...*

She had more to say, but Dr. Oliver's small shot had traveled up my bloodstream to my brain. Her voice faded away like a cloud into the horizon. I stopped stroking Maddox's hand, and I saw the tension release from his shoulders.

"I'm so sorry," I said, gripping his arm a little tighter. He looked down and nodded but didn't respond.

Then, before handing me off to Nurse Addison, he pulled a small silver cross necklace from under his scrubs. "You're not alone," he said simply, pointing his index finger up. "I believe."

# Part IV

## Somewhere In the Middle

# Chapter Eighteen

I told you before that I learned to be what they wanted me to be; in this case, "they" meant both the people around me and the voices within. At White Pines, I learned this more than I ever should have.

The anti-psychotics worked for a bit to silence the voices, but gradually, the effects waned. Dr. Oliver said this was normal as they figured out the right "combination." In the meantime, under Lucy's watchful eye, I learned to be a pinup girl.

She reminded me that I was too heavy and showed me how a simple finger down the throat fixed with that. She insisted that losing weight would make me desirable, that it would make me loveable. We weren't allowed to wear makeup, but she showed me how to mix flower petals with baby powder and a bit of water to make a light rouge and how a pencil's graphite could add a bit of shadow to my eye—according to her, the ancient Egyptians used a similar method to darken their eyes (she loved to reminisce about grinding kohl and malachite powder for eye makeup and missed the green look they imparted, but sighed that the graphite would have to suffice). She fought diligently with Nurse Addison that ChapStick was not makeup and managed to secure some tinted lip balms. She wanted me to look like a poster on the wall, and her tips, along with the natural growth from a girl into young lady, succeeded in accomplishing this.

*She's there with me in the bathroom. Like she'd been the first time I saw her, or at least the essence of her. She always sits on the toilet. I imagine her as girl sitting and filing her nails, although I'm certain she is nowhere near girl aged. I imagine that she pops her gum relentlessly and can almost hear the sound of bubble yum exploding from her mouth. "Not like that." She says as I try to apply the graphite to my flinching eyelids. "You have to do it softly. You don't want to look like any common street walker." I think if she could she'd do it for me, but she doesn't have hands other than my own. Even as she tries to control the makeup brush, my fingers fumble and eyelashes twitch as though they are under assault.*

*I can feel my cheeks burn with frustration. "That's not helping." She chides. She drops the small, angled brush on the counter and picks up a larger, fluffier one. "We'll come back to that." I watch in the mirror as she spins the brush gently in her petal and baby powder concoction. "Like this." She taps the brush into my skin, skillfully pulling it up my cheekbone. Then, taking a tissue from the box on the counter, she wipes away some of the graphite, reducing my racoon-esque appearance. "See, you're actually not half bad."*

*I believe her. Looking at myself I see a glimmer of what others must have seen when they called me by my name the first time. I feel her watching me. There's a strange sense of pride, like somehow, I am finally what she feels I am supposed to be. I both hate the thought and love it.*

While the doctors, especially Dr. Oliver, remained professional (much to Lucy's dismay), the same could not be said of some of the male nurses. Several of the orderlies couldn't resist my charm. Lucy and I came to an agreement: if I let her take the wheel during my remaining time at White Pines, she would keep the others from showing up and causing scenes.

Unfortunately, she wasn't the one in charge (that remained Opi, despite his general lack of involvement), so while outbursts were rarer, they happened often enough to confirm to Dr. Oliver that his diagnosis was on the right track.

I grew sick of the constant changes in medications. While it was nice initially to have a few days or even weeks of relief, adjusting to new medications was exhausting. One gave me diarrhea for a week. Lucy loved the subsequent weight loss; I did not. Eventually, I just started faking it. Forcing a smile here, lying about my wonderful day there. It convinced Dr. Oliver that we'd found the right blend. However, this time when the drugs wore off and my mind started to give way to *them*, I found solace in alcohol—something that shouldn't have been available, but with the right look and the right fluttering of eyelashes to the right nurse, I was able to sneak a few sips here and there. At one point, I discovered that the right touch meant a small, glittery, pink flask of my own.

One of the orderlies, Nick (Lucy loved to call him *Nicky*), became my near-constant companion. He was in his early twenties, a handsome man who reminded me of a lumberjack. He had sandy hair and a matching beard that he kept neatly shaped and tidy. He told me once that, where he was from, there weren't any girls like me.

Lucy worked hard to develop the friendship into something more. Nick knew the building well, including blind spots in the security system and which closets and storage rooms were rarely used or forgotten. His touch became heavier and more demanding. I hated it, but Lucy thrived on it. She arranged for him to bring us ecstasy, and in return, she gave all of me to him.

This became the norm for me: Lucy walking the halls like a Hollywood star, flirting and teasing any male she encountered—she loved making Nicky jealous—then rendezvousing in dark closets, my mind muddied with whatever drug he'd smuggled in that day. At night, she went on and on about how we were loved. About how this was all I'd ever wanted, and how ungrateful I was when she had made me beautiful. Then she'd saunter away to wherever it was they went when they weren't haunting me, and Louis would take her place.

Louis wanted me to know that he would always be there for me. He reminded me that, it was obviously Lucy that everyone else wanted, not me, but he assured me I could stay with him. That he cared for me, even though nobody else did. That he was good.

At one point, there was an epic battle between the two of them. Lucy wanted to be out with everybody at the center of attention; Louis wanted to stay in bed and watch over me. He held my body down while she struggled to overcome my mind. The result was a mind-shattering migraine—think pickaxe to the temple. The pain seared behind my eyes to the top of my skull. I couldn't cry out; I could only wheeze, begging for it to end.

Eventually, Nurse Addison realized that something was physically wrong and called in the doctors. They hooked me up to an IV solution, and Maddox volunteered to monitor me through the night. Nick and Lucy both adamantly opposed, but Lucy couldn't fight the medication, and Nick had no chance against Maddox, who stood at least a foot taller and had a much stronger will, so it was Maddox that sat patiently in the corner of the room, a thick leather book across his lap.

The biggest blessing that night was that the migraine mix included a nice sedative, something they didn't hand out often in that place, so I finally got a good night's rest despite *their* opposition.

At one point during the night, Nick tried to come in. I roused briefly out of the stupor to the door creaking open and Nick sneaking over the threshold. Faster than any man his size had the right to move, Maddox was at the door, a fistful of Nick's scrubs in his hand.

"I've seen the way you look at her," he whispered in the most intimidating growl I'd ever heard. "Enough is enough. The fact that you think of this child as anything less than a child sickens me, and the moment I have proof, you're *gone*. Got it?" Nick whimpered his assent as he straightened his shirt and scuffed away.

Maddox walked back to his chair, and I heard him muttering under his breath, "Lord, I don't know what you have for this girl, but I know it's more than this place. I submit her mind to you, and whatever force comes up against it, I declare its surrender to your mighty name. Thank you, Jesus. Amen."

I felt all of them shudder. They clung to my mind, waiting. Anticipating. A thin flame of hope began to grow as I fell back into the fog of drugs.

When I woke the next morning, something had shifted. Maddox was no longer in the chair, but the thick, leather-bound book remained. *Holy Bible* was etched on the front, and there was a small note tucked into the cover that read, "This is not it for you – M."

As I placed the note back between the pages, Nurse Addison bustled in with all the motion and chaos of a mother hen. "Oh dear, I was so worried when I read about your headache this morning. Let me check you." I think she went over every inch of my body, checking my temperature, my eyes, my ears, my lymph nodes. "Well, you seem fit as a fiddle today!" When I pulled my legs back up on the bed, the Bible hit the floor with a thump.

Nurse Addison leaned down to pick it up. "What do we have here?" Her fingers slowly flipped the pages. "Ah, this makes sense," she said, with no further explanation. "It is Sunday—chapel day. Dr. Oliver told me that you wanted to go—maybe this is the right week. Heck, I'll join you!"

She handed me the Bible and pulled a pair of navy slacks from the dresser and a white and navy striped sweater from the closet. "I won't put you in a dress, but you're certainly not wearing one of those tank tops you like so much." Lucy tried to stick my tongue out; she tried to hiss; she tried to throw the Bible from my hand; but somehow, she couldn't. Suddenly, several of them were there, all trying to toss the Bible away. I felt like the stone, the Bible Excalibur in my hand.

"Well, dear?" Nurse Addison asked.

"Huh?" I responded. I had missed whatever she'd said, too caught up in this strange, new development. "Do you want me to take that while you get dressed?" she repeated, gesturing toward the book in my hands.

"Uh, no," I said, clinging all the tighter to it. "Thank you."

"Alright. I'll be right outside the door as soon as you're ready. And don't think for a moment that you're leaving this room with any smudged pencil on your eyes. Yeah, I know about that." She winked and left.

Without setting the Bible down, I managed to change into the outfit she'd selected for me. I washed my face (Bible securely tucked under my armpit), pulled my hair back into a neat bun, and brushed my teeth. Looking in the mirror, I felt like myself for the first time in a long time. I may have even smiled as I walked out of the room.

I could feel *them,* their resistance. I could hear them, screaming at me to obey, but they couldn't stop me. I was drawn to the chapel like a moth to light.

Midway there, we ran into Nick. He tried to chat with us, but I kept walking. Lucy was furious. She wanted us to stop, to turn away from the chapel and instead go with her Nicky to one of the usual dank places, but I kept going. Nick tried to follow, but Nurse Addison stopped him with a sharp glance.

Once in the chapel, we took seats somewhere in the middle. It was nothing like the church that Father had taken me to. Although, I'm not entirely sure what I expected at a psychiatric hospital. Rather than a skinny man in tight jeans, the music was led by a small choir of inmates directed by a local volunteer—Marcy, as Nurse Addison later informed me. They sang songs I had never heard, accompanied by a booming organ. When the chaplain came out, he wasn't some trendy young man with a vibrant voice and animated personality. Rather, he was an older man, dressed in a thick grey sweater with worn slacks and un-shined shoes. His voice was soft but steady, and he spoke of Jesus as though they were old friends. He told about how God had come to earth, fully man and fully God, in the form of the Son. He shared how, during His time on earth, Jesus turned things upside down—how the Israelites had expected a king with shin-ing armor and an army to conquer their earthly enemies, but Jesus was born the child of a virgin in a town held in little regard. He spoke of how the Pharisees hated Jesus because He didn't obey *their* laws and yet how Jesus came to fulfill *the* law. He spoke about the way Jesus spit in his hand and rubbed it into the eyes of a blind man and he was healed, an affront to the religious leaders of the day. He declared the name of Jesus a holy name (I didn't understand how a name could be holy) and about how all must bow before Him (*they* shuddered at that).

Before ending his sermon, the chaplain explained that we could invite Jesus into our hearts today and accept Him as our Master (*they* snickered at that comment). He welcomed those who wanted to repeat after him in prayer. I couldn't bring my mouth to form the words, but I felt a new presence stir in my heart. *They* hated it, which only made me want it more. Then, after reminding us that the Easter service was only two weeks away and that we were welcome to bring family (Louis huffed at the idea of Mother in this place), he dismissed the group.

"What a wonderful sermon!" Nurse Addison exclaimed as we left our seats. "I always feel such a renewed sense of hope this time of year. I just love how the cross, the darkest day in history, was made our redemption." She squeezed my hand for emphasis. From the corner of my eye, I caught a glimpse of Maddox. He smiled and touched his finger to his head before pointing it to the ceiling knowingly. I don't know how, but I truly believe that he was the first (and possibly only) person to understand what was going on inside me.

19 |

# Chapter Nineteen

For the next several days, I experienced a renewed sense of self. Though I had yet to actually read the Bible, it never left my hands for more than a few moments; even when showering, I kept it within arm's reach, balancing it on the back of the toilet. I flipped through its pages several times, stopping often to glide my finger down the smooth, thin paper and, on more than one occasion, read the thick, bold lettering of Maddox's notes in the margins. It almost felt like an invasion of his privacy, but then I remembered that he had left the book behind for me to look through. Besides, living in a place like that made me realize that privacy was just an illusion.

One morning, while mindlessly turning through the pages, I stopped on a verse highlighted in orange. The page said Revelation, the seventeenth verse of chapter two:

> *Whoever has ears, let them hear what the Spirit says to the churches. To the one who is victorious, I will give some of the hidden manna. I will also give that person a white*

*stone with a new name written on it, known only to the one who receives it.*

A simple note was written in the column: *'New name?' What will I be called?*

I pondered that verse for the rest of the day and through that sleepless night. I had already been given a new name: Beauty. Did that mean I was already victorious? I didn't feel victorious, though. Despite the Bible tucked tightly under my pillow (my fingers grazed it often for reassurance), *their* voices were loud that night. They mocked the idea of victory—*that requires a battle*, they taunted. I imagined them making finger guns and *pew-pew* noises, aiming at my head. I'm not sure what would happen if they did, but I convinced myself that even a *pew-pew* from their lips was enough to make my head explode. I clutched the Bible tighter and fell into a restless sleep, the war on the battleground of my mind keeping me tossing and turning until the sun cast its orange rays across my bed.

The following morning, I told Nurse Addison that I didn't feel well and asked to spend the day in bed. As expected, she performed her normal head-to-toe checkup, her mouth alternating between clicks and *tsks*.

"Well, Beauty," she said once she'd thoroughly checked me out, "I just don't see any symptoms to make me worry. Are you sure you're feeling ill?" I hated lying to her. She'd become like a mother to me (*Like you need another one*, they heckled), but whatever sense of self I'd been feeling was quickly fading, and I needed to cling onto it, which meant limiting opportunities for them to take the strings and play me like a marionette.

I took a quick shower, reaching out at least a dozen times to ensure that the Bible remained safely on its perch (I'd felt guilty laying it directly on the back of the toilet and had instead made a nest with my shower caddy and towels for it to sit in). Although OCD wasn't part of my diagnosis, I'm quite certain that Doctor Oliver would have reconsidered had he seen the way my hand pawed for it, without thought, over and over again.

Once finished, I wrapped myself in a fuzzy robe and climbed back into bed, hair still dripping. I knew I needed to do more than just touch it; I needed to *know* it. If Nurse Addison had become like a mother, the Bible had become my best friend, a confidant, but, like any new friend, I needed to start somewhere.

*With the trash*, they suggested. Once again, their hate for this stack of pages wrapped in leather only made me want it even more.

I tried to start at the beginning but quickly found myself dozing off. Nothing against the creation of the world, but what I really wanted to know was more about the Jesus man—the man Father loved, the man in the clouds, the man whose spit made a blind man see. I fumbled around, reading bits and pieces that made no sense, until I stumbled across a page with his name mentioned in the first sentence. The title read *2 Peter*. I read it eagerly:

> *Simon Peter, a servant and apostle of Jesus Christ, To those who through the righteousness of our God and Savior Jesus Christ have received a faith as precious as ours: Grace and peace be yours in abundance through the knowledge of God and of Jesus our Lord.*

I continued reading, but honestly, I didn't understand much of it. I was intrigued by the idea of a savior but couldn't fathom what that meant for me. I'd never experienced any sort of faith for anything, other than my childhood faith that Father would always protect me—and that proved to be false. I couldn't remember experiencing grace or peace in any meaningful way, and there was no way I could be someone worth saving.

*Exactly*, they agreed.

"For how worthless you seem to find me, you sure fight hard," I verbally chastised them. No response—shocking.

"What was that?" I heard from the doorway. My head shot up. *Nicky*! Lucy squealed. "They sent me to get you for your session—what are you wearing? A robe?" He glanced down the hallway before closing the door behind him.

I couldn't speak. He crossed to the bed and reached out to stroke my knee. Despite the cloth between us, I felt naked. "I've missed you," he cooed. I couldn't respond. I'd never had to talk to him before—Lucy had always done it. Now, with the Bible in my hands, it was just me. "What's that?" he asked, noticing it in my lap.

My hands jerked it away from him, sending it across the bed where it teetered on the edge. A barely audible "nothing" crossed my lips.

"Chill out, man," he said, pulling his hands back to his chest in an "I surrender" motion before switching topics. "I know how much you like Dr. Oliver, but you should change. Showing up to therapy in a robe is desperate, even for you."

I could feel Lucy's flush. She didn't like this. Neither did Priscilla. She squinted my eyes, shooting daggers at him. "What's your deal?" he asked, his hand reaching out once more, this time caressing the silky collar of the robe where it met my sternum. "You go to church one time, and now you're too good for Nicky?" His voice hardened. "Don't get confused—going to church one time won't make you any less cheap or easy. It won't change what we both know you are."

I don't know if it was Lucy or Priscilla—or maybe, just this once, myself—but in a flash my clenched fist went from my side to his face, punching him hard enough to split the skin. "What the hell?!" he screamed, his eyes instantly overflowing and nose running. Gingerly touching his cheekbone, his eyes turned dark at the sight of his blood, and he raised his hand against me.

Priscilla met his gaze, daring him. For an instant I saw recognition in his face. His hand faltered, his fist frozen in the air for a second too long as the door burst open. Maddox barreled through; Nurse Addison close behind.

"*You!*" Maddox roared. Nick jumped back, nearly two feet in one motion, and I sprung from the bed. It was just me now—no Lucy, no Priscilla.

Nurse Addison intervened. "Control yourselves," she demanded, stepping between Maddox and Nick (who was now hunched in embarrassment and fear—a dwarf in Maddox's shadow). "You"—her finger stabbed Nick in the chest, then pointed to the door— "*out.* You"— her finger now pointed at me as she marched across the room and pulled a solid black tunic and leggings from the dresser— "change. You have a session with Dr. Oliver. And you," she said, turning last towards Maddox, finger safely at her side, "don't leave this doorway. Do you understand?" Maddox nodded, following her to the door. Her eyes met mine once again. "Move," she commanded.

I hustled to the bathroom. I could hear her whispering to Maddox as I closed the bathroom door, but I couldn't make out what was said. I quickly dressed and exited the bathroom, making sure to grab the Bible from its resting place on the bed before joining Maddox, now alone in the doorway. He wouldn't make eye contact with me. We stood there, silently, until Nurse Addison returned, bustling down the hallway.

"Let's go," she said, taking my elbow in her hand and guiding me towards Dr. Oliver's office (as if I hadn't been there a hundred times before). She walked me in and plopped me in the chair across from him, something she'd never done before, before grabbing the second chair and pulling it, legs screeching against the tile, to the door and dropping herself down with a dramatic air. I tucked the Bible safely under my leg, somehow embarrassed by my need for it.

"Welcome, Beauty," Dr. Oliver opened, standing behind his chair rather than sitting. "I've heard"—he paused, looking to Nurse Addison, then back to me—"that there's been an unfortunate situation." I didn't know how to respond. My hands were clasped tightly, knuckles sore under the pressure of my fingertips. Dr. Oliver abruptly sat, nearly falling into the chair. Once he composed himself, he scooted to the very edge of his seat, knees a mere inch from mine. Nurse Addison loudly cleared her throat, but he ignored her. His eyes stared deeply into mine, flickering from one to the other. I wondered what he thought about the eye I'd tried to remove. I wondered if he even saw the scar. "Beauty," he started again, "tell me. Tell me what happened."

I didn't know what he wanted. The story I'd be telling wasn't mine; it was Lucy's. Until today, I knew practically nothing of Nick. Or rather, it would be more honest to say that I remembered nothing of Nick. When Lucy was with him, I wasn't—not in the way that people typically are during that sort of thing. I'd swallow whatever concoction of drugs, prescription or otherwise, Nick offered and let Lucy take the reins while I escaped somewhere deep in my mind.

"Let's back up," Dr. Oliver said in response to my silence, leaning back into his seat. "Do you know Nick?" I nodded. "Okay, that's a start. Have you been alone with him before?" I nodded again. He blew out a loud burst of air, and his eyes darted behind me to Nurse Addison. "In your room?" I shook my head. I couldn't tell if his sigh was one of relief or disbelief. "Then where?" I couldn't answer. I didn't know how to. I wished that Lucy was there. She would know; she's the one that met him. But like all those times before, when it was time to fess up, she was nowhere to be seen—that, or she was bound by the Bible tucked snugly beneath my leg.

"Beauty," Dr. Oliver implored, once more on the edge of his seat, "this is important." He was searching my face, looking for something, but I had nothing to give. "Has Nick ever..."—he paused, and in the silence I could hear Nurse Addison breathing, slow and heavy, behind me—"...has Nick ever been inappropriate with you?" Once again, I wasn't sure how to respond. Nick was certainly "inappropriate" (what a word) with Lucy, but she invited it. She thrived on it. She just had the unfortunate luck of being trapped in me.

I could feel my eyes blinking, knew that I was blinking too much, but I couldn't stop. I couldn't draw the line between what happened with Lucy and my role in it. I was there; I felt it. I knew Nick's touch and his weight, but it wasn't me who'd experienced it.

I heard Nurse Addison stand, felt her presence behind me as her hand landed softly on my shoulder.

Dr. Oliver nodded his approval. "Beauty," he repeated, softly snapping his fingers near my face, "has Nick ever acted inappropriately towards you?" My eyes locked on his, and I nodded slowly. Once again, a short breath burst from his lungs. He nodded to Nurse Addison, whose warmth left my side. "Do you want to tell me about your experiences with Nick?"

"They weren't mine," I corrected. I saw his brow furrow, his eyes narrowing as he searched mine once again.

"You'll have to explain that to me. I don't understand." I shrugged. "No, that's not good enough this time. Did Nick coerce you into a physical relationship with him?" I nodded again.

His face fell, and his head dropped. "Oh, Beauty," he said. He'd always been professional, but in that moment, I saw a glimpse of the man he was outside of the office. My confession had broken something in him. Most of the staff considered me a young woman, but not Dr. Oliver. Not Nurse Addison. They both knew that, despite being seventeen, with the life that I'd had I was still very much a girl.

Despite his best attempt to shield it, I saw the rage in his eyes. He stood and started pacing. Some might attribute his reaction to the potential negative press and lawsuits an event like this could spark (and fairly so, as my mother herself later filed one).

I could tell, though, that it was more than that; Dr. Oliver was truly troubled by what had happened under his roof.

"Will you tell me more?" he asked abruptly, pulling at the hairs at his jawline. I shook my head. "Beauty, this is important," he urged, the rage in his eyes merging with compassion. "We let you down." He paused. "I let you down."

"It's not mine to tell," I reminded him again.

"Whose, then?" he demanded. I shrugged, again. He stared at me, again.

A bustling at the door interrupted our staring contest. Nurse Addison had returned. She whispered to Maddox, who nodded and marched away, before gesturing towards Dr. Oliver's chair.

"May I?" she asked. He nodded.

She sat, reaching for my hand. I hesitated, but, like any knowing mother would, she grasped it anyway, covering mine with both of hers. Hers were warm. I stared at them, trying to remember a time when my own mother had held my hands so softly.

"Beauty," she started, drawing my eyes to her face, "your mother is on the way, as are the police. What happened was not okay, and we will be pressing criminal charges against Mr. Meyers." (*Nicky...*) "I know this is a lot to take in, but you did nothing wrong—I need you to know that." She gently squeezed my fingers before continuing, "Nurse Julie and Nurse Gwen are outside the door. They are going to take you to your room until your mother and the authorities get here, then they'll take you to the administrative office. I'll be there too, but first I need to speak with Dr. Oliver. Do you understand?" I nodded. "Maddox will be along as well, but I've instructed him to avoid any contact. Do you understand? *You didn't do anything wrong, Beauty.*" she repeated. I nodded again, watching a bridge of moisture crest over her lower eyelash. She patted my hands and pulled me up from the chair. One hand still holding mine, the other tucked under my elbow, she led me to the door. Just as she said, two young women stood outside, somber-faced. Nurse Addison handed me off to them, turning back into the office with a sigh.

As we started down the hall, there was a sudden shrieking and skidding of rubber-soled shoes against the linoleum. All three of us turned and saw Maddox dragging Nick by the bicep towards the office.

"This is assault!" Nick screamed, digging in his heels, but he had no chance against the mass of Maddox. He yelled even louder when he saw me. "She wanted it. Tell them you wanted it!" When his cries went unanswered, his words turned to venom: "You came on to me!" The shrill cry echoed through the hall.

"*Enough.*" Nurse Addison re-appeared, her sharp tone ending his tantrum. She turned to the two nurses by my side. "Go, now." They each took one arm—as though I was an invalid— and hurried me down the hall. Meanwhile, Nick's voice faded to nothing more than a whimper.

Once at my room, I was directed to sit and wait. Nurse Gwen went searching for a first-aid kit while Nurse Julie intentionally avoided eye contact with me. When Nurse Gwen returned, she carefully cleaned my knuckles where they had split against Nick's face. The sting from the alcohol wipe brought tears to my eyes, and my hand jerked back, surprising both Nurse Gwen and me.

*Witch,* Priscilla accused, staring daggers at the nurse, who slowly backed away. I felt Priscilla reach for my strings again, no longer bound, and that was when I realized that a familiar, leather-bound weight was missing.

"Where is it?" I cried, jolting up from my chair. Panicking, I patted myself down, checking under my arms, my legs, even my pockets (as though it could have fit). Lightning bolts shot across my temple as the anxiety began to rise in my chest.

The nurses looked at each other. It was clear that they'd heard the rumors about me and were uncertain how to handle the situation. "Beauty?" Nurse Julie started, inching towards the door.

"*Where is it?!*" I bellowed. I'd like to say that it was Fred or Annie, but this was all me. I tried to remember the way the leather felt in my hands, the peace and protection I'd felt, tried to recall the words that I'd read, but it was gone. It was all gone.

*Gotcha.* The hair on my arms began to rise along with the dread in my gut as Opi's presence pulled me down. Living free from their control, even for a short time, had let me delude myself into feeling normal. *That's not for you,* they taunted. Their voices swarmed like a tornado, all of them talking, speaking, screaming in their native tongue. I clasped my hands tightly against my temples.

"Stop! Please, stop," I begged. It was obvious that the nurses had not seen and did not know how to handle something like this. Nurse Gwen ran out of the room while Nurse Julie backed up towards the door.

After what felt like an eternity (but was probably only a few minutes), I felt the familiar sting of a syringe and the formidable presence of Maddox. He laid a hand on my head and began to mumble something under his breath.

"Maddox, you can't do that!" Nurse Julie exclaimed. "You know we aren't allowed."

"Look at her," he barked back. "Nothing else is working. She *needs* this." Even though I didn't understand what "this" was at the time, he was right. I later learned that he had prayed over me for nearly ten minutes while the voices raged and the nurses chewed their nails. I also heard that he received his first formal disciplinary action for doing so.

I don't know if it was the contents of the syringe finally kicking in or the words he spoke, but the voices slowly faded away. Subsequently, I was in a meditative-like state when Nurse Addison reappeared at my door. She sent Maddox away, despite his quiet protests.

"This is for the best," she assured him. I was walking on clouds as she led me down the hallway, through large double doors, and to the elevator. The light flashed by each number as we went up, finally landing on level eight.

I'd never been on that level before; it soon became clear why. Long hallways were lined with offices and conference rooms. Despite living in White Pines for over a year, I'd never considered it a place of business, a workplace for as many individuals as it housed. We approached a large door bearing the name *Richard Stone* on a metal plate. As the door opened inward, a tall, lean man beckoned us in—Richard, I assumed, which was soon confirmed.

"Come in, please, come in." He had all the bustle of Nurse Addison without any of the calm. "Please, to the conference room," he said, gesturing to his left. We moved around him, my eye catching his for one uncomfortable moment, before passing through a large office into an even larger conference room. "Take a seat," he said to me, then, "You may leave," to Nurse Addison.

"Not a chance," she responded, plopping into a seat beside me. I could tell he wanted to pull rank, to demand that she leave the room, but instead he simply sighed and relented. Two other nurses—who had apparently followed us in—took their positions along the wall. A moment of uncomfortable silence passed, interrupted by a tap at the door. Marge, whom I'd not seen since my first day at White Pines, slowly opened the door.

"They're here," she announced meekly. There was no sign of the brazen woman who had welcomed me my first night. Richard nodded, and she beckoned to someone I couldn't see, "Please, come in."

Beatrice entered first (I hadn't seen her since my drop-off, either), followed by two men in cheap suits and a third in a police uniform. They shuffled around the table, offering hands with brief introductions.

"I hear they call you Beauty," one of the suits began. He had a strange, Midwestern accent, the type that faded over time but never truly went away. I nodded. "I'm Detective Eddie Weston. This is my partner, Detective Alfred Lewis—he goes by Al. We're part of the Sex Crimes Unit. I'm sorry to meet you under these circumstances." I stared back at him, not sure what to say. This was like an episode of some late-night TV show, not my life. He waited a moment for me to respond, then, when I failed to do so, continued, "We understand that you've been a victim of assault."

I felt my hands press into the table in front of me, Lucy squinting my eyes at him. "He loves me!" she burst out, vaulting from the chair. A flush rose to my face as I was overcome with embarrassment.

Detective Eddie cleared his throat, meeting Lucy's gaze without wavering. "We can talk about that," he answered. "You can tell us all about it."

"I won't. I won't, I won't, I won't!" she declared, throwing me back into the chair with an *umph*. All eyes were on us, but they turned a moment later to a commotion outside the door.

"Please, let us handle this," I heard Dr. Oliver implore. "We just want to do what's best for her."

"Not another minute!" I heard her voice before she burst through the door. "You!" Mother accused. She charged towards Richard, finger ready to meet his chest. "You let this happen. We came to you, and you let this happen!" If she noticed the others in the room, she easily ignored them.

Detective Al quickly stood, placing himself between Mother and the administrator. He swiftly grabbed her hand and introduced himself, catching her off guard and pacifying her briefly. "Please take a seat by your daughter," he instructed. I don't know if she realized I was in the room until that moment, but she quickly came to me, cradling my head between her hands and holding her cheek against my forehead, as though she were checking my temperature. She stayed like that until Detective Al asked if we could begin.

I won't take you through the discussion (let's be honest, it was an interrogation), but I will tell you that Lucy and Priscilla took turns running the show. In this episode Lucy was a petulant child and Priscilla was her typical, defiant self. Oscar may have shown up as well. Needless to say, it was not a fruitful interaction. Several hours later, the suits left, not knowing much more than when they arrived and feeling a bit exasperated at having been involved in the first place.

Mother then took her turn as the inquisitor, demanding answers. I could tell that Richard and Dr. Oliver were exhausted, Richard never having experienced a day with *them* and Dr. Oliver fighting his own emotions and guilt.

"We've told you everything we know," Dr. Oliver said matter-of-factly. "I think it best now if the nurses take Beauty back to her room. We can get her a sedative and revisit this conversation tomorrow." Lucy, who had adored him until that moment, hissed at him. Literally.

Mother groaned while Dr. Oliver's fingers resumed twisting the hair on his jaw. Richard, meanwhile, stared agape at Lucy, then fixed his gaze on Mother. "Well?" he asked.

"Not a chance. She stays with me. In fact, I think she's *leaving* with me."

"That would be a mistake," Dr. Oliver retorted. "What happened is horrendous, and we will deal with it, but like it or not, this is the best place for her."

"She *hissed* at you. You really want to try and tell me that she's better? That you've 'healed' her?"

"I'm not saying that we don't see days like this, but I am saying that we've seen improvement." Lucy scoffed. I wished for Maddox with his prayer and a dose of whatever it was he'd shot into my arm hours before. "Can we please talk in private for a moment? She can sit with Nurse Addison in Richard's office."

Mother tensed briefly before giving in. "Beauty, go with the nurse, please. Just to the office—not a step further, or I'll sue all of you," she informed them icily.

We left, Nurse Addison easing the door shut behind us but leaving a crack at the last minute. Maybe she was nosy, but I'm fairly sure she did it for me.

"What are you going to do?" asked Dr. Oliver. "We only have six months left before she's eighteen and can legally leave, and there won't be anything we can do to stop her. Despite what's happened, she knows this place. She's not been a threat to herself since the day she came to us, and, other than punching Nicolas today—which, from what I understand, she did to defend herself—she hasn't been a threat to anybody else." Even in the next room, I could hear the desperation in his voice. "She *knows* this place," he said again. "Let us continue her treatment. I know we're getting somewhere."

The silence was deafening.

"Fine," Mother relented at last. "But I want background checks on every person that she interacts with. I want limited staff and a dedicated team. And I want *detailed* updates from either you or that nurse out there—Beauty seems to like her. But don't think for a second any of this absolves you."

They spoke a bit more about the terms of my stay before Dr. Oliver again suggested sending me back to my room. This time, Mother agreed, and the two of them, trailed by Richard, exited into the office.

Mother came and knelt beside me. She wrapped her arms around me, whispering her love for me and promising that she would do better.

"It wasn't supposed to be like this," she murmured. I think if she'd had any tears left in her, she would have wept, but her eyes remained dry. As she pulled away, I noticed how much she'd aged in the past year. She looked thin and worn down, a woman left alone in the world after the death of her husband, left with a son who had escaped to college and couldn't be bothered and a daughter who was, well, *me*.

Then she was gone.

20

# Chapter Twenty

The next six months were a blur. Between the legal proceedings (criminal charges were pressed against Nicholas), increased private sessions with Dr. Oliver, group sessions, and the overall renewed sense of urgency around "fixing" me, I was exhausted. All I wanted was sleep and the brief notion of peace that came with it.

I searched my room and everywhere I could think of for the Bible but was never able to find it. *He took it,* Lucy informed me. *He loved me, not you, and you ruined it.* Nurse Addison brought me a small pocket Bible, but it didn't have the same effect as the leatherbound one. I searched for Maddox as well, but he had been moved to a different ward. I don't think she was supposed to tell me, but Nurse Addison said that the higher-ups thought he'd become too attached and, after Nicholas, had decided that it was best for my caregivers to be female. Enter my new orderly: a stocky woman with a thick Southern accent named Alice.

Alice was no-nonsense, matter-of-fact, and, despite her Southern upbringing, very clearly atheist. *They* loved her; I did not. I missed Maddox and the way the voices backed down in his presence. I thought often of the time he'd tapped his head and pointed to the sky. He had known, and knowing that he knew made me feel like I'd had somebody in my corner.

Alice was nothing like that. Alice stuck to the clock. There were no prayers; no church services; nothing of the sort under her care. When Nurse Addison tried to accompany me to chapel, Alice threw a fit not unlike that of Mother all those years ago. At some point, it was easier just to avoid the confrontation, and so I stopped going.

Eventually, I gave way once again to Opi's inky depths. I tried to keep swimming, to keep my head above water, but at some point, I realized I couldn't see the light anymore. It was like being a kid and jumping off the high dive for the first time. You hit the water, and you see the surface getting further and further away. As soon as you stop sinking, you start to kick, kick, kick, and you know you're going up, but, for just a moment, you're not sure if you're going to make it. Your lungs start to burn and scream, and you can't tell how much further you have to go. You feel stuck, trapped just below the surface.

Well, I couldn't see the surface anymore, so I stopped kicking. I drowned in Opi.

I knew, to get out of this place, they (meaning Dr. Oliver, Richard, and the rest of the staff) had to believe I was better (or at least responding well to medication). Otherwise, White Pines could petition the state to keep me even after I turned eighteen. As such, I compromised and stopped fighting *them*, knowing that when I let them have control, there were fewer outbursts. My life became about counting down the days.

Lucy still tried to flirt with any male allowed around us. Most of them avoided us, knowing what had happened to Nick, and those who couldn't kept conversations brief and professional. She hated it. She tried to turn her focus back to Dr. Oliver, but I'm certain he suspected more was happening than I let on, and he managed her quite well.

Eventually, Priscilla grew sick of the constant shutdowns. She shoved Lucy into wherever their void was and brought Oscar back. Those two were always the best of friends, and together they became the prima donnas of the psych ward. Priscilla remained demanding and full of herself while Oscar lashed out at anybody who dared to question her right to be so. I felt the eyes when we entered the room, the way both staff and patients avoided us and walked on eggshells if they had to engage.

The two of them managed to get us banned from group therapy. Priscilla was always one-upping stories or feelings shared by other patients; when chastised for it, the two of them threw a fit that would make a toddler's meltdown seem like adorable puppies napping.

Getting kicked out of group therapy meant more one-on-one sessions with Dr. Oliver. Lucy tried very hard to push her way back in for these, but the other two wouldn't let her; I'm not entirely sure what this looked like to the outside observer, as they often had loud, in-depth arguments in my head during sessions which left me sitting quietly, nursing a headache, or, during brief reprieves, grinding out one-word responses to questions. Around this time *narcissistic tendencies* was added to my file, tacked onto the already-long list of disorders I was presumed to have.

During the day the others controlled me while Louis took over once again at night. He didn't like competing with the others. I'd lay in bed while he told me that nobody would ever care for me or love me. He promised that he'd never leave me—not like everybody else had. Occasionally, Fred showed up too. He was the closest thing to an ally Louis had, always backing up what Louis had to say. *Of course* nobody else would be with me like Louis was. *Of course* I'd always feel this way.

Then the darkness would come, and Opi would fill my nostrils, stealing the very breath from my lungs. Some nights, I'd ask for sleeping meds so I could skip Louis's love song of loneliness and jump straight to Opi, falling into a restless slumber where I relived the nightmares from my childhood.

Six months became five, then four. Three. Two weeks. Then, at last, my eighteenth birthday. *They* counted down the days too, and as soon as I was legally able, they took me away from White Pines.

# Part V

The Time on the Bay

# Chapter Twenty-One

I ran—as fast as I could, as far as I could.

Since I was technically disabled, I was assigned a state case-worker prior to being released. I was supposed to give her an address to check up on me, but I didn't have one to give. I didn't know a home outside of the one I grew up in—which, let's face it, was not much of a home without Father and Brother. Besides, Mother had sold that house and now lived in an apartment in the city. The only other place I knew was the one from which I was now running. Since providing an address was a requirement for release, I simply gave the old address and promised the case-worker I'd update it once I landed somewhere more permanent.

The moment I left White Pines, I made my way to the nearest bus station, a small suitcase at my side and my first disability payment in my pocket. I bought the cheapest ticket, just wanting to get away and not caring where to, and hopped on a bus. It dropped me off in a small, dusty town with only a gas station and pizza parlor within eyesight. The bus I'd came in on was the last one of the day, so I bought a ticket for the next morning (after confirming that it'd take me to a town larger than this place) and curled up on a bench outside the bus stop with only a thin, pink blanket to cover me and a rolled-up sweater as a pillow.

For the first time in my life, I was truly alone. There was nobody to tuck me in, nobody to feed me my pills, and nobody to save me if my nightmares consumed me.

I tried to take my medication (before I left, Dr. Oliver had reminded me a hundred times, with moisture in his eyes, to take it *every single day*), but *they* resisted; *we don't need that anymore,* they insisted. When I tried to put a pill to my lips, my arm betrayed me and threw it to the ground instead. My foot joined in the betrayal, stomping the small, white pill into a small, white pile of dust. I tried three or four more times, all with the same results, before I finally gave up and settled into my makeshift bed.

The night was filled with a strange sense of urgency. The crickets seemed to scream the chorus of a hard rock song; the toads bellowed along, and the cicadas ensured that they weren't left out. If the cacophony of nature wasn't enough, all *their* voices overlapped in my head once more. They spoke hurriedly in their ancient language, excitement building, until my mind felt ready to split. Aware of my frequent migraines, Nurse Addison had insisted that Dr. Oliver prescribe me a supply of medication —"just in case." I'd never been more thankful to have her in my corner than I was that night. Three pills (though the prescription said *one or two as needed*) did the trick. *They* were too distracted with their discussion to notice that I'd taken them.

I faded away, listening to their excited chirps and clicks as the clouds rolled into my brain. Just as my eyelids fluttered shut,

I heard the faintest voice—Father. He was trying to shake me awake, worried sick that I would knock myself out on a bench at night in a town that I didn't know.

In fact, I was shaken awake the following morning, but not by Father; rather, it was a portly man in a blue ticketers uniform whose nametag read *Cal*.

"Young lady," he said with some sort of accent I'd never heard, "you can't stay here any longer. People are going to start arriving soon, and we can't have you out here sleeping on the bench." I mumbled some sort of reply and fished the ticket out of my bag, waving it in the direction of his voice. Even though the pain was gone and the voices still muted, the migraine-hangover clung like cobwebs to every corner of my mind.

He hummed as though expressing some sort of understanding (he probably thought I was a runaway, which wasn't far from the truth) but still insisted that I get up. He said that I could wait until my bus came, but no more sleeping—they didn't want to give the impression that this was a stop for the homeless. I wanted to argue that I wasn't homeless, but at that very moment it struck me that I was.

I quickly sat up and packed the blanket and sweater back into my bag as Cal huffed and returned to his station inside. Oscar was the first to break through the cobwebs, upset by how we'd been treated, and Priscilla comforted him by lifting my middle finger towards the ticketing window. I forced my hand down and hurried to the bathroom to freshen up and change before my bus arrived.

The restroom smelled old and stale, as they often do in places like this. It brought back a memory from a vacation we'd taken when I was five or six.

*We are driving to some relative's house and pause at a rest stop along the way. Mother comes in with me and starts singing some tune from a children's show in the large, empty restroom (I struggle to use public restrooms, and this is her favorite way to calm me). Her voice bounces off the walls echoing throughout.*

*"Sing with me!" she bids from outside the stall. I sing along, quietly at first, worried that someone might hear me, but she simply sings louder. I raise my voice to match hers, and by the time we finish, our song is mixed with giggles and grins.*

*"See, Beauty?" she says. "It's not that bad."*

I stepped into the first stall and locked the door behind me. With that memory in my mind, I started to sing quietly. I sang as I used body wipes to clean up. I sang even louder as I changed my clothes.

*What are you, some sort of bathroom popstar?* Priscilla asked. *Make it stop!* Egged on by how much they hated it, I forced myself to remember the songs I'd learned with Father in church. I could barely remember the words, but just humming the melodies sent them into a rage.

Whatever sense of joy I got from their discomfort quickly faded as they took over once again. Annie forced my eyes to my reflection in the mirror. I felt my body dragged forward from the stall until I was leaning over old, broken tiles, my face no more than an inch from its own reflection. They held me there, staring at myself. *Remember whose you are*, they asserted in tandem. I tried to push away, but they held me there, face-to-face with the part of me that was him. They kept me there until the restroom door squeaked on its hinges, breaking their grip.

Finally able to move, I brushed past the older woman who'd come in without making eye contact. I went back to the bench and sat while they laughed and mocked in their native tongue, mixing in just enough English for me to hear their insults directly: *Potty popstar. Porta-potty princess.* Their laughter was like nails on a chalkboard, and I fought the urge to take a double dose of the migraine medication.

The bus soon arrived. I boarded, their continued cackling now a blade behind my eye. I slipped into a seat near the back of the bus and stuck my hand in my bag. *Just getting a snack,* I promised over and over in my mind. I grabbed a small bag of chips—and the prescription bottle as well.

*Not this time,* one of them said; I couldn't tell who through the chorus of voices squeaking and squealing. Whatever they had talked excitedly about the night before had come up again. I tried to maintain my grip on the prescription bottle, but my hand dropped it back to the bottom of my bag. The pain was now so bad that it brought tears to my eyes. I missed the orderlies who could quickly stick a needle in me and release it. I missed the bed and pillows. I missed Nurse Addison.

*This is what happens when you fight us.* I listened to their mocking as the bus door shut and it lurched forward. I pressed my head firmly against the cool glass window, silently begging them to stop. After four or so hours, they finally relented, and the vice on my temples was released. I sighed in relief and dozed for the remainder of the trip.

The ticket I'd bought took me to a small town by the ocean. As soon as I stepped off the bus, I was overwhelmed by the smell of salt and ˈfish. I was also relieved by the number of people bustling about; people in towns like that always seemed much friendlier than anywhere else, and it proved true here as well. Despite spending my first week sleeping on park benches, eating fast food while sitting on the grass, and waiting out brutal coastal storms in a bank atrium, the locals always greeted me with a smile. Several invited me to their barbecues and offered me slices of birthday cake. They may have kept their children away from me, but none of them gave me a sideways glance when my face froze with rage or when I screamed at whatever happened to upset or offend *them*.

Within a week, the girl who'd left White Pines was gone. I became an erratic rotation of whoever was the strongest that day. Freed from the restricted access to males, Lucy and Priscilla ruled most of my days. Despite our homelessness, they managed to make sure I stayed beautiful. Able at last to access the makeup previously denied by Nurse Addison, Lucy coveted every new makeup, hair care, or style she saw advertised, leading to several trips to the local drug and department stores and spending money on things we didn't have the space or means for. Lucy hated my hair, which was difficult to manage in the humidity, and constantly argued with Priscilla about how to make us look our best. Priscilla was fundamentally opposed to how Lucy dolled us up; she thought it made me look like a clown. She wanted to be more dignified, like a queen, not some concubine.

My first disability check quickly dwindled, and I still didn't have an address for another check or a bank account for direct deposit. Fred took this very seriously and would pop out periodically to count my cash. It became his weird obsession; ten, eleven, twelve times a day, he'd pull my wallet out and count the ever-decreasing supply.

As my money was squandered, tension between him and the girls (an odd thing to call them) increased. When my wallet held less than two hundred dollars, he finally put his foot down. Lucy had seen a new mascara that promised to lift and spread lashes for a "falsie" look. She determined that we absolutely must have it; Fred felt otherwise. I ended up walking to and from the door of the store for at least thirty minutes, mumbling their argument under my breath. People walked by, glancing but not stopping or staring.

This same showdown repeated itself frequently: Lucy wanting to spend, Priscilla demanding we look good enough (she couldn't stand the thought of being judged or found wanting), and Fred stubbornly denying them, worried as he was about money. Lucy even suggested the "old profession" as a means of making money, happily declaring that she'd been preferred by kings back in the day. Oscar then popped up, disgusted with her and her idea, while Priscilla insisted that we just needed to find a rich man.

Their squabbles typically ended with a migraine and, when they allowed it, me taking a double dose of the migraine medication and passing out on my favorite bench, which was partially hidden by overgrown bushes and a large, droopy willow. When they didn't allow it, I'd go what I'd dubbed "full zombie" and either wander about, doing the weird mumbling thing, or find a nook (behind garbage cans, in the allies between buildings, or even inside drain-runoff pipes) to lie in until they finished whatever argument gripped my temples like a vice.

After a few weeks, a local girl adopted me as her friend. Close to my own age, she'd seen me arguing with myself outside the drug store and had given me her mascara and eyeliner when she'd determined my dilemma. Despite (or perhaps because of) the lack of any punk or goth crowd in the area, she'd fully embraced the look: long black coat, spiked collar, and raven-black hair with a bright orange streak.

Ari was her name. She started bringing me makeup and telling me all about the bands that she loved, the concerts she'd gone to, and the band members she'd slept with. Then she started bringing a bottle of fireball, which we took sips from while listening to her music, each of us with one of her earbuds.

*They* loved the music. I didn't really care for it (it was mostly screaming, although periodically there were wonderful melodies), but I loved the relief it provided. They were too busy soaking in the sound to mess with me.

We didn't talk much. As the daughter of the area's only lawyer and local bank-branch manager, Ari didn't have much of a story to tell (which made the whole goth thing all the more hilarious to me), and I had talked enough in White Pines to last a lifetime. Our friendship was based on loud, metal music by bands with names like Nightshade and Suicide Rejects. She also brought me things like blankets, leggings, and snacks. Despite her desperate attempts to fight "the man", she was as soft as the rest of the town. Lucy hated her; Priscilla loved her. Annie was a fan of the music she brought, whereas Oscar couldn't believe she thought we needed her to bring us stuff. Fred simply counted our cash after she left.

At some point, she took me to a large, empty house set up on a hill overlooking the bay. Turns out it was the groundskeeper's house for a lot that her grandmother owned (she later told me that the house had been a part of the underground railroad and was considered a historical site). It was big, it was old, it was dirty, and it was free.

The main floor was large and open. Two antique couches were pushed back against a corner wall. Large hanging lamps flashed when we turned on the lights, illuminating a hole in the kitchen counters where a sink once sat. Ari took me slowly upstairs, telling me how she and her older brother Robert used to play here in the upstairs closet as children. It was a weird little half-room with a tiny door for access. She pointed out areas of the steps to watch for as we ascended: one where she'd stepped on a nail as a child (the adventure that got her banned from playing here) and another where her older brother, Robert, had lost his favorite Pokémon card where the paneling had separated just enough for the tiny card to slip through. According to Ari, this was still a topic of conversation during the holidays. Her brother swore the card had been in perfect condition and would be worth a bundle.

Fred made a mental note of the step.

She walked me past the upstairs closet, a weird half-room with a tiny door for access, reminiscing the times she and Robert had played in there as children, then showed me the master suite, its en-suite bathroom containing a large clawfoot tub and a toilet with a cracked lid.

"You can stay here," she informed me. The next day, she returned with new sheets and bedding. Though I'm certain she could afford it, the bedding still had its security tags attached.

"I can show you," she offered when she caught me eyeballing the tags. Lucy and Fred loved the idea, but I managed to find ways to avoid going with her when she went out for a "haul." I couldn't stand the thought of adding *thief* to my list of titles. Besides, with an official address, I could start getting my disability checks, and with no rent or bills, I had nothing else to spend it on (although I did always make sure to have the migraine medication; I learned quickly that, paired with alcohol, it could knock me out in minutes).

Ari used me and the house as her own fixer-upper. She transitioned my wardrobe from leggings and tunics (common White Pines attire) to ripped black jeans, studded bracelets, black boots, and band shirts splattered with the names of the screaming boys she adored. At the same time, she managed to turn the worn-down house into something almost-charming, completely the opposite of what she adorned herself with: delicate towels with floral decorations, airy curtains that billowed in the breeze, and cozy throw pillows and blankets covering all the antique furniture.

The comfortable living room became our permanent hangout spot. We pushed the couches away from the wall and set a decently-sized flatscreen on a table. She found a Super Nintendo at a garage sale, and we spent our days beating the various Mario kingdoms. She always brought booze—usually fireball or cheap vodka, which we poured into grape juice bottles—and she often offered me weed. We'd sit and drink and smoke and play games for days at a time.

I asked her at one point where her parents thought she was, and it turns out they thought she was attending college. They'd written her several checks to pay for her courses, all of which had gone directly to her bank account. Fred was envious of her freedom to spend; Lucy suddenly adored her; and Priscilla was convinced this was our chance to land a rich one.

One day, Ari showed up with a couple of tattooed and pierced "boys" (I use that term lightly since they were clearly too old to be interested in eighteen-year-old girls). They'd brought some weed that they'd grown themselves called "Lucky Devil."

Ari decided we should use the upstairs closet to smoke, so we all crawled through its miniature door and sat on an assortment of pillows and blankets. With its diminutive size and lack of windows, the room quickly filled with smoke. The boys egged us on, daring us to take in more and more. Ari giggled each time, but I felt my mind give way to something different, a new type of heaviness settling over me. It was as though someone had turned up the gravity, like they do in science fiction movies, pulling me down. From somewhere deep inside my mind, I got the feeling that a doorway was opening.

"I need to pee," I said abruptly. I tried to get up, but my body was stuck to the floor. I felt like I hadn't had water in days (to be fair, I might not have), and my tongue was like sandpaper. I had a sense of being taken over like I never had before. *They* had always taken over my limbs, my voice, my mind, and there had even been times where I had surrendered to them so I didn't have to be present (like when Lucy was with her Nicky), but I'd never felt like this, like I was *behind* them. Now, it was like something else had taken the forefront of my brain, and I was stuck in the background, watching.

Whatever *it* was, it was hungry and thirsty, like it hadn't eaten or had a drink in a thousand years. It tried to push me up from the floor but was held down by the same force that held me. Instead, it crawled to the small door and pushed through. I could hear Ari laughing behind me but didn't know what she was saying. It crawled to the stairs and butt-bounced down, like a child might the first time they encounter stairs.

I felt overwhelmed by it. Its voice, now a cacophony, spoke in many languages. I felt my tailbone hit each wooden step, but it didn't seem to notice or care, too focused on food and water. When we got to the bottom of the stairs, it forced my legs up, each one weighing five hundred pounds. One slow step after the next, it moved to the kitchen. I heard Ari's laugh again from above us.

Once at the fridge, it yanked both doors open and scoured for something to its liking. Its eyes were quickly drawn to a box of Twinkies on the counter. It ripped the top open and shoved a whole Twinkie in. I could feel it rub against my mouth and choked at the way it felt like cardboard against my tongue. Coughing, I tried to force the cake out, but it just pushed another one in. My body retched, refusing to allow it. It made our way to the bathroom sink, box of Twinkies still in my hand, and stuck my face under the running faucet. Like a man stranded on a deserted island, it barely came up for air between gulps of cold water. When it finally did, I saw us in the mirror.

My face was like nothing I'd seen before: one side clearly me, the other a constantly moving distortion of me. I wanted to scream, but when my mouth opened, the noise that came out was like a scratched CD skipping.

The lights flickered, and my voice was freed, releasing a piercing scream that echoed through the house. My body crumpled to the ground, and there was wetness on my forehead where my face had made contact with the cold marble floor.

I heard heavy footsteps on the stairs, Ari calling me. I wanted to call back, to tell her that I was fine, but my tongue was trapped and my mind couldn't reel in the words that it needed.

When she came into the bathroom, she gasped and choked back a scream of her own: "Oh my God!"

"Quick, get her to the couch," one of the boys ordered. "We need to put pressure on that." I felt arms under my legs and neck and, thinking of the weight of each leg earlier, was astonished that he could carry me. I listened for the other voices but could barely hear a whisper.

On the couch, Ari covered me in a blanket while one of the men found a towel and pressed it firmly to my forehead. "I think we should take her to the hospital," he said. "Head wounds bleed a lot."

"No!" Ari barked. "Not the hospital. If my parents find out, they'll kick us out, and then she'll have nothing. Just fix it—weren't you an EMT?"

"I mean, I started training, but they wanted me to take out my piercings, and the band had a tour, so I stopped."

"You must have learned *something*."

I started giggling and opened my eyes. I pushed the towel away and felt a fresh, warm flow of liquid run down my face. I lifted my hand to wipe it away and was mesmerized by the crimson red on my hand. I laughed harder, and they all stared at me, like this was somehow the craziest thing I'd done.

"The demons are in the mirror," I said. "They came through the door. They like Twinkies."

"We *have* to get her to the hospital," the one boy said again.

"I already told you, we can't. She'll be homeless if we do. Just wait—I'll call my brother." Ari left the room with me still laughing. I could just barely hear her from somewhere else in the house.

"Please," she begged. "No, no, don't tell Mom. I just need a first aid kit or something. Or call your friend—what's his name, Paul? Isn't he a doctor? Robert, *please*."

She was back shortly after. I didn't know who Robert or Paul were. At some point, I forgot that she had even left and began mumbling "Robert" and "Paul" over and over under my breath.

"That's it. We're out of here," the one holding the towel said, passing it off to Ari. "I can't be here if someone calls the cops. Just try to keep the pressure on so she doesn't bleed out." With that, they were gone.

Ari may have started crying; I honestly don't remember. I was doing a weird dance with consciousness, and each time I came back, I was giggling uncontrollably. At some point, I blinked back into existence, and there was a beautiful man in the room. He was probably three or four years older than us—Ari's brother, Robert, I assumed.

"You idiot," he said, smacking her gently upside the head. "Paul will be here shortly. He's not technically a doctor and could get kicked out of his med program if anybody finds out about this, so you and your friend better keep your mouths shut." He lifted the towel from my head. "Come on, Ari, this isn't some small cut. That's a gash." I could hear her stifle a sob.

"Fred wants the Pokemon card," I said matter-of-factly. They both stared at me.

"The hell is she talking about?" Robert finally said. "Wait a second, isn't this that crazy girl? The girl from the bench? Mom said she left. You brought the crazy girl here?"

This time, unable to control it, she let out a quiet gag-like sound, and sniffled "I like her! When she's not crazy, she's fun to be around. She was at an insane asylum, but she doesn't take her meds, so I slip them in her food. I have to help her."

"You're an idiot," he said. He turned to flick her but stopped when she flinched. "Oh, come on. That's a bit dramatic, even for you." He turned back to me, looking at my eyes and putting the back of his hand to my face. "She feels warm. Get me a fresh towel, but run half of it under cold water, and wring it out well." Ari hurried to the kitchen.

With the hand not pressed against my head, Robert dialed a number on his phone. "Paul, where are you? Ten minutes still? Come on, man, step on it! Yeah, she's still bleeding. It seems like a lot. I don't know, man—I know head wounds bleed a lot, but she's small. How much blood does someone this small have? Yeah, yeah, pressure. Stop going the speed limit, grandpa. If you get pulled over, I'll work it out with my mom." With that, he hung up and returned his attention to me.

"So, you're the crazy one," he stated matter-of-factly, looking directly into my eyes. "Wouldn't have expected that."

Ari was back with the cold towel and a glass of water. He traded the blood-soaked towel for the fresh one and held it firmly against my head. "Paul will be here soon," he informed her. "What's her name, anyway?"

"Beauty."

"Psh. No way."

"Well, look at her."

"Definitely not what you expect from someone out of a looney bin. I still can't believe you brought her here. What were you thinking? If Grandma finds out, it's over."

"Oh, come on," Ari retorted. "Grandma will love her. She's all about the whole underground-railroad thing."

"That's true."

They were silent after that. He stared at me, and I stared back at him. His eyes were the greenest I'd ever seen, with thick dark rings around the iris and small specks of gold near his pupil. I felt my mind trying to fade away again, but I forced it to hang on, forced it to look back at those eyes.

What felt like an eternity later, there was a light tap on the door. "It's Paul," Robert said. "Go let him in."

The man who entered was nothing like the doctor from that day at the hospital with my father. This was the Grey's Anatomy-esque man I had wanted to see—maybe not a McSteamy or McDreamy, but definitely a Mc-Something. Robert quickly moved out of the way, and his emerald eyes were replaced by deep brown ones under a heavy brow.

Paul was worried. I could tell by the way that his temple furrowed, a deep line forming at the bridge of his nose. "Definitely needs stitches," he declared after examining my head. His gloved hands felt heavy, the palm resting right above my brow bone. "Ari, grab the saline solution out of my bag, and get a couple thick towels if you don't want blood all over your couch." I heard her leave the room and started giggling again.

"Robert?" I asked. His face appeared above mine. "Hi." More giggling.

"What the hell did you do to her, Ari?" Robert asked, his voice angry as his sister handed the towels over to Paul.

"We just smoked a little weed—not her first time. She's never done this."

"You *idiot*," Robert said again, this time halfway under his breath. "Did it ever occur to you that giving a mental patient narcotics wouldn't be the best idea?"

"This isn't the first time, and she's never been like this," Ari repeated, her voice a panicked whine.

"What was it laced with?" he asked.

"I... I don't know..." she stammered. "They grow it themselves."

"*They?*" His voice rose.

"Stop it," Paul barked. "I can't concentrate with you two bickering." He poured something wet on my wound; it ran down my face, making me blink quickly. "Shit. Get another towel, quick." He gently dabbed the clean towel near my eye, absorbing whatever had dripped. "What happened to her eye?" he asked.

"I don't know," Ari said. "She's had it as long as I've known her. She never told me."

"That's a mean scar," Paul murmured.

"It kind of suits her, doesn't it?" Robert asked.

"It was his eye," I mumbled. "I had to take out the monster's eye." I saw all three of their faces above me.

"I think I need to knock her out for this next part," Paul said. "They never tell you how bad stitches actually hurt, and if she doesn't want to look like Frankenstein's monster, I need her to hold still."

"Yes...the monster," I repeated. I felt a familiar pinch in my arm, and their faces faded away.

# Chapter Twenty-Two

When I awoke, Ari and Paul were gone. It was just me and Robert, who was lounged in a chair opposite the couch with a large, leatherbound book in hand; it reminded me of Maddox and the missing Bible.

"Water?" I asked, my tongue like raw wood.

"Right beside you," he replied without looking up. I rolled over to my side, causing a sharp pain to shoot across my temple. "Can't imagine that felt good," he commented, finally closing the book and setting it on the arm of the chair.

I gulped down the water, not caring that it spilled over my chin and rolled down to my shirt. When the glass was empty, I slowly sat up, pulling the blanket over my shoulders and forming a little cocoon. I tried to avoid eye contact, but he wasn't having it. He slid to the edge of his chair, arms resting on his knees.

"So, what's your deal?" I didn't understand the question. "Come on, there's more to you than just a crazy girl on a bench. Who is this 'monster'?" My body started to shake at the question. I felt *them*, angry, like I'd broken some covenant by speaking of *him*. They came from him.

Robert's eyebrows rose. "Nothing to say on the matter today? Okay, then. Let's clean you up, then I need to go." He came to the couch, knelt, and peeled back the bandage from my head. I felt a fresh sting as he wiped around the stitches, applied some sort of goop, and pressed on a new bandage.

I stared at him the entire time. He was the exact opposite of me: statuesque, with a sharp jawline, high cheekbones, and a perfect chin. His forehead was almost too large, but somehow it matched him perfectly. With his hair tousled across it, he looked half Greek-god, half surfer boy. Every move he made was calculated and confident. I wondered what it was like to be like that; I wondered what it was like to be him.

As he tidied up the medical supplies around him, I reached out and grabbed his hand. He looked at our hands for a moment before meeting my eyes with his. They were so clear.

"Beauty," he said, halfway under his breath, before releasing my hand to me.

He left right as Ari entered the room. From her smudged makeup, I could tell she'd been crying. Later that night, over cheap wine, she told me that Robert had made her reveal everything to their parents. They were outraged—not by what had happened to me, or Paul risking his career, or even their daughter's lifestyle, but rather by the possible rumors that could circle through the community. Specifically, as prominent figures in the small town, they worried about the negative effect association with me might have on their reputation.

Ari was disgusted by their response. Apparently, her grand-mother was as well.

"She fought for you, Beauty. I didn't think she would, but she did. She said she'd work to have the house cleaned up and that, as long as we didn't have any more 'incidents,' we could stay." She paused to take a long guzzle of her semi-pink liquid (so different from the crimson that Mother used to sip). "She said you have to notify your caseworker, and you have to stay on your medication, but she doesn't have a problem with you being crazy—although she's convinced you just need a good exorcism or something." I didn't know what an exorcism was, but it sure made all of them squeal. She started laughing; I don't know why, but I started laughing too.

Ari also informed me that, during this family talk, it came out that she had been staying at the house as well, and she told her parents that she'd be moving in full time. Her mother was distraught, which delighted her. I traded to a smaller room down the hall and helped Ari move her belongings into the master suite.

For the first time since leaving my childhood home in a white van, I felt like I belonged somewhere. Despite their grandmother offering to fix up the place, Robert took on the task himself, beginning with the missing kitchen sink. At first, I tried to avoid him; I was embarrassed by the previous incident and didn't think he had any interest in hanging around his little sister's crazy friend. Lucy, however, had different plans, and Robert seemed to be okay with that. After sizing the hole, he brought a catalog for us to look through. He stood next to me—almost too close, which Lucy loved—flipping through the pages and pointing out sinks and faucets he thought would fit.

After the sink was installed, he determined that a new backsplash would spruce up the place. He showed up with a box of sample tiles and laid them out on the kitchen floor. We sat together, each with a glass of iced tea, knees touching, looking at the various options.

I was almost happy, and, for some reason, *they* let me be. I was always waiting for the next explosion, but it didn't come. I wondered if it was as simple as taking my medications and began to do so like clockwork.

After the backsplash came a bathroom remodel. This time, he took me with him to the hardware store. I remember running my hands over tiles and hardwood and walking down aisles surrounded by lights, chandeliers gleaming and sparkling. At one point, he took my hand and danced me down the aisle, singing "Beauty and the Beast". I think everyone in the store stopped to stare at us, but he didn't think twice. His eyes remained on mine, bright and clear, every single bulb reflected in them.

His confidence was contagious. For as long as he danced me down the row, I couldn't think about anything other than his hand on my waist and the ease with which he spun me around. When his song and dance ended, I felt fire rush to my face, acutely aware of all the eyes on me. I was horrified; *they* loved it. That day, he bought me a small glass chandelier for my room. He said that he'd love to see the diamonds in my eyes.

When it was time to replace the bathroom flooring, he recruited my help: "Can't live here for free, Beaut." We spent the next several weeks cramped in the small bathroom, peeling up old tiles and laying new faux hardwood. After that, we retiled the shower. Finally, we painted the walls a light mint color.

Robert was edging around the toilet while I was painting above the new shower tile, feet balanced on the edge of the tub, when suddenly, one of my feet slipped, and I began to tumble. With the speed of Superman, he jumped into the tub, catching me before I cracked my head open again. I looked up to thank him and was shocked to find his lips on mine.

"*Beauty.*" I heard my name spoken sharply and twisted to see Ari in the doorway, mouth agape. As quickly as he'd caught me, Robert released me and returned to his task. Without another word, Ari turned and walked up the stairs to her room, each step heavier than it should have been.

First came Priscilla, furious that we'd been called out—an unforgivable offense. Then came Fred; he reminded me of the nights spent on the bench. Last came Lucy, who rejected both offense and fear, instead stepping out of the tub and winking at Robert before sauntering up the stairs.

Ari's door was closed, and she didn't respond to Lucy's knocks. In hindsight, I'm grateful for it, as Lucy's not exactly the best conversation partner. Lucy quickly gave up (she wasn't one for a long battle), and I ran to my room, crying.

I didn't understand why Ari was mad at me. I'd thought, for once, that I fit in, yet somehow, my only friend didn't want me as part of her family. I'd never had a close girlfriend, but I'd seen on TV where the best friend becomes the sister-in-law, and I wanted that. I'd let myself believe that it could happen—that in some reality I could live in this house with Robert and Ari and it would all be "happily ever after." My own personal 90s sitcom, full of laughter and joy, with fights that were always somehow just a misunderstanding and ended with a group hug.

This didn't feel like that.

# Chapter Twenty-Three

The twinkling lights in Robert's eyes when dancing down the aisle turned to pools of Opi's ink, merging with his pupils before dripping down his cheeks like oil. The aisle turned into a slide of black goop, and I slipped, arms outstretched, begging him to save me. Somewhere deep in my spirit, I heard the truth that I'd never admitted reverberate: *He can't save you.* The lights and chandeliers suddenly had faces—twisted, angry cartoon faces that mocked me.

A low tapping sound. Then, my name: "Beauty?"

I jerked up from the bed. I didn't remember falling asleep, but when I wiped the dream from my eyes, Ari was standing in front of me. Without her makeup, fishnets, and black clothes, she looked so innocent—almost angelic. "Sorry, did I wake you?"

I nodded, scooching up to the headboard and patting the bed beside me. "I'm sorry–" I started, but she cut me off.

"No, it's not your fault. It's Robert." She paused, looking at me, her hands twisting together in a knot. "Beauty, he's married."

The words were like a punch to the gut. Every memory, every thought that I'd had of him, was covered in ink. It was all tainted. She stared at me, waiting for something, but I didn't have anything to give. I waited for *them* to show up, but, like all those years ago in the classroom, laying on cold linoleum with a sore head and arms and legs stretched out, they weren't here.

It suddenly clicked that *they* had known. They had allowed me to become an adulteress—or at least dream about it—and hadn't tried to stop me. The freedom that I'd thought I'd felt was, in fact, a trap that they'd set, one where I'd happily walked through the door. I felt like I was looking through bars, serving a sentence. They brought up memories of how I'd acted towards my parents, teachers—anybody who had shown me kindness— and the end result was the same: I lashed out, and I lost them.

And now, here I was, facing the exact same situation with the only friend I'd ever know, looking over a never-ending precipice into my future

"Beauty?" Ari asked, interrupting my ruminations. "Are you okay?"

"I'm sorry..." was all I could muster.

"No you don't, not this time. I cleaned your blood off the same floors you and Robbie got all sorts of comfortable on. Talk to me."

Priscilla hated her—*How dare she speak to us in that way!*— and Annie completely agreed. The two of them plotted, but Fred and Louis won in the end, reminding me of the park bench, of the bank terminal in storms, of gazing out into nothingness as lightning lit up empty roads.

"I didn't know..." I murmured. "I just thought..." I was too embarrassed to go on.

Echoes of my daydreams flashed through my mind: an engagement, a bridal party thrown by Ari, a wedding where she was my maid of honor, me walking down the aisle in white, people looking at me and thinking that I was...

"Beauty," Ari nudged, pulling me out of the made-for-TV romance playing in my head. "Come on, we're friends. You can tell me anything."

"...I thought, maybe, I could be normal." I couldn't bring myself to meet her eyes.

She sighed and pushed herself up from the bed. "This is just Robbie, Beauty. It's what he does. He collects beautiful women. He always has. You should see his wife—if he's a ten, she's a twenty. Even so, I'm pretty sure the only reason he married Cate is because of pressure from Mom and Dad. Her father is a senator or something—I don't know, but she fits."

I stared at her. It made sense. Cate fit in a way that *I* didn't, never could.

"He's charming," she continued. "It's why he gets away with shit. If it makes you feel any better, you aren't the first toy he's pined after, and I doubt you'll be the last."

It didn't make me feel better. Of course it didn't—I felt again like a marionette doll, always manipulated, never moving for myself.

"I'm sorry," Ari finished, making her exit.

Annie burst first. She hurled the bedside lamp across the room, releasing a guttural scream that felt like it was going to rip apart my vocal cords. Anything she could grab and throw, she did, until there was nothing within her grasp.

When she finally stopped, I collapsed into a chair by the window, my body sweating, my arms sore from her tantrum. Looking down, I saw Robert standing by his car, looking up. Our eyes met. He winked, then left.

We hated him, yet we wanted him, and so, more than anything, we hated his Cate—his beautiful, perfect, "fits in" Cate. The girls began to plot, entertaining the type of thoughts you see in True Crime documentaries.

First, we had to find her. We had to know more about our enemy. Scouring the phone book, scanning local news articles, and probing Ari revealed that Cate was a singer and even more, she was considered somewhat of a local celebrity. She often played at upscale bars, clubs, events, and even weddings, but calling her a mere lounge singer wasn't giving her enough credit.

When I finally tracked her down, my heart broke. She was everything I wasn't: graceful and kind, gorgeous and glamorous. Watching her perform, I wanted to hate her (*they* all did), but I couldn't.

I started to go to more of her shows, lurking in the background. *They* assumed I was on board with whatever schemes they were concocting, but really, I just wanted to see her. The way she moved was so light and free. She'd swing her arms out, and bracelets with little charms would catch the light, sending twinkles dancing around her.

I wanted a bracelet like that; Oscar needed a bracelet like that.

Soon, to Lucy's great joy, I ditched the black wardrobe that Ari had purchased for me and replaced it with something more like Cate's. Garage sales, rummage sales, donations—I took every opportunity to remake myself in her image. I even got an old straightener and curling iron at Goodwill. I'd never learned how to do my hair, so I enlisted Ari to teach me. I could tell she wasn't happy about my makeover, but beyond grumbling under her breath, she kept it to herself.

Robert noticed, too. I tried to stay away from him, but I was drawn to him. Although, I suppose I can't say that I truly tried or even wanted to stay away. I convinced myself that this whole transformation was for me, but really, it was for him. It was a desperate attempt to make him think differently of me, to see me as more than what I was. I was drawn to him like a moth to a lamp—or maybe it was less him, and more the life that he represented. The life that I wanted.

*They* loved it. Louis even stopped visiting at night. He'd always loved to tell me that it was just the two of us, but I guess even he thought that would change. After the bedroom destruction drama, there weren't any more outbursts—at least, for a while.

# Chapter Twenty-Four

Our flirtations quickly crossed a line.

Ari knew but never said anything. More and more, she found ways to avoid me (not that I blame her). She'd said before that I was just a toy to Robert (which was true), but I was just as much a novelty to her. When that wore off, I became a burden, a decision that she was stuck with.

Despite knowing in my heart how wrong it was, I couldn't stop. Lucy loved it; she thrived off it. I didn't have the strength (or the options, as Fred often reminded me) to end it. But even beyond that, beyond the pieces of them that kept me in it, I just truly believed that there was more there.

Tale as old as time, right? Married man meets young, pretty, impressionable girl and promises to leave his wife. Then enter whatever excuse works best that week: "There's too much going on to break it to her," or "I just need time to figure out how to explain to my family." The list goes on. I was intriguing, dark, sporadic—fun things to have in a side chick, not so fun to share a life with.

Through all of this, I continued to spy on Cate. I Continued to lurk in the shadows as she performed and watched as the light drained from her.

One night, I remember creeping through the crowd and taking a seat on an old wooden barstool right as she began to sing. The joyful smile was gone, replaced with a tight jaw and tired eyes. The upbeat melodies had disappeared, replaced with a heavy and haunting piano:

*What is it that we long for, every moment when we wake?*
*To spend minutes and hours applying masks to our face*
*So that true love will be drawn to us, but not to who we are*
*We must hide each insecurity, each flaw and each scar*
*What's been done it's been done; you do it for fun*
*To forget; I regret that you won't ever let*
*Let it be, let it be, not only for me*
*Who am I?*
*No one knows*
*No one asks you to go*

I couldn't take it. I couldn't watch her anymore: the spotlight shining down on her golden hair, the waves falling long and loose; her graceful hands, holding so tightly to the microphone; her gray eyes, cloudy and moist. She sighed audibly into the mic before continuing the song; I couldn't stand to hear it. It was accusatory, and I knew it was my fault—I had taken her joy.

I snuck quickly out the back. My hands were shaking as I turned the corner into the alley behind the bar. A group of hippies were hanging out, smoking cigarettes.

Surprisingly, I'd never been one to smoke (outside of the asylum, where it was more an act of defiance, combined with Lucy's old-school beliefs of what made a woman look attractive), but I was suddenly desperate for one. One of the tassel-vested men gladly offered and lit one for me. I took a long drag, hand still shaking, and fought the urge to cough as the bitter flavor filled my mouth. I dropped a quick thanks and walked, head down, away from the group, taking long, slow drags. Once out of sight, I dropped to the cold cement, back against the building.

There was a new type of battle brewing. I knew what I was doing was wrong, but even beyond their influence, I *liked* it. I had convinced myself that the stories he told me were true, that he'd only married her because of his family's influence and what it meant for the two families to be associated, that he didn't love her, that he wanted me, blah blah blah.

But I could tell she loved him. In the short few months I'd been stealing his attention, she'd gone from a flourishing sunflower to something withered and wilted.

Hearing footsteps in the alley, I looked up. It was her, walking determinedly towards me, cowboy boots click- click clicking on the pavement.

"Can you just stop?" she demanded, finally coming to a stop ten feet away from me. "You don't have to rub my face in it. You think I don't see you, sneaking around like some sort of *rat*?" She spit the word out with venom. "Is it not enough that you've broken my marriage? You can't let me have peace in the only other thing in this life that brings me joy?" She glared at me, mouth twisting into a grimace, the moisture in her eyes spilling over.

Priscilla was not having it. She pushed my body up in one fluid motion and positioned us within inches of Cate's face. I watched as the anger in her eyes quickly transitioned into fear. I tried to fight off Priscilla's control, but Annie was there too. She'd always maintained the ability to control my limbs that the others didn't have, and in that moment, she clenched my fists. I looked into Cate's cool gray eyes and felt a rage inside me, but it wasn't my own. I had wronged this woman, and I knew it, but *they* didn't care.

I knew I couldn't give them my voice, so instead, I let them hold me there, clenching my teeth so tightly I felt an ache in my jaw. Slowly Cate backed away, facing me the whole time, until she was in line with the cross street, then she turned and quickly walked away.

I felt more exhausted in that moment than I ever had before. I wanted to cry; I wanted to laugh. I was at the intersection of their will and my own, and I didn't like how closely mine aligned with theirs. As I made my way back to the house, I could hear them arguing in their old language, though every once in a while they'd slip into English and I'd catch something like, *Don't worry, she'll do it,* or *We can up the pressure.* Fred lingered close by that night, distracting me, and once I was home in bed, Louis showed up. This time, he didn't tell me that he was my only friend; instead, he warned me that he'd leave me too. His threats filled me with an unnerving sense of dread.

You might ask why losing him would impact me in such a way; this is another one of those times when I don't expect my response to make sense. At eighteen—nearly nineteen—years old, I'd known *them* for as long as I could remember. Despite their outbursts, they were my constant companions. The idea of losing something so close, even if it wasn't necessarily a good thing, was terrifying. And they made sure that I knew it. They'd never threatened me like this before, and it rattled me.

So, I did what any eighteen-year-old would: I ignored him. When Louis hung threats of his leaving over my head at night, I whispered nursery rhymes until I fell into restless sleep. My relationship with Robert became more than it ever should have, and I allowed myself simultaneously to forget Cate while also listening to Priscilla and Annie plot her end.

Lucy was in her happy place. Robert showered us with gifts and affection, and she ate up every second of it. As he spent more and more time with us, I felt like I had to worry less about Cate (imagine thinking that way). After six months, he was spending nearly every night at the house. Then, about eight months in, something weird happened.

I don't know when I realized it, but their voices were gone. Occasionally, I'd think I heard them, but it was more like an echo of a monster in a dream. For the first time since I could remember, I felt like me—just me. Finally, after all those times that I'd seen happy, carefree people and dreamt of what it would be like to live that way, I felt it. I felt *free*. Somewhere below the surface I slowly suffocated on the guilt that threatened to spill over, but I wasn't willing to lose this chance at an ordinary life, and I knew that if I allowed myself to consider it, I'd spiral into a nightmare of my own making.

Ari and I started to rebuild our relationship, despite her disapproval of Robert and me. Now, when she talked with me about it, I didn't have to fight Priscilla and Annie to respond, I could step back and acknowledge her feelings and share my own thoughts rather than pushing back their sarcastic and biting remarks. For a couple of months, I was in this half-light, half-dark sort of bliss. I knew what I was doing was wrong; I knew that it was one-hundred percent my choice to continue; and I knew that I had every intention of doing so. Then, I started to get sick.

At the time. I thought that *they* had made good on their threats to destroy me. It felt like my body was being eaten from the inside. I had nightmares, reminiscent of *The Mummy* movie, wherein the voices consumed me, little bugs tearing my flesh away from me. I'd wake with soaked sheets and hair plastered in a sweaty mess to my face. Then, I started having horrible pain in my back and legs. I tried to stretch and move, taking walks along the beach every day for hours, hoping that it would end. It didn't. At times, I felt like I was starving. I would smell something and immediately need to consume it (or vomit, or both). I put on weight from constantly eating and ran more along the beach to fight it—to no avail.

At some point, I stopped taking my medications. They added to the nausea, and I think, in some way, I was trying to appease *them*, a sacrifice to invite them back.

It didn't work. Nothing worked. Finally, Ari dragged me to the urgent care center, convinced I'd caught a tapeworm or something.

It was definitely "or something."

A small, older doctor came in, hmming and hawing and listening intently as I described my symptoms, Ari filling in details I missed (or intentionally left out). He asked about my family history. I started to share that Father had died from cancer, then realized that his medical history would have nothing to do with my own. I quickly corrected myself, saying through tears that I didn't know the medical history of either of my birth parents. The doctor ordered blood tests and an ultrasound; I assumed he thought I had a tumor.

Ari thought differently. Her entire demeanor changed; she moved away from me, pressing herself into a corner of the room and chewing her fingernails until they bled.

When the doctor returned, he directed me to lift my shirt and squeezed out a cold gel onto my stomach. Then he pressed the little wand against me.

After less than a minute, he exclaimed, "Just what I thought!" He turned the monitor so I could see. There, on the screen, was a tiny little thing, arms and legs wiggling and moving. Heart beating. A baby. *My* baby.

The whole drive home, Ari didn't speak to me, and I didn't care; I was too infatuated with the fact that I would be a mother—*could* be a mother. There was never a time in my life where had I considered such a thing probable. My mind wandered again to that perfect future, where Robert and I would live with our baby in our cozy house by the bay, our nursery tastefully decorated with those plastic glow-in-the-dark stars plastered to the ceiling.

As soon as we parked in the driveway, Ari jumped out, slammed her door shut, and stomped up the steps and through the door, all without speaking a word to me.

As I watched her march away, I felt *them* for the first time in months.

Fred told me that the baby would be just like the monster I came from—just like *me*. Opi was there, twisting my stomach so hard that I gagged. Worried I would vomit in Ari's car, I opened the door and fell onto the pavement, where I sat, legs splayed in front of me, for several minutes, waiting for the nausea to ebb. When Opi finally released his grip, Lucy and Priscilla arrived. They didn't so much speak to me as they mumbled to each other: *I hate it,* Lucy said. *It'll be more beautiful than us,* Priscilla agreed. *We should just end it. END IT!*

The very thought made me sick again, and I quickly let loose my lunch on the driveway. I desperately needed to escape but, unlike my lunch splattered before me, couldn't think of a way to purge *them*. I ran down the road, breathing heavily and dry heaving the whole way, my body trying to outrun my mind.

I finally stopped, out of breath, in front of a small stone chapel I'd passed by many times but never entered. I remembered that church had always been a place the voices couldn't be. I ran up the steps and bolted through the door.

A group of ladies sat around a small folding card table; books opened in front of them. They looked up at my entrance.

"Oh, dear," one of them tutted. "You look a mess. Can we get you some tea?"

"Here," another one chimed in, "let me get you a chair. Maia, bring a wet towel from the kitchen, please."

I was quickly surrounded by middle-aged women in bright pastel clothing. I don't think I've ever been more uncomfortable in my life, but they quickly calmed my nerves with tea (which I'd never had before) and reassurances.

After getting me settled, the first lady, Abigale, put her hand on mine and, with the most sincerity I've ever witnessed, asked, "What is it, darling? What had you so flustered?"

Before I could answer, I burst into tears. Crying wasn't new to me—I often cried myself to sleep—but this was different. This came from some well, buried deep within my soul, that had suddenly been tapped. Tears and snot rolled down my face, and my mouth twisted as I fought the urge to let a sound escape from the deepest part of me.

Once again, I was enveloped in pastels. Hands landed on my shoulders, my hands, my head, and then something strange happened, the women started murmuring. It was like when *they* spoke in their weird language all at once, only I wasn't scared. I felt a strange sense of peace settle over me as I realized that they were praying (I hadn't heard a prayer in so long, I'd forgotten it was something people did).

Not a single one of them asked me what was wrong. Rather, when they finished their prayer, I was handed a tissue and another dainty teacup of Earl Grey, and they returned to their discussion, as though some strange girl hadn't come flying in out of the blue.

They eagerly included me in their conversations—I swear there was never just one—but they were all focused on happenings at the church. What flowers should they have for the Easter ceremony? What color should they wear to so-and-so's upcoming wedding? Who had started which devotional with who, and what book should they pick for the next book club meeting? I didn't know if these were the things they were talking about before my arrival, but they managed to make me feel like I was one of them and that my input was welcomed. I felt this surreal sense of belonging (and a familiar sense of longing) but never allowed myself to answer with more than a few words: peonies; certainly not white; I'd never been a part of a devotional group, and I hadn't read a book in ages.

One of the women (I couldn't remember her name) handed me a little card for my name and number and said she'd love to follow up. At that point, I excused myself to the restroom, then snuck out the door without handing it back.

Somehow in leaving, I felt like I was betraying them, but more so, I felt like I was betraying myself. I wanted to run back in and confess: "It's me—I'm the monster under the bed!" I wanted to yell, "I'm the one you tell your kids to stay away from!" I thought about the way that people had walked past me in the park and on the streets, and suddenly, their faces weren't cheerful anymore; they wore tight frowns instead. The memory of park-goers offering me barbeque rearranged itself into a Salvador Dali painting, with melting smiles turning into grimaces.

My world was closing in on me. I ran back to the house, avoiding the roads in case any of the pastel ladies happened to drive by. I snuck into Ari's empty room (she must have left shortly after I did) and took a small handful of sleeping pills—I just needed to not exist for a while—before collapsing into the bed.

As the pills took effect and my vision faded like the screen blacking out after an old-school movie, I heard *their* voices again. I couldn't hear them clearly, though; for some reason, they couldn't break through the surface. It was more like they were in a room down the hall with the door cracked. I imagined them, floating heads, around a conference table – that made me chuckle in my drugged daze. At first, I thought they were talking about me, but nothing they said made sense: they were talking about *her*, how *she* would destroy them. They fretted that she could be the one who took me back and vowed to end her before she could end them. With the weight of their words on my mind, I fell into blackness.

## 25

## Chapter Twenty-Five

Suddenly, I found myself in the woods. There was an old cabin where I was apparently staying. I couldn't remember how I got there, or why I was there, but I knew it was where I was supposed to be. Inside, the furnishings were old but comfortable, and they were mine. On the back of a worn couch was the blanket that used to hang from my father's recliner. On the wooden dinner table was a glass of wine, crimson reflections dancing along the table, and next to it, a small tumbler of honey liquid—Father's whiskey. I called for them, knowing they must be near. I ran down hallways that I didn't know as though I'd been down them a hundred times before. I could smell them, but I couldn't see them.

There was a quick tap-tap-tap at the door. I flung it open, eager to see them, but when it swung open, it revealed an old, worn woman instead. Her face was like leather, worn down from untold hours working in the sun. Her limp hair was braided in two strands down either side of her head. Her lips had tight lines, the type smokers get after decades of smoking, and her heavy denim jacket reeked of stale tobacco.

I assumed she was someone's grandmother, so when she asked me for help unloading her groceries, I couldn't refuse (I was many things, but never intentionally rude). As I walked to her truck, I let my hand rest on my stomach. Flat mere minutes before, it was now bulging with life. A tiny foot met my hand from within. I was overwhelmed with love for it.

"Well?" the woman asked, pointing to paper bags, heavy-laden with groceries, in her truck. I lifted one; she handed me another. I felt their weight and thought that it was too much, especially for someone in my condition. My back strained as the extra weight pulled me down, and I stumbled. She laughed: "Don't drop it, girl."

I followed her awkwardly up a long pathway to her door. The house, a weathered log cabin, had been painted teal at some point, but the paint was now peeling and poking up, betraying the rotting wood beneath. Flowers that had been carefully planted along the walkway were worn down with weeds. Wilting, they fought to get the nutrients they needed, but most were no more than stiff, dried carcasses. I stumbled again, this time on a crack in the walkway that lifted one side away from the other (*don't step on a crack, or you'll break your mother's back*). She snickered again. It sounded old and deep, as if rising from the caverns of the earth. I felt like I should drop the bags and run, but she beckoned me forward through her doorway, leaving it open behind her.

I didn't want to go in. I was certain if I went in, I would never make it out again. "Come now, girl. No more diddly-dawdling.

Didn't your daddy teach you any manners?" As I crossed the threshold, a shiver ran up my spine. I followed her voice down a thin, dingy hallway lined with doors that I assumed led to bedrooms (I didn't want to think about the type of people she might have living with her). At the end was the kitchen and, across the bar, a living room. Another shudder ran through me, this one begging me to turn and go, but my feet were frozen in place.

Her living room wasn't filled with couches, chairs, and a TV. Instead, it held walls of bookshelves bearing tanks and aquariums. Snakes, spiders, and scorpions twisted and writhed in their jails. She laughed again as I watched them move. Her laugh coming from an even deeper place. Somewhere older than the earth itself. "Scared, girl?" she cackled.

I dropped the bags on the ground, making her shriek, and ran for the door. The walls began to close around me, and a bony hand wrapped around the doorframe of one of the dark rooms ahead of me. I yanked on the front door to get outside, not remembering closing it, and heard it creak and fight back in my hand. The hand crawled across its door frame, a crooked wrist appearing, and then a skinny arm partially hidden by flowing black fabric. I knew I couldn't see it. I knew it was Death, and he'd come to take my child from me. I yanked again; this time, the door flew open, nearly pinning me against the wall.

I could feel the figure creeping towards me. Wrapping my arm around my stomach, took off down the walkway. I had to protect the life inside.

The weeds in the flower beds were now vines, reaching, grabbing at my feet and trying to trip me up. I ran. The cabin I'd been in before was gone, along with any trace of Father and Mother.

I wished that I'd stayed put; maybe, if I'd just sat at the table, they would have come. Instead, I found myself running down a two-lane dirt road, stumbling over rocks and branches. Then I saw them: people.

Sweet relief swept over me. "Help!" I screamed, running towards them. They turned to face me, and I recognized them. All of them. The nurses and orderlies from White Pines, the pastel women from the church, my old teachers from school. As one, their smiling faces twisted. Mummering, they raised their fingers to point and, forming an army-esque marching line, advanced upon me.

I turned to flee, and the old woman was right behind me. Her hand, now its own bony representation of death, reached towards me. I screamed and spun away, this time racing back into the woods. I tripped and tumbled over roots, felt branches smack me in the face, yet I kept my arms folded around my stomach.

As I entered a clearing, I felt the weight of exhaustion overtake me. I fell to the ground near a rotting stump, my knees sinking into the soft soil, listening as the crowd paraded closer and closer. They burst into the clearing, chanting my name, followed closely by the old lady.

"You can't escape him!" she crowed. They drew nearer and nearer, surrounding me. I dropped my face to the ground, curling my body around the small life inside me. With the deepest breath I could muster, I let out a window-shattering scream.

"Beauty! Beauty, wake up!" I felt my limbs flailing, and my fist connected with flesh. The nightmare still fresh, I felt a sense of accomplishment at having taken one of them down—until my eyes opened and I saw Ari instead, standing back, away from me, rubbing her chin. It reminded me of Mother's look of betrayal as a bruise formed on her face.

"What *the hell* is wrong with you?" she hissed.

I couldn't clear the sleeping pills from my mind. "Sorry, sorry..." I heard myself mumble as I fell back into blackness. Luckily, this time I didn't dream.

When I woke the second time, Robert was there, standing at the window. The blinds were mostly drawn, but I could see raindrops hitting the glass and could hear the wind dancing in the trees.

He must have heard me move because he turned from the window and walked towards me. His face was tense, his mouth showing no trace of its usual smirk.

"Is it true?" he inquired. At first, I didn't know what he meant; I couldn't shake the feeling of boney fingers clinging to me, trying to steal the life in me. Then it clicked, and I nodded. I watched him drag his hands down his face. He aged ten years in a matter of seconds. This isn't what I expected. It isn't what I'd imagined in the brief moments that I was able to enjoy being what I was.

"How could this happen?" he asked flatly. I'd rather yelling and screaming, instead I got this. If Lucy was there, she'd have smarted off, telling him that he surely knew about the birds and the bees after all the times we'd played house. If Annie was there, she'd have hardened my eyes, told him he was to blame. If Priscilla was there, she'd have turned up my nose and replied that I was better without him, that I could find someone better.

But they weren't there. It was just me.

"You *are* going to end it, aren't you?" he asked. I didn't understand what he meant, but *they* cheered in agreement with him. "Don't act dumb, Beauty. You know what I mean. I'm *married*. I can't have a bastard child with…" He paused, looking me over. He didn't need to say anything for me to know what he meant.

I rolled over and pulled the covers over my head. "Beauty," he demanded, his voice rising as I continued to ignore him. "This can't happen. You have to end it." That felt like a threat, but I still couldn't bring myself to respond. I wished Annie would show up; I'd feel safer if she were there.

*End it,* I heard echo somewhere within. It finally clicked, and suddenly, I didn't need Annie there anymore.

"End her?" I leapt from the bed, surprising Robert, who startled backwards against the wall. He caught himself with his elbow and winced. "*End her?!*" I yelled again, advancing towards him. A fierce protection had risen up in me. "*Nobody* will *ever* touch her!" I was nearing a manic scream. Tears flooded my face again, but these weren't tears of sadness—they were pure, righteous rage.

His face was frozen, braced as though he were expecting a physical outburst. Instead, I fell softly back into the bed, hands behind me to hold me up. "Out." I ordered.

"Beauty…" he started.

"Out!" I repeated, this time a roar.

I watched as he left the room and listened to his footsteps trudge down the stairs. Ari must have heard the conversation— or at least a part of it—because she also had some choice words for him. She came into my room a while later and set a plastic sack on my end table.

"If you are going to have my niece, she needs to be healthy," she stated, leaving my room and returning to her own.

I opened the bag and wept as I pulled out prenatal vitamins, a small pink onesie with *Mama's Girl* emblazoned on the front, and hemorrhoid cream with a sticky note stuck on it: *For all the times you've been a pain in my ass, it's about time you get a pain in yours.*

Our relationship changed that day. We could never again be friends after I'd betrayed her family, but at the same time, I was carrying her family, and I knew that she'd go as far to protect the little girl inside me as I would.

Ari was with me at all of my appointments, and the months began to pass in a blur. Sometime later, Robert's wife discovered that I was pregnant, and she kicked him out. He didn't want his parents to know about his crazy mistress, so he made a deal with her to keep quiet and avoid a public scandal. In this arrangement he would continue to pay for their mortgage and her day-to-day life, and in return, she would appear at family gatherings with a fake smile plastered to her face. Cate, in turn, added two stipulations: one, she never wanted to see me again, swearing that if she ever did, she would scream to the entire town that I was his whore and was carrying his bastard; second, once the child was born, she wanted us both gone.

Of course, Robert didn't tell me any of this; Ari did. She grew increasingly uncomfortable at family dinners when they showed up together, despite the fact that Robert was staying at a hotel a town over and Cate could barely stand his touch without grimacing. Eventually, Ari gave up on family time, choosing to go only when one or the other of them was absent. She created a new family time for the three of us instead, where she would bring home take-out and adorable baby items. We would sit in the "nursery" (a large closet off the upstairs hallway), eating, painting, and decorating.

The closet soon became the fanciest place in the house. I even brought in the small chandelier, delighted at the thought of my little one watching the lights bounce off the layers of diamond-shaped glass onto the pink walls, now cleverly decorated with hopping pink bunnies.

Despite our weekly family time, I could still feel the tension with Ari. When she returned from a family event, she'd go on for hours about the fractures in her family, ranting and raving about their hypocrisy, slandering her brother for his choices, and desperately wishing that he and Cate would split up already.

"He'll never actually leave her," she stated matter-of-factly one day. "He can't. She's too good for him, and if they split up, he'd have to admit that, and his ego would never let him."

I don't know if my face betrayed me or if she finally realized that her complaints against her family were in fact directed at me, but she clamped her mouth shut and returned to folding tiny clothes while I ate tacos in silence.

Then, out of the blue, Robert showed up at the door, carrying gift bags and balloons with a big smile painted on his face. I don't know why it seemed so fake to me, but I let that thought dissipate as I slid back into his charm: "I know you can't have a real baby shower, so I thought I'd at least give you a tiny one."

(I think this was his way of apologizing, even though he never actually apologized.)

He set the balloons around the living room and hung pink and white streamers delicately across the four corners of the room. He made me a "princess chair" by wrapping a dining chair in more of the pink streamers. He sat me in the chair and placed a plastic tiara with pink gems on my head while I giggled with delight. Then he presented flowers and a half-dozen wrapped gifts.

I was ecstatic. My excitement woke Ari from an afternoon nap, and she came down the stairs heavy with sleep.

"I thought I heard a rat," she commented when she neared the bottom and saw her brother, sitting near my makeshift throne.

"Come on, Ari!" I laughed. "Come join our baby shower! It's for Little Girl." Ari rolled her eyes, grabbed her jacket off a hook by the door, and left without another word.

Later, after cleaning up the gift wrap and streamers, I spotted her standing on the dock, stoic and so still. I watched her for several minutes out the kitchen window, and I don't think she moved an inch other than her shoulders sagging at one point. Then Robert came up behind me, pulling my eyes from her, and told me he wanted to stay.

He said he missed me. He claimed that he wanted everything out in the open, but that Cate had held him back, jealous because she had never gotten pregnant in all their years together. He swore that I was what he really wanted, consequences be damned.

I was thrilled. All my daydreams were coming true. It would be the three of us, a little family. I imagined a world where I was a member of the community, with an adoring husband and beautiful baby girl. I even pictured wearing pastels and joining the ladies for book club at the church, now that the voices were gone—after all, it had been several weeks since they'd shown up in any meaningful way. I was certain that that phase of my life was over. Everything good was coming my way.

The dream soon became a nightmare—but I'll get to that.

# Chapter Twenty-Six

Robert moved into the house, into my room. He initially tried to fight Ari for the master suite, saying that it made sense since there were two of us with a baby on the way. He argued that, as a family, we should have the larger space. Ari quickly retorted that if his *wife* (the word shot out like a bullet) would like to come stay, she would gladly give up the space.

Robert set his jaw and gave up that battle. Instead, he settled for redoing my room. He claimed that it was childish and needed to be more representative of a lady. He preferred black furniture with straight lines and tempered glass. All linens were to be white, with no color. Even color on the throw pillows and blankets was forbidden. He decorated our little house by the bay like it was a high-rise apartment in New York. Slowly changing the cozy and charming environment that Ari had made, into some cold and uninviting.

I hated it. My room, which had been soft and full of life, was now hard.

I started to spend more and more time in the nursery. What father could deny his little girl a colorful room with hopping bunnies and fluffy pink pillows and blankets? I'd never really been one for pink, but the idea of a little baby girl in a pink tutu melted my heart.

When I wasn't in the nursery, I found myself avoiding Robert, preferring to pass the time by myself, often taking walks along the bay. Ari would periodically join me; she was also spending less and less time around the house. Occasionally she'd bring home takeout and sit in the nursery with me, but only when Robert wasn't around. I could tell that she was tense and unhappy, but I hesitated to ask why, afraid of breaking our tenuous alliance.

One day, while walking together by the water, I heard her sniffling and looked up to see tears running down her face. "What's wrong, Ari?" She was such a steadfast person—I never expected to see her cry (or really react much to anything).

For a moment, she couldn't speak; when she opened her mouth, only sobs escaped. When she finally could, she choked out, "I'm leaving, Beauty." I stared, astounded. She was my family now—how could she leave? "I just can't handle *this*"— she gestured at my growing stomach—"anymore." My heart dropped.

*You'll always be alone,.* Fred's voice rose up from some inner dark place. "You're such an idiot," She continued, stopping in her tracks and turning on her heel to face me. "Do you honestly think he'd leave her for *you*?" I wondered if this was what she'd been thinking about when she'd stood on that dock, motionless and alone. "Beauty, Cate is *good*. She doesn't deserve this. And" —the tears were flowing faster now— "it's my fault. I know it is. I just wanted to keep you safe, to keep you away from people who'd judge you because you're crazy. I didn't mean to destroy my family."

She took a long, shuddering breath before repeating: "Do you really think he left his wife for you?"

I just stared. I didn't know what else to do. If Priscilla and Annie were there, they would have knocked Ari out right then and there and buried her the sand. I was glad that they weren't, but I couldn't help but miss the way they stood up for me.

Instead of lashing out like *they* would have, I turned on my heel and walked back to the house. I don't know where Robert was, but the house was empty when I returned. I stomped up the stairs, nearly begging for one of them to show up and validate my anger, they did not. I marched to the nursery and plopped down cross-legged on the floor, a pink teddy bear in my hands. There I sat, in that same spot, for hours, stewing in my anger and hurt, letting it consume my mind and pervert the memories I had with Ari.

Eventually, she came home. I heard the sounds of her dresser drawers opening and shutting; heard the crinkle of garbage bags as she stuffed her things into them; listened as her steps, heavy with her packed belongings, trudged out of the house and out of my heart.

When the door shut behind her, I finally allowed myself to weep. While I'd wanted Robert since the moment I met him, I'd never considered the cost. It was easy to miss the impact of my actions when there was a barrage of voices cheering me on; now, in the silence, I could see that the consequences of our choices went much further than the little island I'd built around myself.

I'd allowed myself to forget that Cate was a real person, with feelings just like mine—that she had married a man and that I had come between them (at this point I nearly *prayed* to have *them* back—ironic, right? But I craved their reassurances, their support). I'd never considered that outside of these walls was a world where Ari had a family—a family who had allowed me to live in this home. A family who, in return, I'd torn apart.

Then, in my despair, I felt the prickly fingers of Opi running down my neck. I ran to my bed, crawled in, and stayed there until Robert came home.

I told him of the disagreement Ari and I had had and that she was gone, for good. Without hesitation, almost gleefully, he began to move our furniture into Ari's room.

I hated it. Even though the room was bigger and had large French doors that opened onto a deck with a glorious view, it didn't feel like it was mine to take. I wondered if the kings of old ever felt this way when walking through a conquered land.

Robert shoved all of Ari's furniture haphazardly into my old room. For some reason, it felt like we were throwing her away. I couldn't stand it, so I carefully rearranged everything and remade the bed. Every few days, I went out and picked fresh wildflowers to put in a vase on her dresser. If she did come back, I wanted her to know that I missed her.

Robert transformed into a different person. Half the time, he was so loving and over the top about the baby that it was suffocating; the other half, he was cold and aloof. It was like he was stuck on some pendulum with no moderate space in the swing. Moreover, as my belly grew, so did my ankles, my appetite, and, most of all, my emotions. I remember, after a particularly distant day, lying in bed with him and just *hating* him. He was lying with one arm under his face (that perfect face) the other stretched out, nearly touching me, and I felt myself shrink away from his touch.

Even sleeping, he looked aloof.

I rolled out of the bed and walked down the hall to my old room. With Ari's furniture and bedding, it felt as though she could walk through the door at any moment, and I wished desperately that she would. I missed my friend and our time together. I missed feeling like there was somebody in the world who understood me, with no expectations. I plopped into her bed, pulled the covers over my head, and began to weep.

I wept that she was gone; I wept that it was my fault; I wept that Little Girl wouldn't know her aunt in the way that I desperately wanted her to. All I'd wanted was a family, and I'd betrayed hers by trying to force my way into it.

My mind began to race, and I began to miss *them* again. I felt this overwhelming sense of guilt that gnawed at my stomach and rose up my throat like bile. I think some people would say that what I felt was shame, but really, for the first time there was a voice louder than theirs. A Jiminy Cricket. A conscience.

The weight of this new voice—which was less a voice and more a feeling—felt like it would crush me. At some point, I'd excused myself from accountability because it wasn't *really* my fault, it was *them*. Yet the warning bells had gone off in my head: *Don't take the cookie; taking the cookie is wrong.* Well in the end, I still took the "cookie". Lucy certainly didn't keep me from it, but there was no denying that I had wanted it and had resolved very quickly to have it.

At this point, I was about eight months pregnant, and I started to feel like I had a split personality (again: ironic, right?). Part of me clung to the dream of life with this family, with Robert and the supposed love that would come with it; at the same time, this new side of me opposed it. My conscience, which spoke with Father's voice, would remind me that this was wrong, that Robert was a married man. His voice would often merge with Ari's, who'd then urge me to think about Cate and how she didn't deserve any of this.

The constant battle was exhausting. I could barely stand to look at Robert but couldn't stand to be away from him either. I'd spend all day in the nursery, looking at cute little pink things, or walking by the water, where Ari's voice still rang through the trees. I'd collapse at night into the bed that Robert and I shared, only to jolt awake and run in a guilt-stricken panic to Ari's bed, where I'd sleep through the night.

Then, around nine months, I became obsessed with cleaning. Most people would shrug it off and say that I was nesting— Robert certainly did—but I wasn't. I was trying to scour away my guilt from any surface where it might have landed. Every day was the same: I'd shower, nearly burning my skin and scrubbing myself raw with a loofa. Then, starting in the nursery, I'd work my way through the house. I scrubbed baseboards, backsplashes, toilets—everywhere my eyes landed had to be cleaned (I'm sure, had Dr. Oliver been there, he would have diagnosed me with OCD). By the time Robert got home, I'd be on the floor in the kitchen, washing everything down with a sponge and a bucket of soapy water. He'd make some comment about it being clean enough— "You sure are taking this nesting thing serious"— then walk out of the room, mumbling something about me being crazy under his breath.

I quickly began to resent him. I loved this little girl I was carrying and wouldn't change anything that would take her from me, but how I wished it was possible to undo some things without erasing others! As my due date drew closer, I stopped sleeping in bed with him altogether. I blamed it on the hip pain and claimed to need space to sprawl out, which he believed, but in reality, the perfect world that I had dreamed of was steadily crashing down. Now, when I pictured us all together, our little girl in my arms, I found the man in the room with us was a warped version of Robert: eyes slightly skewed, skin off-colored, mouth twisted. As much as I'd dreamt of a future with him, I now dreamed about running away with my baby and living in a tiny house, working as a maid or something to make ends meet, and just being happy because she was mine and I was hers. But, as I had to acknowledge, she was also his.

Annie would have thrown a fit over that; she would have stomped my feet and insisted that Little Girl was ours and ours alone. Priscilla would have lifted my head, daring anybody to defy her sole claim to our child. In my loneliness, I missed them even more. As I lay in bed at night, I missed the voice of Louis, insisting that he'd never leave me. Yet even he had.

Everyone always left.

# Chapter Twenty-Seven

Days began to blend together, separated only by a big, bold mark on the calendar: *Due Date*. Each day Robert left, and I went about reorganizing the nursery. I'd walk by the water, pick wildflowers, and find something to clean in the house. His workdays dragged longer and longer until he started to stumble in after I'd gone to bed. *You think he'd pick you?* Ari's voice rang in my head.

I was desperate for something more—some purpose to make my life mean something—and she was growing inside me.

Summer turned to fall as my stomach grew, stretching until I couldn't see anything beneath it anymore. My walks became scarce as putting on shoes became a chore and the days grew too chilly for sandals. I felt like a bird trapped in a cage. The house was clean, the nursery organized in a way that felt right, and I was left with nothing to do. I spent most of my days sitting by a window, watching leaves lazily drift to the ground and talking to Little Girl.

I told her about Father and Mother, how they had taken me in. I told her that I came from a dark place, but Father and Mother had found me and saved me from a big, mean monster. I told her that she would never meet Father (this made me weep) and that I hadn't spoken to Mother in some time but promised that, one day, we would.

I dreamed of my beautiful baby and how she would grow. I imagined the promise that she would have and the dreams that she would chase because she would be *free*. I pictured her running through the leaves, laughing and giggling, calling out "Mama, Mama" to get my attention. I saw her twirling in a pink tutu in the kitchen as I made dinner—"Look what I can do," she'd say as she spun.

Never in these fantasies did Robert appear.

It was early fall when I felt something strange—a pain in my back. I tried to shake it off and go about the morning, but while I was making eggs, it happened again, stronger this time. I dropped the spatula and leaned my hand on the counter, my body doubling over. I worried that there was something wrong with Little Girl, and immediately began to panic.

I remember slipping on my sandals and a sweater, leaving the house and, for some reason, feeling pulled to the little church, certain that someone there would be able to help. I slowly waddled up the road, toes bitten by the morning chill, forced to stop periodically as my body twisted and contorted. At one point, I almost sat on the road, but my will to go on fought through.

"I've got you, Little Girl," I repeated over and over, my mantra to keep going.

When I got to the church, however, my heart fell. No cars sat waiting in the small parking lot. The lights were off, and the building was dark. I walked as quickly as I was able to the door and pulled the handle. Locked. I pounded on it anyway, yelling, "Help! Please, somebody, help!" No answer.

Exhausted, I slid down and sat on the damp welcome mat. My eyes closed as another wave of pain washed over me. I felt for certain that Little Girl was in trouble and that I'd failed her. Tears chased each other down my cheeks.

I'd failed her.

I don't know how much time passed before I heard the unmistakable sound of an old truck. It reminded me of the excitement that I'd felt as a child when I heard Father's truck pull into our driveway.

That nostalgia turned to bile when I remembered the dream and the old lady: they were coming to destroy me. My eyes popped open, and I turned to face the sound. An old, mint-colored truck pulled up in front of me. I felt fear rising as the door opened. I pictured the crone's old, leathery face and remembered the boney fingers reaching for me from the shadows of my mind.

"Oh, dear," a shaky voice said. "You look like you could use a hand."

The man who stepped out of the truck was nothing like the woman from my dream. He was short and squat, a circle of shining scalp showing where his hairline had betrayed him. His eyes were deep blue and sparkled, like I'd imagine Santa's would. He wore olive-green coveralls that had *Al* embroidered over the breast pocket.

He came around and knelt down in front of me. "Hello, girl. What's going on?"

Something about him immediately calmed me. He was like the grandparent I'd always wanted and never got.

"I–I think she's in trouble," I stammered.

He made a thoughtful noise, looked me over, then said, "You may be in labor." He took me by the arm and pulled me to my feet. He opened the truck door and helped me climb in (it didn't cross my mind for a second that I shouldn't get into a stranger's truck). He crossed the front of the truck, one hand on the hood like a horseman keeps his hand on a horse's behind when walking around it, and then settled into the driver's seat with more mumbling sounds.

"Well, I'm Al," he said, putting the truck in gear. "Let's get you to the hospital, and then we can call your folks or whoever."

I thought for a moment before telling him, "There's no one to call."

More mumbles. "Okay. We can call Maia—she'll know what to do. She runs the women's group at the church, and I figure she'll know more about how to help you than I will. Never had any kids of my own. Had a wife once, but she died." He shrugged his shoulders. "Sorry, I'm rambling. You look pretty young to be having a kid, though." Another rush of pain gripped me from inside, and I let my body double over in the seat. "I think that means it's close. Who's your doctor?"

I just shook my head. I hadn't had steady care since Ari left and wasn't there to take me. In fact, it occurred to me for the first time that I had no idea what was about to happen. My knowledge of childbirth was limited; I just knew that someone went to the hospital and came home with a baby.

I was suddenly overwhelmed with fear. It gripped my heart, squeezing the life from me. I tried to breathe, but my lungs refused to expand. I wheezed, a low, heavy creak escaping from my lips.

"Breath, girl!" Al demanded. "You have to do the heh-heh-heh thing—haven't you ever seen a show?" I knew what he was talking about but couldn't get my body to cooperate. Panic was running the show. I felt his cool hand take mine and squeeze. "I said *breathe*." He turned to me, his peripheral vision still on the road, and demonstrated: "Like this: heh-heh-heh. Do it with me."

With his hand in mine, I did as he did. Slowly, the panic receded. Although the pain increased as we neared the hospital, as long as I held Al's hand, I felt like everything would be okay.

As we pulled into the Emergency Room entrance, I spotted a short, stocky woman in purple pastel waiting at the door: Maia. She ran (as best she could) to the passenger side of the truck and opened the door. "Hello, dear. It's wonderful to see you again." She helped me down and yelled for Al to get a wheelchair from inside.

"I can walk," I protested.

"Not on my watch!" she declared.

The rest of the morning was a blur. Al kept back but remained available, as demanded by Maia. She was like a mother hen, bustling here and bustling there. She'd had four children at this very hospital, she proudly informed me, and had supported numerous churchgoers in their deliveries. I watched, amazed at the way she commanded attention, even from the doctors and staff.

I won't go into all the details, but very shortly after arriving, I held in my arms the tiniest little girl I could ever imagine. Her face was squishy, but I could tell that she was beautiful. The nurses wrapped her in a tiny pink blanket and placed a tiny pink cap on her head. I stared at her, heart filled with love, until they insisted that I rest. I tried to resist, but Maia, in that mother-knows-best tone, said that she'd take the baby.

As soon as she was out of my arms, I fell into a deep sleep. I dreamed again of the cabin and the old lady, of racing through the woods as bony fingers stretched out towards me, desperate to pull me into them. This time, though, I wasn't alone; this time, I carried a tiny bundle, wrapped in a pink blanket, in a pink cap with its little pom-pom sticking out.

Willing myself not to trip, I dodged my way through the trees. I knew I had to stay away from the clearing, so I tried to avoid the path I'd taken before, intentionally turning left where before I'd gone right and vice versa. Yet despite my efforts, I stumbled again into the clearing. For a moment, there was silence. No birds chirped; no squirrels shouted their alarm. There was only my breath and the breath of the wind. For a moment.

Then I heard the crowd crashing through the woods. The earth itself shook as they came nearer and nearer to me. I looked down at what I held and knew that I had to protect her. I had to hide her. I found the partially rotted stump in the middle of the clearing and dug dirt out of its roots. Gently, I placed her in the hole and covered her with leaves and small sticks.

"Shh, Little Girl," I implored. They were close now, just beyond the edge of the trees. I quickly spun on my heels, taking several steps to the right and forward to draw them away from the stump. Then, I saw *them*—not the people from my past like before. *Them*, their floating heads joined to bodies. I saw Priscilla stomp through the tree line, followed by Annie, Louis, Lucy, Gus, Fred, and Oscar. Behind them all, a thick black fog rolled through the trees. Opi.

*She's ours,* they chanted. They said it in English, then repeated it in the old tongue. They pressed closer and closer, their arms dragging along the ground, fingers long and boney. Their faces were nothing like they'd shown me as a child; they were Death, and I knew I had to draw them away from her. I turned feet from them, shoes digging into the earth and ran. This time not worrying about what might trip me, knowing that even if they caught me, she'd be safe. I sprinted and stumbled until I was out of breath, finally stopping near a precipice overlooking the bay. I glanced across the horizon and spotted my little cabin, but not the cute, clean house that I'd cared for. Even from this distance, I could see the paint peeling off the siding. I could see cracks in the windows and dead plants spilling over pots near the porch.

I heard a branch snap as their chanting drew closer. They came towards me, their arms reaching out—searching for her. I could let them consume me, or I could throw myself over the cliff.

Without hesitation, I leapt.

# Chapter Twenty-Eight

When I came to the surface, I blinked and blinked, fighting the water from my eyes. Only there was no water—just the overwhelming brightness of luminescent hospital lighting. I gagged, fighting the urge to puke, then felt my body fill with panic.

"Where is she?" I screamed. "*Where is she?!*"

Maia hurried into the room, followed by the rest of the pastels. "Settle down, dear," she said. "I have her." She gently placed Little Girl in my arms. "Are you feeling okay? You look pale. Let me get a nurse." She bustled out of the room while the others swarmed around me. I was overwhelmed as they formed a semicircle around the bed, flashing back to the woods, the way *they* had surrounded me, but this was different. The pastels were like lanterns; I felt that somehow, with them around us, the others couldn't get through.

When Maia returned, she was nearly dragging a young nurse behind her. "Look how pale she is." she implored. "Make sure she's okay."

The nurse squeezed through the circle and took my vitals. "Hmm...your pulse and blood pressure appear to be elevated. It's not that uncommon after birth, but it's been a few hours now, so I'd expect it to have normalized. Let me grab the doctor."

When the doctor arrived, he tried to make me hand Little Girl off while they looked me over. "No," I whined, feeling like a petulant child. "She's mine."

"We need to examine you, and we can't while you hold her. She can stay right next to you," he insisted.

Begrudgingly, I handed her to Maia. "She's mine," I repeated.

"Yes, dear," Maia responded knowingly. "She is all yours."

*She's ours,* I heard them say, clear as day. "No, no, no, no, no!" I began to scream. "She's mine! She's *mine*! Please, *please* let me have her!"

Maia brought her to me, her brow wrinkled with worry. "Yes, dear, of course she's yours."

"*Please*," I begged again. Maia shot a concerned look to the doctor, whose brow was also furrowed.

"You can get her right back," he assured me. "This shouldn't take long." He turned to the nurse. "Let's get blood while we're here."

*She's ours,* they crooned again. My heart raced; my eyes darted around the room. "No, no, no..." I repeated, more moan than shout.

"Easy, easy," Maia said. "Look, look at me. She's right here."

Pressure built in my chest. My racing heart was an engine, trying to start up. *Tick tick tick tick tick.* My mind wandered; my eyes tunneled in. *Tick tick tick tick tick.*

"Breathe," the doctor commanded me, then, "Out," he ordered to the pastels.

"No!" I screamed, afraid Maia would leave with Little Girl.

"You stay," he told Maia. He turned to the nurse: "Benzodiazepine. Now."

The drugs quickly took effect. They didn't completely knock me out, but they left me feeling like I was sitting on a churning ocean, my body rocked as each wave pushed me about. I could feel Maia's hand clutching mine, could hear tiny noises coming from the tiny form cradled in her arms, could catch the back-and-forth between Maia and the doctor, but all of it was distant, disconnected from me like the shore from the sea.

"We can't find anything wrong with her," I heard the doctor say. "I'll call for a psych consult, but our on-call psychiatrist is about two hours away. For now, all we can do is keep her sedated so she's not a threat to herself or her baby. Does she have any family you can call in the meantime?"

"None that we know of," Maia responded. Her normally chipper voice was heavy with strain. "I think we can contact the child's father—at least, whom we all suspect is the child's father."

Sometime later, in my daze, I heard the pastels return to the room. "What type of man...?" one whispered. "To just leave her here, the mother of his child? I just can't..." They continued to murmur, most of their words too low for me to hear, but I did catch pieces: "How do you forgive that?", "Poor girl", "Poor child", and so on. Then I felt them surround me again. My eyes flew open to a sea of pastel. Each placed one hand on me, the other on each other.

"Lord," Maia started, "we pray for Your mighty hand of healing on this girl. Only You know what ails her, and only You can calm her fears. We pray for this dear girl—Your daughter—that You would find the places in her mind that hold anxiety and release her from them. We pray that You are the loudest voice that she hears, that she would know that the words You speak are peace and truth."

She paused, and another spoke: "Yes, heavenly Father. We don't know her circumstances, but we do know that she belongs to You. We submit her to Your mighty name and ask that You bind any forces that come against her. In Your timing and Your will, we trust that You will meet her, and she will know You. From the time she was formed in her mother's womb, You knew her and the battles that she would face. Now, as she carried a child and delivered that promise into the world, we ask that You are with her as you were with Esther—that as she enters into this unknown season, she would be covered by Your grace."

"Yes, Lord!" another spoke up. "Let every chain that binds her be broken in Your name. May fear and doubt dissolve in Your presence. May any spirit against her be purged from her"— I felt goosebumps rise on my arms— "and your Holy Spirit rise like a flame in her heart."

With their words echoing in my mind, I surrendered to the fog and fell into a deep sleep.

This time when I woke, I felt something different, like a heavy blanket of snow was covering me. I didn't fully understand it, but I didn't question it, either.

"Hello, dear," Maia said in that way of hers. She sat on a chair in the corner, a Bible in her hands, the small table lamp casting its soft light over her."

"Little Girl?" I croaked.

"She's sleeping in the nursery. We can get her if you'd like, but she's just fine."

"No, leave her there," I sighed, sinking back into my pillow. I felt like, if she were with me, my dreams would become hers, and I didn't want her to face them.

"Speaking of..." Maia started, "Little Girl is adorable, but it's not much of a name. Should we give her a real name?"

I nodded. In all my time talking to her, I'd never called her anything else. "Someone said a name—Esther. Who is she?" I asked.

"Ah! Yes, Esther. Esther is one of two women to have a book in the Bible named after her. She was a Jewish woman, originally named Hadassah, who changed her name to keep her heritage hidden from the king. She ended up becoming a queen and saving her people."

"I like that," I said. "We can call her that."

"Wonderful choice! Esther is a good namesake; God was always with her. What about a middle name?"

I paused for a moment. "What about Tindra?" I asked. "It is —well, it was my biological mother's name. I never knew her."

"I think that's a great idea. Although, if you didn't know your biological mother, can I ask who raised you? Your father?"

I shuddered, remembering his eye in my own. "No," I responded fiercely, feeling the venom that came out whenever I thought of him. "He was a bad man. A very, very bad man."

"I see. Then who?"

"I was adopted. My father...well, he died. Cancer. My mother is...somewhere. I haven't seen her in a long time." I felt tears well up. More than anything I wished they were there: Father. Mother. Even Brother. I tried to contain the tears, but I couldn't, so I pulled my knees to my chin and sobbed into them.

Maia was quickly beside me, her arm on my back, murmuring something I couldn't understand. It almost sounded like *their* language, but it was different—softer. I felt like I almost knew the words that she was speaking, like they were translated somewhere deep within me and sent to my heart. The tears stopped, and I wiped my face with the sleeve of the hospital gown.

"I miss them," I admitted, sniffling.

"I imagine so. Why don't you call your mother? Or I can call her for you."

"No," I said, choking back a sob. "She doesn't want to see me. I wasn't good."

"Oh, dear. Does she know about Esther?" It was weird to hear Little Girl called by her name. But it also felt right.

"No. She doesn't know anything."

"Well, as a mother myself, I can promise you that a great deal from the past can be forgiven, and she would run to you with open arms! She's a grandmother now, and that's a wonderful gift."

*She'll never take you back,* Louis warned.

"No," I parroted, "she'll never take me back."

Maia clicked with her tongue, which I noticed she often did, and squeezed my hand: "Get some rest. We'll figure the rest out tomorrow." She didn't leave my side that night.

In fact, she stayed by my side for the next few days. The psychiatrist came and went; just a bout of postpartum, he declared, and prescribed valium, suggesting I take a pill when I felt anxious. I don't think that my doctor agreed with the diagnosis, so he kept me in the hospital a few more days. During that time, Maia and the pastels taught me how to care for Esther: how to nurse and burp, how to change diapers (I hadn't thought about that part either) and how to rock her to sleep. They asked me what I already had and what I needed and took turns going shopping to make sure that I would be thoroughly prepared when I was released.

Through all of this, Robert never called; he never showed up. I tried not to think about it, but it clung to my mind like gum on shoes.

*They*, however, came back. Not as loud as before, but every bit as defiant. When the pastels were present, they went silent, but once the pastels left, their voices returned, whispering as though behind a curtain. I tried to brush it away: I was tired; I'd just had a baby; this was probably normal. But it wasn't.

When my doctor concluded that my initial outburst had been a fluke, he brought the discharge papers and I was finally able to leave with Esther. Maia had her husband pick us up and load the piles of stuff in their car while she showed me how to safely tuck Esther into her car seat and click the seat into its base. Then she climbed in the front, and I sat in the back next to the only thing in the world that was truly mine.

I stared at her the entire drive home. Her eyes were bright blue like my birth mother's. Her nose was perfectly plump, a teardrop sitting on her face. Her hair was dark like mine, but her features were light. Only a few days old, and she was already striking, the type of baby they modeled dolls after. Soft and delicate, her tiny fingers curled around mine as she yawned, letting out a tiny squeak.

Maia chatted the whole drive. I wanted to be polite after all she'd done for me, but I couldn't make myself listen, so I responded vaguely, keeping my eyes on Esther. Finally, I felt the car roll to a stop. Looking up, I saw the house, it seemed somewhat brighter than before. When I'd left, there had been leaves covering the ground and walkways; the empty planters had been overturned by the wind, and weeds had taken over the flowerbeds. Now, it looked clean and fresh: leaves raked, weeds removed, planters set right and filled with mums.

Maia noted my surprise and explained: "Al and the girls wanted you to feel like you were coming home to a fresh start. They tidied up out here and a bit in the house. Don't worry, they knocked—nobody was ever home." She blushed slightly. "I know it seems odd, but we just wanted this for you."

I nearly cried, overwhelmed at their thoughtfulness. For people who barely knew me, they'd been kinder to me than anybody I'd ever known. "How can I ever repay you?"

"Oh, dear," Maia responded as she opened her car door, "we don't do this to get something back—we do this because we love you. The best gift that you could give us is to take care of that little gift from God. Put her above yourself, and always do what is right by her. And if you need a babysitter, call us!" she added, grinning.

Half laughing, half sobbing, I jumped from the car and wrapped my arms tightly around her. I couldn't remember the last time that I'd received a hug, let alone given one, and there was something powerful in it. As she squeezed back, I felt my shoulders fall; I hadn't even realized how tense they had been.

Somehow, that hug made me feel like everything would be alright.

"Do you need help getting settled?" she finally asked, breaking the hug. Her husband had already unloaded most of the stuff into the house.

"No, no," I waved my hand, "you've done enough. You've done more than enough."

She hugged me again, this time kissing the top of my head, helped me unload the car seat and base, and then, blowing a kiss, got back into her car. She waved as they drove away.

I looked down to Esther in her car seat. "It's just you and me now."

*And me.*

*And me.*

*Don't forget me!*

*Or me, sugar. I'm here too.*

Their voices rose – a chorus in my mind.

I felt the panic rise as their voices grew louder and louder. "No, no, no..." I grabbed the car seat, leaving the base in the grass, and ran into the house, slamming the door behind me.

I had to keep it together—had to get Esther settled in. Then I could figure out what to do about *them*. I carried her up the stairs, humming to keep her (or maybe more myself) calm. Once in the nursery, I felt safe. The pink ruffles and bunnies reminded me that I was home now. Even if nowhere else in the house felt like home, this room was hers, and she was mine, so *this* was home.

I picked her up and removed the pink cap from her head. I checked her diaper, which had been changed right before we left the hospital. Satisfied that she was still clean, I sat with her in the rocking chair and started talking.

I told her about Father and the man he was. I told her about the Jesus man that he had known and how I thought the pastels were friends of Him too. I sang her bits and pieces of the songs that I remembered from the radio all those years ago and watched as she drifted to sleep.

Then I continued just to sit there, rocking her, even as the sun began to set and the room darkened. Vibrant colors from the sunset lit up the walls with hues of orange and pink. Esther's face glowed in the light's reflection.

She was beautiful.

*I hate it,* one of them (probably Priscilla) growled.

*It can't stay.* The sassy voice of Lucy was clear.

*Get rid of it!* demanded another.

All at once, they began to speak. I couldn't discern the words as they went in and out of their native tongue, but I could feel the way they despised her. I quickly set her in her crib and ran down the stairs.

I found my purse in the pile of baby goods and pulled out the pill bottle. It said to take one or two tablets as needed, but I decided that three would be good. I took the pills and sat on the couch in the dark. The bright colors were no longer painting the walls; instead, the deep purple and navy of night set shadows through the room. As *they* continued to spew their hatred, I imagined each of the shadows as one of them. A branch out the window waving its shadow across the wall matched the tempo of Lucy's sarcasm as she talked about how *the little thing* would be better than us. The lamp casting a thin, tall silhouette suited Louis, who claimed repeatedly that *she can't stay*. A fake fig tree in the corner moved slightly under a vent's air flow, twitching with Annie as she plotted how to *end it*. And, ever stoic, the deep, dark shadow of the kitchen door frame was reminiscent of Opi's ink: a great, yearning chasm ready to swallow me whole.

I tried not to listen to them, not to stare at the shadows. I tried to will them to go back to whatever pit they came from. But I failed. They switched fully to their language, and the movement of the branches on the wall, along with the valium, lured me into a trance-like sleep.

# Chapter Twenty-Nine

Hours later, I jerked awake to Esther crying from her crib. I leapt from the couch, my mind still a blur, and took the steps two at a time, worried that somehow *they* had managed to act while I slumbered. I threatened them, dared them to try anything, begged them to leave her alone. When I got to her door, I hesitated for a moment as Fred whispered what I would find inside. He told a gruesome tale that made my stomach clench as bile rose to my throat. I gagged, forcing back the contents of my stomach and, after one deep breath, pushed myself through the door.

In three quick bounds, I made it to the crib. She was there, perfect. Her face was red from crying, and an unmistakable stench oozed from her diaper, but she was okay. I clung her to my chest and rocked as panic gave way to relief. Even as I held her, I felt *them* demand her. I quickly changed her, then ran downstairs again to the radio. I remembered how music had kept them at bay before and clicked through various stations until I found one that filled the room with something more than just noise. I fed Esther, then sat her down on a blanket next to me while I rummaged through the bags to keep my mind preoccupied.

*They* were furious. I felt their threats, their rage. Goosebumps rose on my arms as they hissed and seethed at me. Yet in this room with this music, their voices came through muffled, as though from behind some hidden veil. They were there, and they were determined to take out ten months of discontent on me and Esther, but for the moment, they had no power.

I decided to set up a makeshift bedroom for us. I found a small pack-and-play in the pile of boxes and set it next to the couch. In another bag were new sheets and blankets, which I used to ready the pack and play for Esther, before gently placing her in the makeshift crib. Unwilling to leave the room even for a moment, I tossed a throw blanket over the couch cushions and pulled another one over me.

That night, I didn't sleep. It was like having a mob right outside the door. *They* yelled and screamed, demanding that I give her up. They spoke curses in their language. Twice I turned up the radio, which it drowned them out some, but I still knew they were there. Esther, thankfully, was blissfully unaware. She woke several times during the night, as I was told babies do, but quickly fell back asleep after being fed and changed.

Finally, as dawn started to cast its light in the room, my eyes fluttered and gave way to sleep. I'd thought about taking another valium, but I couldn't allow *them* the opportunity to take my mind. I hadn't forgotten Fred's vivid description.

I woke to a key unlocking the front door. I rubbed my hands against my eyes and blinked away the sleep, despite my brain's protest. When I sat up, I felt a presence in the room. My eyes quickly focused and saw him—Robert. He was staring down into the playpen where Esther lay peacefully.

"That's her?" he asked. I nodded. "She's lovely."

I nodded again. "You can hold her," I offered, immediately feeling like a fool.

He shook his head. "I...I can't." He sighed heavily and sat on the edge of a chair. "Cate said she'll take me back. She..."—his pause was deafening—"she didn't know I was here, with you. Still doesn't. I told her I was staying in a hotel in town—God, can we turn off that awful radio? I don't know how you slept with that." He practically ran across the room and, rather than turning it off, yanked the cord right out of the wall.

Immediately *they* were back. I felt Annie clench my fingers into a fist. Priscilla lifted my head in defiance. I can only assume that Robert noticed the difference because he remained several feet away from me and began pacing, keeping the furniture between us.

"This isn't right," he continued, his breathing labored. "It was never right. See–see, Cate's good, and she didn't deserve this. It was me—I just got confused." He paused again, resting his hands on the back of the couch opposite me. He met my eyes—or rather, he met the eyes of one of *them* through mine. Maybe Gus. Or Annie, or Priscilla. He blinked twice and looked away. "I'm going back," he exhaled and began pacing again. "My parents know—Ari told them. They want you out. Said they'd write you a check for ten thousand, but you have to leave. They know about the baby, and they'll find you an adoption lawyer. " He stopped again, and I watched as his hand started to lift towards the playpen, then dropped, defeated. "I just–I can't be this."

"You...don't want to be a dad?" I asked—hurt, confused, and, above all, angry.

"You don't understand." His eyes met mine, pleading. "I'm *going* to be a dad. Cate's pregnant. Finally. You have to understand..."

He kept going, but I didn't hear him. My blood was boiling, and I heard the beating of ancient drums as my heart pounded in my ears. *This is her fault,* Lucy hissed. Annie climbed up my throat, like she had all those years ago. I stomped twice, fighting her as she inhabited my vocal cords.

"...We tried for so long and she couldn't, and now she is. That's my family, Beauty—"

"And what are we?!" we snapped. I stepped towards him, my palms sore from where my nails had dug in. Esther began to cry in her crib, woken from her pleasant sleep by our shouting. "*What are we?!*" I roared again; her stifled cries became a scream.

He looked to the crib and back to me, as if asking if I were going to soothe her. "She's yours, too!" I screamed; my voice empowered by Annie's presence. He stared at me, then settled his gaze on Esther.

"One month," he said, so quietly I could barely hear him above the noise in my mind and Esther's wails filling the room. "You have one month to be out, or they will get the police involved. Once you're out, their lawyer will meet you with a check and a copy of documents saying that I've signed away my parental rights. She will no longer be mine."

With that, he tore his gaze away, turned on his heel, and left. The echo of the shutting door hung heavily in the room. I felt like I was going to black out. My head was suddenly so heavy that my neck couldn't support its weight, and I stumbled and fell into the arm of the couch. I managed to catch myself and staggered my way to Esther. I tried to soothe her, tried to quiet her, but my hands were shaking so badly that I could hardly support her. I put her back in the crib as she screamed, and I ran instead to the bedroom Robert and I had shared. He'd put in a landline to catch any work-related calls—and, I now presumed, so that Cate could reach him.

I dialed the number Maia had given me, which I'd easily committed to memory. She picked up on the second ring.

"I need help—" was all I managed before letting out a wail. I'm sure she replied, but my mind was going dark. I dropped the phone and nearly fell down the stairs trying to get back to Esther. I floundered through the living room, knocking over a light and the end table holding the radio. It crashed to the floor, and her screams magnified, filling the house.

I leaned over the pen, careful not to put my weight on it, and set my hand on her stomach. "I'm so sorry," I blubbered, over and over again. I needed her to hear it, to know it.

She kept screaming. *Just shut her up!* I heard them say. Over and over, they said it. I wept as I pleaded with them to stop, with her to stop.

My ears were ringing so loudly with their combined cries that I missed the sound of a car pulling up to the house. Maia came storming in, a warrior ready for battle in her bathrobe and rainbow slippers, curlers still in her hair.

"Come now, come now," she ordered, lifting me by the arm and, gently but firmly, settling me into the couch. She scooped up Esther and began to bounce her, whispering words I couldn't hear. After a few minutes, Esther's screams shifted to choked gasps. She fell into a fitful sleep, one marred by the events of the morning, which caused her to periodically gasp and her whole body to shake. Maia handed her to me on the couch and started to dig through the bags still stacked by the door. I was nervous to hold Esther. I didn't trust my hands—didn't trust that they were mine, and I never wanted her to be touched by *them*.

Maia's efforts uncovered a container of formula and a bottle. In the kitchen, she started a pot of coffee while making the bottle. Coming back in, she set a mug on the coffee table before me and handed me the bottle. "Feed her," she instructed as she went to work setting the room right.

I felt *their* hatred for her. They hated Maia almost as much as they hated Esther. Priscilla wanted to challenge her. She wanted to rage, to tell Maia where to shove her help and where she could spend eternity. I clenched my jaw shut, biting down so hard on my tongue that I could taste blood.

Right then, the room filled once again with songs; Maia had plugged in the radio. Whatever magic the music held immediately sent them back to whatever place they came from. Knowing now that they couldn't do anything more, I pulled Esther to me and hugged her tightly as I wept.

Maia came back from the kitchen with another mug and sat opposite me. "Oh, dear," she said. "Quite the first day, hmm?" I nodded through tears. "They normally are. Do you want to tell me about it?"

I nodded again. I wanted to tell her everything: I wanted to tell her about *them*, how they hated Esther and how they'd planned terrible things; I wanted to tell her how much I hated them but also missed them when they were gone, and how now they were back, and it was as though they'd spent every day of the past ten months in the floating-head-gym or doing steroids. I wanted to tell her how they yelled in my mind and filled it with smoke that clouded everything. But I couldn't. So instead, I told her about Robert. She listened intently, nodding her head here or sighing there, but never interrupting.

When I'd finished, she clicked her tongue (a sound that I'd become quite fond of). "Well, that *is* a lot. Let's make breakfast and talk it over." She gently took sleeping Esther from my arms and placed her back in the pen. "Come now," she said, taking my hand to lead me to the kitchen.

"Wait, the radio." I turned, pulling my hand free. I didn't want to unplug it, even for a moment, but I needed it. I quickly pulled the plug from the wall and nearly ran through the doorway between the two rooms, sighing with relief when the music filled the space again. I set it on the floor at the edge of the doorway.

Maia watched all this without saying a word. I could see that she was processing, but she refrained from commenting, instead moving forward with making breakfast. I tried to help her cook, but she was far more efficient than I was, so eventually, feeling in the way, I sat at the table and spun my coffee mug as she asked me questions.

"What do you want to do?" she asked, whisking eggs and frying bacon.

"About what?"

"About Esther. Is adoption an option?"

I stopped spinning the mug and looked at her, shocked she'd even ask such a question. "*Never*," I said definitively. "She's *mine*."

She nodded knowingly. "How will you care for the two of you? It's much different being homeless with an infant. There are places, though even at the church, we have people who have room to help. You know I'd take you both in a heartbeat if I only had the room, but we sold our house when our children were grown and now have a one-bedroom condo." She seemed to chastise herself for that decision, as though she should have anticipated that I would blow into her life like a hurricane.

"I'll take the money and leave."

"And go where?"

"I don't know. I didn't know this place before I got here, so I guess I'll just find somewhere new."

"How are you going to get there?" She piled the bacon on one plate and the eggs on another and brought them both to the table where she sat across from me.

"The bus, I guess."

She clicked her tongue again, shaking her head. "You're going to take all of your stuff—all of her stuff—on the bus?"

I hadn't thought about that. "I'll just leave it then. All I need is her."

"Oh, dear," she said, a bite of bacon in her mouth. "That's not how children work. You'll need those things, and it's far too expensive to buy it all over again somewhere new. Do you have a phone?"

"Upstairs in the master bedroom."

"Excuse me." I heard her check on Esther, then meander up the stairs. She came back down after five or ten minutes with a look that said she'd figured it all out.

"It's terribly cold in that room," she commented, joining me at the table again.

"I can turn up the heat," I suggested through eggs.

"No, no, I don't mean temperature wise. I mean, it's lacking life in that room."

I nodded in agreement. "I preferred to sleep in Ari's room— she was so kind and colorful, despite the way she dressed. Her room reflected that—it always felt like a better place to be." We chatted some more as we finished breakfast, Maia expertly turning the attention away from my troubles. With the radio on, I felt almost normal.

Once we finished eating, Maia asked me to do the dishes while she excused herself. She went to her car, grabbed an overnight bag, and spent the next thirty minutes or so in the bathroom. When she emerged, she was once again a pristine pastel: hair curlers removed, makeup expertly applied, and slippers replaced with kitten heels. As she came out, tires treaded their way up the road.

"Right on time!" she declared. I'd just finished feeding Esther and set her back in her pen, anxious about whatever Maia had planned

I looked out the window and saw a fleet of cars coming up the drive. A sea of women exited cars, their excited voices like birds chirping in the trees. Maia opened the door, and one by one, they entered. They each hugged me (some kissed me) and made their way to Esther, where they cooed and aahed at her.

After they'd all piled in, Maia lifted her hands and drew all attention to her: "Alright, ladies. As you know, Beauty here has had quite a time of it lately and now has a darling little girl to care for. She will be leaving soon and wants to make a go of it on her own. We're here today to pray over her and the child and to bless her with a collection." Immediately the others began to chirp excitedly. Maia calmed them and beckoned the group to gather around me. She handed me Esther, and one at a time, the ladies prayed.

Being conscious this time around, I found their prayer circle to be the strangest thing I'd ever experienced, but wonderful at the same time. I still mostly thought of prayer as something people did before eating or what the pastor did after a service; even my previous experiences with prayer (with Father first and Maddox later) were different from this. Surrounded by these women, I felt like I was a part of some sort of ancient ritual. Whatever the ritual was, I could feel it in the deepest parts of myself, and I hoped, in some way, that Esther could too.

After they finished, Maia brought a vase from the kitchen and passed it around the room. One by one the women dropped cash into the vase until it was overflowing. Then the doorbell rang, and Maia opened it to a delivery. A man in a white vest came in and set platters of food and two large jugs of tea on the coffee table. I'd never seen such a spread: rolled deli meats, cheeses of all shapes and colors, crackers, olives—it was like something out of a movie. He left as quickly as he'd come, and the ladies went to work on the trays.

I was overwhelmed and thrilled at the same time. I felt like I was part of something that mattered and had an unusual feeling of expectation as I chatted with each of them, feeling like a queen as they asked me questions (nothing too heavy or personal, though). Then Maia called for their attention again.

This time, she turned her full focus towards me. "Beauty," she started, "you've shared some of your past with me, and I have to say that I am absolutely amazed at the young lady that you are. You have had your fair share of trials, and I guarantee that they're not over yet." My heart dropped at the reminder. "We are so limited in what we can do for you, but you have a good Father who cares for you, and we believe that He put you with us for this very day and this very purpose." Her eyes held mine, her gaze steady, and then she smiled. "We have one more surprise for you."

She grabbed my hand, asking one of the ladies to watch Esther, and led me outside, the other ladies following. As she stepped to the side, I saw Al and Maia's husband standing by an old Honda with a bow on it.

"It's not much," Al explained humbly, "but it's clean, and it works." Maia's husband came and took my hand from hers and walked me to the car.

Maia followed, stating, "A bus just won't do for you and the baby. This way, you can load up as much as you're able, and anything else you can't, we'll store until you find a place."

I couldn't speak. I couldn't imagine how a day could start like this one had and, just a few hours later, turn out like this. I now had a freedom that I'd never had before. I dropped to my knees and wept. The women quickly surrounded me, speaking words of encouragement and demanding that I check in when I got to wherever I was going. I nodded and promised each of them I would.

Soon after, they began to leave. The house grew quieter until, once again, it was just Maia, Esther, and me. "If you need me to stay, I'd be happy to," she offered.

I don't think I'd ever wanted anything so badly, and yet I knew I couldn't ask more of her, so I shook my head and, choking back tears, walked her to the door.

There, she took my hand, looked me straight in the eyes, and said, "I need you to know that *you* are a child of God. Somewhere or sometime, something told you otherwise, but I see you like He does. You are His precious child—don't forget it." With that, she left.

It's amazing how the absolute presence of people amplifies the absolute absence of them. I desperately wanted to stay with them. I wanted to take up the offer of a room from any of the several who'd extended it. I'd even be willing to trade my wardrobe for pastels. But I knew it would end; Louis reminded me that it always did. He reminded me of my biological mother, who was forced to leave me; of Father, who was gone; of Mother, who had so easily let me drive away in a white van; of Ari, who I'd driven away, and Robert, who'd run away on his own. He told me that this was my curse: I would always be alone.

*They* would see to it.

I cleaned up the plates and tucked the leftovers in the fridge. Then, after feeding Esther, the radio still on, I took my solitary place on the couch.

# Chapter Thirty

For the next month, my life was like a haunted roller coaster. Since *they* couldn't control me, they took to randomly destroying things around the house instead. The first victim was the nursery. You might try to tell me that the following is insane (like everything up to this point somehow wasn't), that these things only happen in horror movies—and they do—but they also happened to me.

It was late one night, around two in the morning, when I heard an awful commotion above us. Esther slept through it, but I shivered with fear under the covers until the noise passed, nearly an hour later. The next morning, I quickly moved the radio to a plug by the stairs and turned up the volume. With each step, I ran back down to turn the volume up a bit more, needing to make sure the music would reach the top. When I was finally confident it would, I climbed the stairs. I wished I had grabbed a fire poker or umbrella or something, but I didn't want to walk all the way down the stairs again—my nerves couldn't take it.

I pressed my ear against the nursery door. Satisfied that there was nobody in there, I slowly opened it.

The room looked like a dresser had violently vomited pink. Every item of baby clothing was torn from the drawers and strewn about. Stuffed animals had been shredded; their cotton fluff scattered across the floor. The crib was turned on its side, the rocking chair askew next to it.

*Told you*, they taunted. I shuddered and ran out of the room, back to the safety of the music. That night, I asked Maia to take Esther for a few hours so I could pack. I couldn't stand the idea of leaving her downstairs by herself, but I also didn't want her anywhere near the pink catastrophe that was her room.

After watching Maia's car drive away, I unplugged the radio and, singing one of the songs I remembered, hurried up the stairs to plug it back in in the nursery. I sang along to the songs as I cleaned and tried to act like everything was normal. But every moment I felt like I was being watched. I kept glancing over my shoulder into the next room, expecting to see *them*. Waiting for them to walk in. Not as floating heads, though; after that one dream, they must have permanently graduated to full-on bodies. It was the only explanation for the chaos they'd wreaked on the room.

During my final month there, this became my new normal. During the night, they'd throw their fits and destroy something; the next day, I'd ask one of the pastels to watch Esther for a few hours and would use the time to pack and clean up whatever mess they'd made.

Once I'd retrieved everything that I wanted from upstairs, I let them have their way with it. During their rampages, it sounded as though a pack of wild monkeys was set loose. I could hear crashing and tearing and could only imagine what they were doing. Several times I was tempted to peek, but then I would remember the boney hand from my dream. No need to get any closer.

When our stuff was all packed (minus the things that we'd need until the day of our departure), I started to practice driving. On the first ride, I was dismayed to discover that the car's radio didn't work. Using some of the cash from the collection, I purchased a CD player and a tape-adapter for the car as well as a handful of CDs from the Christian/Religion section. I didn't know any of the names on the shelves, but I didn't care; I just needed to be able to hear them, to take in whatever it was that made a dome around me that *they* couldn't penetrate.

I nearly flew into a blind rage, that I'd love to blame on Annie, when the radio still didn't work, even with the adapter. I sat in the parking lot, banging my head against the steering wheel, as other patrons looked on, those walking by the car hurriedly crossing away from it. I drove home, singing what words I could remember, but for some reason, it wasn't the same. *They* flooded my mind again with their gruesome plans.

By the time I made it back through the door, sweat was pouring down my face. I grabbed the radio and ran to the bathroom, where I sat it on the counter and plugged it in. I had an hour before one of the women would be dropping Esther off, and I needed to scrub their thoughts and words from my mind. I stood in the shower, letting the steam rise and the heat fall on my shoulders, begging it to burn away the imagery. I couldn't understand why *they* hated her so much—she was so lovely, so pure.

I reminded myself of Maia's words: *I am a child of God*. I didn't know what it meant, but I felt the weight of it.

What's more, if I was a child of God, then Esther was a granddaughter of God, and if he loved his grandchildren anything like Maia loved hers, then Esther would have to be okay.

That became my mantra during that final week. Part of me felt like I was about to drive into a never-ending tunnel of darkness, but elsewhere, deep inside me, I felt this odd burning, a coal that indicated something different—something hopeful.

At last, the day came. Maia came as support; despite her trying otherwise, I'd specifically requested that it was only her. I'd relented that her husband could stay in the car, but I didn't want the other women here. They didn't know about Robert or the conditions behind my pre-determined departure, and I didn't need any more witnesses to this.

Robert arrived with a wormy-looking man next to him—his lawyer. When they got out of the car, the lawyer attempted to shake my hand, but I refused. His outstretched fingers were thin and boney, and I felt certain that if I touched them, he would transform into something different and consume me. Robert remained a foot behind him while Maia stood steadily behind me, holding Esther.

"Can I see her?" he asked, peering past me.

"You had your chance," Maia barked in a shame-on-you tone that only a mother can pull off.

I glanced back at her, almost grinning. For the second time, I saw that a blush had risen to her face. I don't know why she was embarrassed; she'd taken the words from my heart.

"The papers?" I requested instead.

The lawyer pulled a manilla envelope from his briefcase and handed it to me. Inside were the official documents declaring that Robert was no longer legally a parent to Esther. He'd already signed them. I stared at his signature, unable to understand how someone so normal could do something so cavalierly. How do you just give up on something that you made?

But then, as I continued to study it, I noticed that the first "R" of his name was written twice. The first was light, shaky, whereas the second was written so forcefully, it indented the page. What it meant, I had no idea, but nevertheless, it settled something in me.

I nodded and looked up, asking, "And the money?" From his briefcase, the lawyer pulled out another envelope, small and white this time. I couldn't believe that so much cash fit in such a small envelope. When he handed it to me, I could feel that it was only about an inch thick. From the movies, I had half-expected him to hand me the whole briefcase, which would click open to reveal neatly stacked rows of green.

I looked back at Maia, confused. She nodded affirmingly.

"That's it, then," the lawyer said.

"That's it," I agreed, turning to leave.

"Beauty—" Robert started, but there was no radio out here. Annie was in my eyes like a flash of lightning. Priscilla held my head high. My shoulders lifted as I felt my body rise—not levitating off the ground or anything like that but straightening from the posture of a beaten and bruised girl to that of an ancient something-or-other. It was times like this that I didn't hate them —when I felt like, if they weren't plotting to kill my child, we could be friends.

He saw the shift too. His jaw clenched, and he turned without another word.

"Not a word of this. Ever." reminded the lawyer before backing up.

I clenched my mouth shut as Priscilla tried to respond; I knew nothing helpful would come out. I looked to Maia once again and saw that her face was locked as well.

I wondered who she was holding in.

When they'd driven off, Maia and her husband helped me tuck Esther into her car seat and load up the last few bags. Maia hugged me and made me promise to call every stop along the way. She even threatened, only half-joking, with tears in her eyes, to send the police to find me if I failed to check in.

Then I climbed into my car and, blinking away tears myself, turned the key. I put my headphones on and started one of the CDs before setting the car in gear and beginning to drive.

Leaving the driveway for the last time, I saw that Maia had only partially kept her promise. The road was lined with cars, with a woman in pastel colors behind every steering wheel.

They honked and waved as I drove towards my future—and the last part of this story.

# Part VI

It Is Finished

# Chapter Thirty-One

Rain started to fall as I turned onto the highway out of town. It fell harder and harder until the windshield wipers could barely keep up. At the same time, my eyes were flooded with emotion. In my short time in that small town, I'd had three families. First was Ari. No matter what, she had been my friend, and we were now permanently linked through Esther. Next came Robert. Despite all that had happened and how much I wanted to hate him, he'd given me the most precious thing in my life: the tiny baby contently sleeping behind me. And finally, through Esther, I'd met the pastels and, most importantly, Maia. She'd been more to me than I'd ever be able to explain, and through her, some kind of flame had planted itself in my heart (although I didn't yet recognize it). I wept as I drove, running my sleeve across my eyes and nose and blinking out the remnants of remorse and regret so I could see the road.

I drove all day, pausing every few hours to find a rest stop or fast-food joint to feed and change Esther, walk around with the stroller, and get food for myself. That first night, I stayed in a cheap hotel, one that boasted cable and a free breakfast. Then, paying cash at the front desk, loaded what little we had into the dingy room. Maia had warned me to keep only a small amount of money in my wallet, with the rest hidden and locked away in my suitcase. I'd taken her advice to heart; that first night cost the full amount in my wallet, so later, I cautiously pulled out a bit more so I could order dinner from the diner across the street.

That night, I ate buffalo wings and a piece of cheesecake while lying across the bed and watching *I Love Lucy*. I hadn't watched TV in so long, I'd nearly forgotten how wonderful it could be to be completely absorbed in something. Behind the TV, the radio I'd brought along was tuned in to the local Christian station. I'd been careful to look up local station numbers in advance so I could immediately tune in wherever I was. The laugh track didn't pair well with hymns, but I barely noticed after a while.

Thus, a new routine was born. I'd drive all day, periodically pausing for snacks and to tend to Esther, then would find a cheap hotels near the highway at night, where I'd fall asleep next to Esther with the TV and radio both on. Gradually, I was able to release some of the initial sorrow. I knew that my time before had been important in that it had started to mold me, but I also felt the importance of this new season. I was figuring out how to be alone and care for my child. For the first time in my life, I had to be the adult.

After the first month, Esther started sleeping less, so we couldn't travel as far during the day. She also began to hate new places, so I would stay in the same hotel for several nights in a row before moving on.

While those parts were hard, she more than made up for it with gummy smiles, coos and other weird noises, and an astonishing alertness. I fell more and more in love with her every day, and I desperately craved somewhere more permanent where we could live for the rest of our lives. I knew that a hotel was no place for a baby to live, but I hadn't found a better solution, so I kept on.

I didn't have any clear destination in mind, so I drove haphazardly across the country, trying to find a place that felt like home. I quickly learned that the Midwest was not for me (entirely too much corn, plus the eerie sense of something lurking in the fields) and headed back to the East coast. As soon as I saw the ocean again, I knew I'd made the right decision.

I did my best to stay away from large cities. Being young with a baby, it was dangerous for me to stay in any of the areas I could afford, so I often pushed a bit farther to find a smaller town with motels right off the highway. One particular day, though, Esther had the blowout of all blowouts right as we were driving through a large city. The stench stung my nostrils and made my eyes water. I'd planned to keep driving through, but dusk had already settled, and I knew I wouldn't be able to get her changed and clean and make it to another town before the blackness of night consumed the highway. Even more than I dreaded staying in a city, I feared driving on unknown highways in the dark.

So I was driving the city streets, one hand plugging my nose, and Esther screaming, when I saw a beam of hope up ahead. The sign promised a room, breakfast, and a pool for only sixty-nine dollars a night. I quickly found my way to its parking lot. I paid a burly, sour-smelling man at the front desk and drove around the side. It was one of those places where all the rooms have doors on the outside, so I backed the car into a spot right in front of my room and quickly unloaded.

I immediately plugged in the radio and turned it to a local Christian station. Then I changed Esther, gave her a bath, and wrapped her in warm pajamas. Most of the time I put her in the playpen for sleep, but tonight I decided to lay her on one of the queen beds, surrounded by pillows. I didn't want to take the extra time to unload the pen in this area. It was the type of place they showed as the "other side of the tracks" in movies: dirty, crumbling, and stinky.

I ordered a pizza and soda and ate quickly before snuggling next to Esther. I had no desire to stay in this place any longer than I had to, so I turned in early and set the radio alarm clock for six the following morning.

Then, during the night, I felt something shift. I heard *them*. Not quietly, either—they were screaming. Furious. I blinked away the sleep and slapped my hands over my ears, desperate to block them out, but they pulled my hands away, making them clench into fists instead. I rolled off the bed, knowing that I had to get away from Esther, fearful what they might do to her with my limbs.

I hit the ground with a thud and tried to push myself to my knees, but it was like being caught in quicksand; despite the floor beneath me being solid, I could not push up from it. Their voices rang in a chorus of English and their old language. I tried to tuck my head under my hands, but instead they brought fists to my face, striking again and again, until I felt blood trickle from my nose.

I didn't understand. I'd been so careful; I'd done everything right. Why had the magic stopped? Beyond their screaming, I heard a strange sound—not the music I expected, but static. I army-crawled to the radio, fighting to turn the knob to get the music back.

*Not this time,* Priscilla hissed.

*You're OURS,* they chorused in harmonious unison.

I knew I had to get away. I pushed my body towards the door. Clinging to the doorknob, begging it to hold my weight, I dragged myself up and managed to twist it open.

Outside, the freezing air stung at my face, biting my lips and ears. I clenched my eyes shut against it, but that only amplified the *thud-thud-thud* of my heart and *their* voices, accusing: *You did this.* I staggered to my car, but it was locked. I moaned; I knew where the keys were, but I didn't know if I could risk going back for them.

I leaned against the trunk, fighting to control my body. Every muscle I had was quivering, tense, and under their control. I moved slowly, deliberately, around the car, checking all the doors in case one was unlocked.

When I got to the front passenger side, to my shock and dismay, I found the window shattered, shards of it scattered over the ground and seat. I cried out, pushing through the pieces, desperate to find the precious CD player, but it was gone, along with the headphones I'd purchased when I returned the adapter. The inside of the car, now illuminated, revealed a mess. In a desperate search for valuables, the thief had torn apart the car. The glove box was open, its papers strewn about the front seat. They'd even dumped the garbage bag that I used to keep the car tidy, spilling fast food bags and wrappers across the floor in the back. Thankfully, they'd left the car seat, but everything else was taken, likely to be pawned.

My disappointment cut deep, and I began to weep. *You can't do anything right*—I could no longer tell if it was my own despondency or *their voices* echoing through my mind; either way, it was effective, pulling me down, twisting the knife of despair.

Suddenly, I heard Esther scream. I wrestled back control of my body and ran to her, slamming the door shut behind me. She laid on the bed exactly where I'd left her, face beet-red and squinched with fury. As I neared, the stench hit my nose. I breathed a sigh of relief—just another blowout. I lifted her up and fought the urge to squeeze her hard.

*Just once,* they said. *Just once, and you'll be ours again.*

I nearly gagged at the thought. I stripped her clothes from her as she wiggled and wailed while I tried to wipe her clean, but she needed a bath. As soon as I thought about filling the tub, though, I saw *them*, holding her under the water. Unable to force it down this time, I ran to the wastebasket and violently retched up my partially digested pizza. Esther continued to scream as I slumped to the floor.

I couldn't touch her. If I touched her, *they* would touch her, and I couldn't let them. I couldn't give them even a moment's opportunity to harm her. I reached for the radio again, turning the dial, each time meeting only static. No stations, no sounds. Then I remembered the radio clock by the bed. In a flash, I was on my feet, stumbling over to it.

*No!* they shrieked. *End it! END IT!* I felt bile tickle the back of my throat. My feet tripped, and I fell, hard, but at the last minute, I managed to stick my arm out and grabbed the clock, cradling it tightly even as my elbow hit the floor, sending a sharp pain all the way up my arm to my shoulder. I blinked through the pain and hit the FM button on the radio.

*NO!* they screamed again, their voices a migraine behind my eyes. My vision went blurry, and the walls began to cave, but I managed to turn the knob to the station I'd found earlier.

A hymn, one I knew, filled the room.

Immediately, like a puppet whose master had dropped the strings, my body fell to the floor. The tension released, my mind filled with silence—which lasted only a moment before Esther's mighty screams broke through, now paired with the sound of banging on the wall.

"Shut that kid up!" an angry voice yelled.

"I'm sorry..." I stuttered to the man behind the wall. I shuffled across the floor on my knees to my daughter and lifted her, still covered in filth, and held her against my chest. I tried to comfort her but couldn't get any words through my own weeping. Instead, I simply bounced her in my arms. When her screams finally subsided, I let myself sit on the edge of the bed. I'd never felt so tired in my life. It felt like I had just gone to war, but I certainly didn't feel like the victor.

When I finally was confident that their voices were gone and my body was my own, I took Esther to the bathroom and rinsed her with warm water and soap in the sink. I couldn't bring myself to use the bathtub; the picture of *them* holding her under flooded my mind, and once again I wept.

"I'm so sorry," I said to her over and over. What type of life was this for her? What kind of mother was I?

Once she was clean, I clothed and fed her. Lying her on the other bed (fortunately the room had two), I stripped off the comforter and sheets. I rolled them neatly in a bundle on the floor and wrote a note to housekeeping (assuming there was something like that here), which I left with a twenty-dollar bill on top of the pile.

I left Esther for a moment on the bed and went around to the backside of the building where I'd spotted a dumpster earlier in the day. I found a box and a partially-chewed roll of duct tape in the trash; it looked like a dog must have gotten the brand-new roll and chomped through most of the layers of tape. Back at my car, I pulled off the useless layers, uncovering the usable bits below, and taped the cardboard inside and outside until I was certain it was secure. By the time I'd finished, my fingers were numb from the cold.

Back in the room, Esther was once again sleeping peacefully, as if the events of the evening had been merely an inconvenience in her sleep schedule. I gently swaddled her in several blankets and placed her in the car seat. Then, for good measure, I laid another thick blanket over the top of her. Once she was secure, I stuffed all my belongings in a bag, grabbed the clock radio as an extra precaution (stealing, I know), and threw it all in the passenger seat. Desperately singing any songs I could remember, humming the parts I didn't, I hopped in and began to drive. I needed a super-store—one that stayed open all night and would have a CD player.

I sang as loudly as I could without disturbing her, although I'd have woken her in a heartbeat if it meant keeping *them* away. I could again feel them in my mind, like when you walk through a spider web and it sticks, invisible, to your skin. You pull and wipe at it, but no matter how you try, you can't get free from it. I felt them mock me and laugh at their own clever cruelty. They dared me to drive into the oncoming traffic, each set of head-lights an invitation to just end it all. I sang louder, nearing a wail now, desperate to silence them. They laughed even more.

*You have no power here,* Lucy squealed with delight as she projected images into my mind of my car bashing head-on into an oncoming semi-truck.

My hands clenched the steering wheel tightly. I forced my-self to stay focused and was rewarded with the bright sign of a supercenter up ahead. I peeled into the parking lot and parked in a handicap space right outside the entrance. I grabbed my purse and keys and, locking the car with Esther inside (I honestly couldn't imagine anything more dangerous to her than me in that moment), I ran directly to the electronics department. I grabbed a CD player, headphones, and batteries, and raced to the checkout aisles. Only one lane was open; fortunately, the store was empty at that time of night—or rather, morning.

I slapped cash down on the counter and barked, "Scissors," to the young cashier. I can only imagine how I must have looked. I hadn't taken time to brush my hair or teeth or wash my face. I was too panicked to feel shame in the moment, but later I won-dered what he thought. He hesitantly handed the shears to me, and I quickly snipped the plastic off the top of each case before slamming the scissors down and racing out the door.

Back at the car, I used my teeth to tear the rest of the plastic off, then fumbled to pop the batteries in. I pulled a CD from my purse and slapped it in. Closing the player, I put the headphones on and let my body sink down the outside of the car until I felt the cold, wet parking lot through my jeans. I sat through at least two songs, letting the music push away the voices. Only when I could stand the biting wind no more did I unlock the door and climb back into the car.

For the first time on this trip, I knew exactly where I needed to go. Luckily, I wasn't too far. I hopped back on the highway and took the on-ramp north, to the place I'd run from years ago.

Home.

# Chapter Thirty-Two

Driving down familiar roads, I realized how much a part of me this place still was. Even after all that time, I knew every building, every store, every alleyway. What I didn't know was if Mother was still in the same apartment she'd been in when I left White Pines. She'd sold the house after Brother had joined the military, and she and Father had always talked about finding a smaller house on the edge of town once they were empty nesters. I didn't know if she'd followed through on that plan or if it was yet another dream that had died with him.

I stopped at a gas station across from the hospital where my father had died, stifling tears at the memory, and picked up a phone book. Skimming through the white pages, I found her name, a new address listed underneath. I drove to the neat cul-de-sac, nestled amongst pleasantly bright evergreen trees, and stopped in front of the house that matched her numbers. It was smaller than our old home—only one floor—but clearly well cared for. Even in the harsh winter months, it was tidy.

I sat in the car with the lights off and the heat on until the sun began to peek over the horizon. If she'd maintained her normal sleeping habits, she'd be up with the sun. While I waited, I wrote a note on a piece of the car's owner manual that had been ripped out by the car thief. One side talked about the car's power steering, and on the other, blank side, I told my mother about my daughter. At the end, I wrote, "She is Esther Tindra. Make sure she knows that I loved her, but never let her know what I am."

When I saw a light upstairs turn on, I grabbed the lock-bag from my suitcase, pulled out five thousand dollars (leaving myself the remaining three to live on), and placed the cash and note into an envelope—the same one that the lawyer had given me. Tucking the envelope into the car seat next to Esther, I kissed my baby on her forehead, then I unclicked the car seat, walked to the door, sat her down, and knocked. I ran back to my car, killed the engine, and sat until Mother came to the door.

She opened the door slowly—understandable at this time of day. The sun had just crested the hills, and it shone a brilliant orange puddle over the house. At first, I could tell that Mother was confused. From somewhere in the house came a light bark, and a small yellow dog came bounding out. It saw the car seat before Mother did. I couldn't hear it, but I saw her gasp. She knelt down, holding her bathrobe closed at the knees, and tucked the blanket around Esther's face. She pulled the note out and began to read. I watched her face fill with emotion as she saw a glimpse of what had happened to her daughter. Then I watched as she gently lifted her grandchild and clung her tightly, weeping.

When they'd gone back inside, and I knew that my baby was finally safe, I turned the car on and drove away. Back on the highway, I took the headphones off, turned the CD player off, and gave up. Whatever father Maia had talked about must have abandoned me, as I now abandoned my child. Whatever spark of hope had been lit died that cold morning. *Their* voices filled my mind again, and this time, I didn't try to stop them.

# Chapter Thirty-Three

For the next two years, I lived out of my car. I returned to the bay, staying a town over it. It was the only place that I could remember feeling happy, so I was desperate to keep it close but needed to stay far enough away to avoid Maia, the pastels, and Robert.

I hopped from one urgent care to the next and developed my own ritual prescription usage to block out the shame and regret in my life. Valium and opiates kept me numb as *they* did what they'd always wanted to do. I earned money in the oldest way and spent it doing everything I could to stay numb. Periodically, I'd find a motel to stay in for a couple of nights where I'd cry myself to sleep, riding a wave of vodka and valium. When I woke from a restless night of nightmares, I'd go about the day at their whims.

One night early on, while scavenging the trash of a restaurant that threw out good food and (as long as I didn't make a commotion) didn't chase me away, I heard a familiar voice coming from a small, country-themed venue across the way. I crossed the street, staying clear of a group of smokers, and peeked through the window.

She was as beautiful as I remembered: her hair long and wavy, her movements smooth and graceful. *Cate.*

She was sitting on a stool, but when she stood, I saw that she was heavily pregnant—just as Robert had said. I felt my blood boil. *She stole him from us,* Lucy accused. *The whore,* Priscilla agreed. Gus and Annie showed up, best buds like all those years ago, and punched the glass.

It was strong, so it didn't shatter, but it did crack, and the webbed fissures tore like seams up the side of the window. She paused her singing and looked towards the window. At first, she only saw the glass. Then, with a sharp inhale, a glimmer of recognition crossed her face. I watched her clutch her stomach to protect it, as I had once done with my own. Covered in a new layer of shame, I turned and ran, the smokers yelling behind me.

*They* pushed me to a liquor store, where the cheapest bottle of vodka immediately met my lips. They reminded me of everything she'd taken from me, how she had *ruined* me.

I *hated* her. Every part of me wanted to drive my car through that same glass window and watch her face lit up in the headlights. *They* showed me it, as vivid as they'd shown my own collision with a semi-truck. They dared me to do it. Instead, I crawled into the backseat, took a handful of valium with a shot of vodka, and fell asleep.

From then on, I avoided any area where I might be recognized. I bathed at community centers, attended AA meetings (just to feel like I had something to do), and ended my days with valium and vodka.

A year later, I saw her again—this time in early spring. She pushed a stroller through the park and walked side-by-side with a tall, handsome blonde.

*Robert.*

I lost it. From the back of my car, where I'd slept the night before, I felt *them* push me over the seat. one leg awkwardly flying upward, to climb into the front. I felt them turn the key in my hand, felt their feet go to the gas. I felt Priscilla, or maybe Lucy, push down, the lever giving way until my foot was on the floor. The car made a horrendous sound, but luckily, they'd forgotten to shift it out of park.

A moment later, I realized what they'd tried to do. They'd tried to destroy a family.

*They destroyed yours,* they reminded me. I'd become so accustomed to vomiting after binging, I didn't even try to force down the disgust. I quickly rolled down the window and let it out the side of the car.

Without rolling the window back up, I put the car in reverse and started to drive. I drove to a truck stop near the edge of town. I'd come to know one of the cashiers, who'd let me use the shower periodically. Luckily, she was working. As I entered, she nodded and tossed me a key. I made my way back to the shower room and let the hot water run over my body. *They* screamed in my mind, enraged at what I'd taken from them. It was the first time in a long time that I'd defied them, and they were furious. My head began to pound as their voices, shrill and heavy, filled it with chaos. Behind the chorus, I felt Opi. He rarely showed up, but when he did, it filled me with a new type of dread.

I sat on the shower floor, letting the water burn my back, until I heard the cashier knock on the door. I immediately turned off the shower and dressed, pulling my hair into a tight bun and brushing my teeth. Then, feeling at least somewhat human again, I walked to my car.

Somewhere between the parking lot and my car, I heard something familiar; the beat of a drum and a certain melody caught my ears. Looking around, I saw a large building across the street. I was immediately drawn to it. *They* started to object and fight, which made me want it even more. I crossed the street haphazardly, cars honking as I did. I walked behind a group of giggling girls, one who held the door for me while smiling. I nodded my thanks and walked into the foyer. As I followed the group of girls, others patted me in welcome or shook my hand in greeting. I tried to nod politely but felt pulled in the direction of the music.

As I entered the sanctuary, the music filled me immediately. Not a single eye drifted away from the stage, where a thin woman with perfectly tanned skin stood with a microphone. A light lit her from above. The instruments started to fade as her voice rose and her hands reached toward heaven.

*What if we believed You are who You say You are?*
Her voice was crisp and bright, her song filling the room.
*What if we believed You could do what You say You can do?*
A few cheers were let loose in the audience.
*What if we believed He gave up his life for us?*
*Every sin, every shame. What if we believed?*

Her voice was melodic and silky as she pumped her arms and fists, calling out, "Declare it! Declare it!" She paused, looking across the rows and aisles, her eyes landing on mine.

The air felt weighted with anticipation.

The band joined her once again. This time the lyrics weren't questions, but statements. She sang.

> *God, we believe You are who You say You are*
> *God, we believe You can do what You say You can do*
> *God, we believe You gave up Your life for us*
> *Every sin, every shame*
> *We believe*

I wanted that; I wanted to *believe.*

I felt something familiar winding its way up my spine. It brought goosebumps to my arms and rode the shiver like a wave to my heart.

*I know you,* it said. Like one of *them,* only different. This voice was soft and gentle. It asked me to come and know Him. It didn't demand; it didn't expect. It offered.

At first, I could feel *them* resist, but they held no ground against it. Then, I felt myself fight it. It was familiar, but I was *theirs*—for always and forever.

It chuckled softly, not cruel, or malicious: *You've always been Mine.* I immediately knew it was true. *Ask Me,* it beckoned. *Ask Me to show you.*

Fred tried to rise up. He tried to clench my heart, to make me run.

*Fear has no power here,* the new voice said; I realized it reminded me of Father. *Ask Me.*

"*Please?*" I breathed, unable to muster more. It was barely a whimper, drowned from any nearby ears by the clear, strong voice from stage that continued to rise into the rafters, echoing a promise.

*That'll do*, He said. I felt a wave, beginning at my toes. It was as though I was being stripped of clothing. Garment after garment was peeled from my form. My fingers lifted to the sky, and I felt each of *them* pulled from me. Some were like stripping the top sheet, coming loose easily. Others, like Priscilla, hung on for dear life. It felt at times like the seams of my very being were being ripped and torn from me. I wanted to vomit, to purge all of them from me. I imagined myself as a squid, expelling the ink of Opi over the patrons around me. Their beautiful Sunday best, covered in my sin.

I gagged and ran from the sanctuary, desperately looking for a bathroom. The new voice was gone, but I felt Him still. Reaching a wastebasket, I violently ejected every last part of *them* from me. Shaking, I slid to the ground, one arm still linked over the side of the trash. I saw several forms running towards me. At first, I panicked, thinking it was *them* trying to get back in, and I pushed my free hand up in front of my face, intuiting that they would crawl back in through my mouth.

*Settle, child*, the new voice said. I let my body fall to the floor as the group surrounded me.

# Chapter Thirty-Four

They put a cool rag on my forehead and led me to a couch in a small library off the main entrance. A woman, maybe five years older than me, spoke to me softly. She asked where I was from and if I needed help. I couldn't respond; I was overcome with emotion. I couldn't fathom an existence where *their* weight wasn't on me. She patted my hand knowingly and called for someone out the door. A tall, skinny man with red hair and a red beard came in.

"My husband, Noah," she said by way of explanation. "He's a paramedic. We just want to have him look over you, if that's okay." I nodded in agreement and let Noah check my pulse and temperature. As he finished, I saw a girl, maybe three or four, come through the door and wrap herself around the woman's legs. The child had her father's bright red hair and the softness of her mother.

She left her mother's side and came over to her father's, where she placed one hand on his shoulder as he knelt before me. Shyly, she looked up and said, "Hi."

"Hello," I responded, my heart melting. I wondered if Esther was speaking yet.

"You're pretty," she stated, putting her hand on my knee. "What's your name?" Her chubby fingers found a hole in my leggings, and she giggled, not maliciously.

"I'm called Beauty," I said.

She giggled again: "That's not a name!" I smiled, agreeing.

Her mother called her back with the look that only mothers have mastered. "She's too young yet to have a filter," she apologized.

"Everything seems normal," Noah interjected, putting his tools and instruments back in a bag.

"Excellent news!" his wife said. She came and sat with me on the couch. "Noah, stay with Joy for a bit. I'll be out after a while." He took the little girl and exited.

She sat with me in silence for a moment before sharing, "I think I was expecting you." I was shocked by her frank statement and unsure of how to respond, but she just nodded confidently: "Yes, I'm quite sure of it. Oh, don't worry," she said, seeing my brows furrow. "I think you know Noah's mother—Maia?" I nearly began to weep. Over the past year or more, my biggest regret had been breaking my promise to Maia. She was the only person who I felt would understand everything in my life. I'd wanted so badly to call her so many times, but they kept me from it.

"He's ginger," I stated, matter-of-factly.

She grinned so big, I couldn't help but smile with her. "He is. He was adopted." Again, I was astounded. I knew that Maia had children, but she'd never told me, even after I'd revealed my own origins, that she'd adopted a child as well.

As if reading my mind, she added, "Maia refuses to use words like 'adopted.' As far as she's concerned, he is a child from her heart. Just as the Lord invites us into His family as children, she did the same." I felt something stir in me; that new voice was there again. It must have shown on my face because she asked, "Are you okay?"

I nodded. "Is–is she here?"

"No, she and Papa Phil are with our youngest—she's only about eight months old. Noah is the worship pastor here, so we try to be here on Sundays, even when he's not on the team. I can call her if you want, though. I'm sure Phil would manage just fine for a bit without her."

I nodded again; my insides were about to burst in anticipation of seeing her.

"I'm sorry, what's your name again?" I asked as she was walking out of the room.

"Adina," she said. "But you can call me Addie."

The service ended, and the church quickly emptied. When all that remained were a few stragglers, I heard a voice like that of an angel, echoing through the foyer: "Where is she?"

I bounced from the couch and threw myself through the doors, bumping one shoulder into the frame in my eagerness. I caught my balance and turned the corner. When Maia saw me, she let out a sob. I ran to her and clung to her as she enveloped me and we fell into a puddle on the floor. I was filled with something I'd never felt before: a mixture of hope and love and joy and, more than anything, *belonging*.

Adina came over and helped us both up, her eyes moist. "Come on, I've started a pot of coffee. Let's sit at the bar in the kitchen." She led us down a hall and through swinging doors. In the kitchen, two women were wiping down the counters and drying dishes. "I'll finish this up, ladies. May we have the room?" The two nodded, said their farewells, and left.

Maia sat by me on one of the stools, and, keeping her hand on me as if to prevent me from running, demanded, "Talk."

"I think I met Him," I started.

"Who?"

"Your Father God."

That day, I told them *everything*. I told them about the first time I remembered seeing the floating heads. I told them about how *they* told me to take a cookie and how they sometimes controlled me, and how nobody knew. I told them about my biological family and the horrors that seemed to have followed me from then until now.

Somewhere in the middle, Adina called Noah and asked him to bring the other two pastors and their wives. Maia offered Phil up for babysitting, and Adina brewed a fresh pot of coffee, commenting, "You don't have to start all over, but you should share enough with them for them to understand. We are going to pray over you and break any chains or bondage that still stands. To-day, the voice of God claimed you, and we're going to help you now as your journey begins."

# Chapter Thirty-Five

And what a journey it's been. I think part of me always thought that once someone knew God, that was it: life got good, all on its own—which, in many regards, it did, but knowing God didn't end my addiction overnight; it didn't shake away the nightmares; it didn't make me any less *me*. But it did change me, all at once and over time.

I ended up moving in with one of the pastels. She and her husband had a son who had gone off to college, leaving an empty bedroom behind, and they said they'd love to have me around. I was always under the watchful eye and graceful hand of Maia. She set me up with a new Bible as well as a journal, devotional, and books on spirits. She said that, if I was going to win this war, I needed to know my enemy. I went to church every Sunday morning and a study group Wednesday night. I also joined Maia's book club and grew close to the other pastels (I'd let my fond nickname for them slip at some point, and they now cheerfully referred to their group as such).

Slowly but steadily, my brokenness healed. I had, for the first time in my life, a community of people who knew me—the real me. They didn't all know my complete story, but they knew enough, and there was freedom in that. I stopped looking over my shoulder and stopped hiding from what I had been. More than community, I was starting to find my identity.

After a few months, Maia insisted that I call Mother. I tried to push back, but she was relentless. When Mother picked up the phone, I barely knew what to say. I tried to say hello, and it came out as a squeak, caught in my throat. Maia, being Maia, gracefully took the phone from my hands and introduced herself. She told Mother where I was and that I was more than safe.

When she asked about Esther, my heart exploded. Then I heard her in the background: my little girl, my baby, laughing and giggling, her voice clear and pure. I laid my head on the table and wept. I felt that regret again, that pain that sits below your belly button, heavy like rocks in your intestines.

Maia, again being Maia, flicked me on the arm. When I lifted my eyes to meet hers, she reminded me, "You did what you had to do to keep your child safe. That is the very best thing that you ever could have done for her."

A moment later, I heard Esther on the phone. "Mama?" she asked.

Grabbing the phone back from Maia, I said, "Hi, baby."

"Mama sad?" she asked.

"No, baby, Mama is happy—so happy to hear you."

She giggled, that baby giggle that makes everything right in the world, and promptly dropped the phone.

"I tell her about you every day," Mother said after reclaiming the receiver. Tears filled my eyes again.

"Hi, Mama," I said, echoing my own child. I let my body collapse into Maia, who supported me with ease. I couldn't carry the weight of the past few years anymore, so Maia carried it for me.

Shortly after that call, I moved back home. With my permission, Maia told Mother everything. I was hesitant at first, but she insisted that, to continue my new life in Christ, I had to come to terms with the death of my old one. She was right when she said that secrets only lead to destruction.

The morning of my big move, Noah and Adina threw me a surprise going-away party at the church. They served cake and coffee, prayed over me, and made me promise to come back to share my story. Then, with hugs, kisses, and tears, I left my home for the second time.

This time, though, I left with purpose and promise.

The drive was long but filled with music; this time, when I sang along, it was a joyful praise to my Heavenly Father. As I drove, I heard His voice. It was never as loud or as bold as *they* had been, but it touched my heart in the way that only He could. Now, when the music ended, I didn't panic because I knew the power wasn't in the mere words of the song—it was in that of Whom they spoke.

When I finally arrived at the house, I stood in the driveway for a moment, uncertain of how to move forward. Before I had time to decide, Mother came running out, my beautiful Esther in her hands and a small barking dog at her heel. Mother threw her free arm around me, and together, we wept—not as broken people, but as people reunited in truth.

"I'm so sorry," she whispered. "I never knew—I should have known."

We stood like that, arms wrapped around each other, until a little voice asked, "Gammie sad?"

We both laughed, and my mother handed me the most beautiful child that I had ever seen. She was the unexpected outcome of so much pain and so much evil, but here she was before me, filled with so much joy.

"Mama?" she asked.

"Yes, baby. I'm Mama!"

# Chapter Thirty-Six

Two years later, I got a call from Adina and Noah, reminding me of my promise to tell my story. That day, I heard *their* voices for the first time in years:

Fear whispered I wasn't saved enough to be used by God.

Anger told me that I'd blow it.

Pride said that I made it through this life by my own strength, not God's.

Loneliness warned that none of this would last and that nobody could relate—that I was alone in my experience.

Lust suggested that if I looked good enough, everyone would listen to me.

Greed chastised that I'd never be as good as the other women speaking.

Offense muttered that this church would let me down, that everyone would judge me.

And finally, Oppression promised that he'd be waiting in the shadows when I failed, that I'd become his again.

I mentioned identity before, and it took me two years from that day of salvation to truly find mine. They called me Beauty, but really, I was Broken, Fractured, Shattered, Abused, Isolated, Addicted, and, more than anything else, Desperate For Love.

But all that has been erased...

Because He calls me Redeemed.

# Epilogue

Thanks to the kindness and generosity of the church, Esther and I have been able to move into a small place of our own near Mother. Esther is so wonderfully full of joy and happiness and sees the world in a way that I only wish I could. Her curiosity and love for everything around her shows me daily the true heart of God.

Each step of this journey has been marked by sadness, and once upon a time, I would have told you that I regret certain moments. It's certainly safe to say that there are things that happened that I wish hadn't, but I know that each of those things led to this point.

Romans 8:28 promises that God works all things together for our good. I've struggled with that for a long time: *If this was my outcome, why did I have to endure?* I often asked this question, and there have been many nights when I've been angry with Him —even a little disappointed. At first, this worried me. I thought it meant that I couldn't truly love Him. But in His compassion and in His grace, He tells me that it's okay to be angry, that it's okay to be disappointed. He reminds me of a time when I let anger control me, and, with a gentle spirit, He teaches me how to be different.

Every day, we grow and learn more together. I'm in my Bible daily (and Esther is in her children's Bible) and am learning about the people who came before me—people who, like me, had to endure incredible hardships and hurts. People, like me, who were found by a Father and called home.

Esther doesn't know her biological father, and she likely never will. However, she does know her Father God, who loves her and cares for her. She knows of my adopted father, whose heart she would have stolen, and she has Maia's husband, Papa Phil, who speaks into her life as a father should speak into the life of a little girl. She will face her own troubles, but she will know that she is never alone.

When I look back on my life, it's hard to believe that anybody else could experience what I have. It's hard to tell a story that seems more like something you'd see in a horror movie than in the people around you. But it's there; *they* are there. I see them in the faces of people that I pass at the grocery store, or when Mother and I take Esther to the mall for pretzels, or in comments on social media. I see them in people who are listening to the wrong voices, people who are struggling to swim in the darkness. I know now that everything that has happened to me has shown me the truth about this world: we truly do not fight against flesh and blood, but against spirits—*demons*. When you start to see that, you start to love a little bit more and just a little bit better.

I can look at my past and see the spirits that Mother and Father dealt with. Maybe they didn't go by the same names as Lucy and Priscilla, but I can see them. I can see them in the faces of the men at Grandfather's funeral. I can see how they settled on Brother. Somehow, that knowledge brought more healing than I ever thought possible.

In our little home, we come together once a month after church (which I'm shocked to say that Mother is now attending): Maia and Phil, Mother, Brother, Esther, and me. There are no secrets in this place; there is no judgement. We know that the devil works in the darkness, and we refuse to let *them* get a second chance.

In this house, we sing the praises of the God Who saves, and when we come together, we are called by His name—the Name that is above all Names.

Yours Truly,
*Redeemed*

A special thanks to the people in my life who were willing to answer texts  or calls late into the evening when I suddenly panicked about who-knows-what on the journey that is publishing. You know who you are and I hope you know that you mean the absolute world to me.
J.Hieb